Deadly Obsession

ANGUS BRODIE AND MIKAELA FORSYTHE MURDER MYSTERY
BOOK SIX

CARLA SIMPSON

OLIVERHEBERBOOKS

Prologue

〜

OCTOBER, 1890, LONDON

AMBER LIGHT GLOWED SOFTLY in the darkened room, the smell of chemicals thick in the air as the sheet of paper was dipped into the last basin and the image of a young woman appeared.

She was pretty like the others who carried an air of privilege and wealth, with that certain expectation of young women who were seen in the society pages of the Times newspaper.

There had been no protest, she hadn't made a sound or cried out. There was only that startled expression, surprise perhaps. But no words came with her last dying breath.

There was only that air of sadness about her, her image caught in that photograph.

"Soon," she was assured as if she could still hear beyond death as the photograph was removed from the basin and carefully hung to dry alongside the other photographs.

"Soon, the others will join you."

One

"GOOD AFTERNOON, MISS MIKAELA," Mr. Cavendish greeted me as I arrived at the office at #204, on the Strand.

"It's a fine day."

Fine might be open to argument as the drizzle that had set in earlier in the day, had settled into a steady rain.

Mr. Cavendish, a colorful street person more commonly known as the Mudger, lived in the alcove just below the office on the Strand. He worked with Brodie from time to time, and had become a good friend over the course of our investigations that included the disappearance of my sister.

I stepped down from the cab and immediately felt the warm greeting of a wet tongue on my hand from Rupert, the hound. He kept company with Mr. Cavendish and was also a resident in the alcove on the stairs. Although he was out and about the streets scavenging for something to eat which was usually quite disgusting.

He greeted me with the usual wag of the tail, what appeared to be a foolish grin on his face— I was often reminded by Brodie that hounds did not grin. However, I chose to ignore that. Rupert then dropped to the sidewalk and rolled over onto his back for his

3

usual belly rub much like someone I knew, I thought smiling to myself.

I gave him a biscuit that my housekeeper had sent. Mrs. Ryan was more than familiar with the hound since he was often inclined to accompany me.

Although she considered him to be quite disgusting—covered as he usually was from head to foot in soot and grime, I was aware that she had taken to slipping him food left from a recent meal or one of the biscuits she fixed in the mornings.

When I questioned her about it, she had simply shrugged. "Better than throwing it out." She was also prone to giving him a scratch about the ears from time to time when she thought no one was looking.

Now, the biscuit quickly disappeared, and there was that grin before the hound set off on his rounds of the Strand.

I handed Mr. Cavendish some of Mrs. Ryan's lemon sponge cake.

"The woman is a saint," he replied with a gleam in his eye.

I wasn't certain about that, since my housekeeper was unaware that I had absconded with a good portion of her cake. Had she known, there would have been the evil eye and a lecture about the time it took to prepare and the suggestion that I might learn to prepare it myself if I was simply going to give it away. However, cooking was not one of my talents.

In fact, I had been known to very nearly burn the house down over a game hen that I had undertaken. It was a lesson well learned and I had crossed off cooking from my list of accomplishments. It was much safer for everyone.

I had spent the morning with my sister, Lady Lenore Forsythe as she now insisted on using our family name after her divorce from her husband following a dreadful scandal and his imprisonment over the affair.

In the aftermath, she had at first retreated to our great aunt's residence at Sussex Square where we were raised after the death of our parents. However, in more recent months she had recovered from the difficult situation, and had purchased her own residence that she was now renovating.

It was quite obvious from the look about her recently, with a completely new wardrobe, not to mention the attentions of someone we both knew quite well, that her new residence was not the only thing that had been renovated.

Months earlier, concerned that Linnie might be wasting away, closed off from her circle of friends with boring efforts at redecorating, I had determined that she needed to get out more.

I had introduced her to my publisher, James Warren, when she accompanied me to an event for my latest novel. To say there had been an immediate connection was an understatement in the least.

I thought the event might be turned into an inferno as I had attempted to carry on conversation with them and had finally given up. They had been thick as thieves ever since. It was the only way to describe the situation.

I had then attempted to include her for an evening at the theater to see my friend Templeton's latest performance. However, she had declined somewhat mysteriously.

Somewhat put out by her excuses and with genuine concern, I had taken myself off to her residence where I discovered the obvious reason— James Warren.

It seems that she had thrown caution, along with the threat of scandal, to the wind in their growing *relationship*. To be more precise— their affair.

Her reasoning, when we had met for luncheon the following day, was quite well-thought, articulate, not to mention most entertaining.

"Do say something," she had finally insisted. "I would understand if you do not approve..."

I had burst out laughing, which brought considerable attention from other guests at the Savoy.

"What are you laughing at?" Linnie had demanded somewhat put off.

"Seeking my approval?" I finally managed to reply after sufficiently recovering. "You are a woman of independent means, quite capable of making your own decisions and choices..." I had pointed out.

"It is not necessary for you to have anyone's permission," I continued. Most certainly not mine, I thought, considering my relationship with Angus Brodie.

"You're not angry?" She had been genuinely surprised.

"Good heavens, no!" I had replied. "Why do you think I introduced you to him? He is intelligent, well-respected, and quite knowledgeable in the world of art. You have a great deal in common."

Linnie was very talented as an amateur artist, but had been forced to give that up as her former husband felt it was not appropriate for the wife of a peer to hold showings of her work at a London gallery.

"And he is quite handsome," I had added.

"He is, isn't he? she had responded before catching herself. The sudden color in her face spoke volumes.

"He's been most encouraging about my taking up my painting again," she had quickly added as if she needed to convince me.

"You must do that, of course," I replied.

"Then you don't disapprove..." She had still been hesitant.

Of her painting, or the affair? It really was too tempting, but I didn't say it.

"It is about time," I replied, quite pleased for my sister, and I had managed to avoid any discussion about my relationship with Brodie which had taken a turn at the conclusion of our previous case.

We were both recovering from mishaps on my great aunt's property in Scotland. I could have blamed it on too much of my aunt's very fine whisky that was produced at Old Lodge, however neither one of us had had any at the time.

"I understand yer hesitation," Brodie had explained, and I knew that he did.

The man knew quite a lot about me by then— my habits, quirks, and shortcomings— my *stubbornness and taking myself off into dangerous situations* had been mentioned. But notwithstanding that, what followed had definitely left me speechless— he had proposed!

I had been taken aback to put it mildly. I had spent the better part of the past several years avoiding such things after an engagement that I had called off when I realized that I didn't want to be the usual society hostess for someone else's ambitions.

Over the intervening years, I had taken myself off on my various adventures, established myself as a successful author, and happily ignored the whispers of those in my great aunt's social circle about my unmarried status.

I had succeeded quite well in convincing myself that I didn't need or want the usual trappings of marriage. My parents' disastrous marriage as well as my sister's were examples of situations to avoid.

Then, there was Brodie.

He could be stubborn, opinionated, old-fashioned in many ways, and yet... he valued my opinions and ideas, and as my great aunt once said, was the only person "for the situation, and he could be trusted."

There was that other thing, of course, something I had never experienced before... Something my great aunt assured me was worth its weight in gold. He made my toes curl.

So there it was. In that uncompromising way, he had left me quite undone with his heartfelt and quite stirring proposal. Who else would have cared or told me that he knew where my hesitation came from?

"I'm not the same sort of man as yer father," he had told me that day at Old Lodge.

I knew that, of course. One didn't pursue the cases we'd worked on over the past two years, often in dangerous situations, and not learn the true character of someone. And it was not the difference in our social status that might be an obstacle. I didn't give a fig about that.

"It's not enough for me to be with ye, in that way, if ye get my meanin'," he had said then. "I want more, even as I stand here knowin' that I have no right and fully expect ye to say no, or at the very least to argue with me."

That did seem somewhat of an unusual way to propose by emphasizing my faults.

As for no right to ask me? If that wasn't enough, I had come completely undone at his next words, even though at the time I considered that it might have been my weakened physical condition in the aftermath of that last case.

"I want ye," he told me. "God help us both, and I have nothing to give ye, except meself and *this*."

This had been the one thing that was most precious to him, the St. Christopher's medallion given to him by his mother as she lay dying.

And then, knowing me quite well, he had simply added, "I will give ye time, Mikaela Forsythe..."

"So," my sister said, as we talked over luncheon days earlier. "What is your answer to Mr. Brodie going to be?"

I was quite surprised as I had not mentioned his somewhat unusual proposal to anyone upon our return to London.

"You'd be quite foolish to turn him down," she had announced before I had a chance to reply.

"Particularly if you insist on pursuing these cases with him. He is undoubtedly the only person who can put up with you, aside from myself and our aunt, of course. And, he is wickedly handsome." She had proceeded quite calmly to take a sip of wine.

"There's no need to look so surprised," she commented. "Aunt Antonia mentioned it some time ago, and you may close your mouth now," she added. "You look like a cod at the fish market and people are beginning to stare."

So much for keeping things to myself.

I loved my sister. But it seemed she had gone through some sort of transformation, emerging much like a butterfly from a cocoon. Or, possibly a bothersome insect most particularly with her comment about my resemblance to a fish— cod to be precise.

Now, speaking of *wickedly handsome*— I looked up to find Brodie descending the stairs from the office rather urgently.

Wicked was most definitely an appropriate description with his dark hair overlong at the collar of his coat and that dark gaze that softened as it met mine in that way that spoke of other things we shared.

"We will need the driver," he informed me as he motioned for the man to wait.

"Has something happened?" I asked as he assisted me up into the rig, then climbed in beside me.

"There's been a development in the matter of the photograph that was received by Sir John and Lady Mainwaring."

That sounded quite ominous.

"It seems that their daughter, Amelia, did not arrive at the home of an acquaintance yesterday evening as planned," he explained. "And this was delivered this morning to the Mainwaring residence." Brodie pulled an envelope from the inside pocket of his long coat and handed it to me.

At first glance, it seemed to be a photograph much like any common photograph. The young woman, who appeared to be Amelia Mainwaring, was sitting on a park bench with hands folded on her lap as if awaiting the arrival of an acquaintance or possibly the driver of a hack or cab.

"Someone playing another prank?" I commented.

Lady Althea Mainwaring, an acquaintance of my aunt, had contacted me some weeks earlier while Brodie and I were in the midst of another case, regarding a photograph of her daughter they had received.

In that odd way of connections, Sir John Mainwaring was the cousin of the former foreign secretary whom we had encountered previously. Lady Mainwaring had contacted us because of that unfortunate circumstance as well as her acquaintance with my aunt.

Now a possible turn in what had initially seemed a rather innocent if bothersome situation. The first photograph appeared to have been taken without their knowledge in the gardens of the Mainwaring estate at Portman Square, Marylebone.

It had been disconcerting for the family and they were unable to provide any information that might have led to the identity of the person who took it.

I had made the usual inquiries on their behalf as Brodie was up north in Scotland at the time. But there had been nothing to indicate who might have taken the photograph.

With no possible clues to indicate the meaning of that first photograph, or even when it might have been taken, it seemed to have been more of a prank.

"Take a closer look at the second photograph," Brodie said now. "And this note accompanied it." He handed that to me as well.

I read the cryptic message. "And then there were three...?"

What was that supposed to mean?

Upon closer inspection, I realized the photograph in my hands was not merely another casual picture taken by a friend or other acquaintance.

Amelia Mainwaring's eyes were open staring fixedly, her head bent at an odd angle, not the usual way of someone who was possibly awaiting the arrival of an acquaintance.

In spite of the evening shadows in the photograph, a nearby street lamp revealed her expression, completely void of any emotion as she blankly stared ahead perhaps in the direction of whoever had been holding the camera.

It appeared that I was looking at the sort of photo that had become quite common among those who had lost a loved one, most particularly an infant or child, a last remembrance or keepsake of someone who had passed on.

I had always thought the gesture to be somewhat morbid and

off-putting. For myself I thought it much better to remember someone as they were in life, full of energy, laughing, that sort of thing.

Admittedly, I had been accused of being cynical of such things, undoubtedly an influence after the funeral service for my father whom I had discovered dead as a child in the stables.

I had taken one look at him in his finery when he was laid out in the formal parlor of our home— soon to be taken by the bank to pay his gambling debts, and listened to the words spoken over him at the service, a pathetic contradiction to the man I had rarely seen those last months before he took his own life.

I supposed witnessing such a thing as a child did have a bearing on the way one viewed such things. However, I was not without sympathy now.

"She was found in Hyde Park near the royal fountain by police constables. According to Sir John's man who delivered this. She was identified by a calling card in her possession and the family was contacted."

"Oh dear," I said as I studied the photograph.

It seemed that whoever Miss Amelia had set out to meet, or whatever reason she had gone to the park, she was in fact quite dead.

Two

THE ESTATE at Portman Square in Marylebone was a two-story brick manor in the late Georgian style with dormer windows that looked out onto the circular drive. Fanlight windows over the entrance were framed by twin columns and the estate was surrounded by an expanse of lawn and gardens.

"What do ye know about the family?" Brodie asked as we rode through the gated entrance to the manor.

"Sir John is the Deputy Governor of the Bank of England, and a distant cousin of the former foreign secretary," I replied. "Lady Mainwaring is from the Armstrong-Burton family." There was the faint lift of a dark brow. It obviously meant nothing to him.

"They are a longtime family in the import and export trade."

"Are there other members in the immediate family?"

"There is a son from Sir John's first marriage. He is away at university," I replied, sharing what I had learned in my initial conversation with Lady Mainwaring about that first photograph.

"The young woman's age?" Brodie then asked.

"She turned nineteen years this past summer."

"There are obviously potential suitors," he commented.

"She had her coming out this past April," I added. I had also learned that from that initial conversation with Lady Mainwaring since it seemed that the photograph might have been taken as a jest or from an admirer.

"It was expected that she might become engaged at the Christmas season."

"That could be useful," he replied. "As well as any young men who might have been turned down," he added. "Sir John has an important position, to be certain," he commented thoughtfully.

I knew the direction of his thoughts. It was a position that might attract the criminal sort. A possibility of blackmail or extortion that might have gone wrong at the last minute for a man of Sir John's position and authority?

It was Brodie's way of thinking, looking at every aspect of an inquiry case. He called it an affliction, a natural suspicion of everyone, from his years as an inspector with the Metropolitan Police, and now in private practice.

He asked our driver to wait as we stepped down from the cab.

The doorman at the Mainwaring residence appeared as we presented ourselves at the entrance. He escorted us into the formal drawing room. There the head butler asked us to wait while he went to inform Sir John of our arrival.

The room was quite opulently appointed, as opposed to the less formal garden room where I had met with Lady Mainwaring after that first photograph was received. There was a fire in the fireplace, but it failed to warm the expansive room with cold marble floors, dark furnishings.

"What is yer aunt's acquaintance with Lady Mainwaring?" Brodie asked as we waited.

"Through Sir John," I replied. "He had overseen my aunt's financial affairs with the bank for over thirty years before he was appointed to the new position."

Those affairs were quite substantial with the family fortunes that went back several hundred years that had grown considerably with business interest across the empire along with the properties she owned in England, Scotland, and France. It was said that she was wealthier than the Queen.

My sister and I were her only family. However, neither of us cared a fig about inheriting our aunt's wealth. I was quite capable of supporting myself, and Linnie had received a substantial settlement including her now former husband's estate upon her divorce.

More power to our aunt if she was able to spend every last farthing indulging whatever whim took her fancy. And there were several whims that included travel in spite of her age, a growing fascination with automobiles, and renovating her home at Sussex Square.

She was at present deeply involved with the architect in that regard, and I suspected that it had more to do with the man than his designs for the house. As I said, more power to her.

But returning to the matter at hand, I then asked Brodie about his suspicions.

"Do you believe it might be someone in the family?"

"Or possibly a connection of the family who might have access to the young woman," Brodie replied.

It was then that Sir John arrived. He was quite tall with graying hair and side whiskers, his features drawn. Brodie introduced himself and expressed his condolences. Sir John nodded in my direction.

"I appreciate your meeting me this afternoon," Sir John told us. "Obviously this is a very difficult time. Lady Mainwaring is indisposed. You understand, of course."

We were directed to those chairs. A servant silently appeared, and Sir John requested tea.

Over the next hour, he explained when that second photograph had been received earlier that morning, sent in an envelope by one of the courier services.

"I thought nothing of it, as I often receive dispatches from the central office. But when I opened it…"

He hesitated, then continued.

"Our daughter was to have spent the evening and then a stay-over with her friend, Miss Beatrice Ainsley-Townsend. We have subsequently learned that their daughter received a message that Amelia was not feeling well and cancelled the plans."

However, the Mainwaring's daughter had still left their residence as originally planned. There were several very obvious questions.

Where had she gone after leaving the Mainwaring residence? Obviously a driver would have accompanied her. Where had he taken her, if not to the residence of her friend?

What had happened afterward, as it seemed that second photograph was taken at some time during the previous evening? And by whom?

And when was the poor girl's body found?

"After receiving that photograph and the note, I contacted her friend's family and learned that Amelia never arrived at their residence."

"What of your coachman?" Brodie asked. "Have you questioned him?"

"Of course," Sir John replied. "Amelia directed him to Kensington where she told him she was to join Miss Ainsley-Townsend at Harrod's for a bit of shopping. She assured him that they would hire a driver when their purchases were completed and continue on to the young woman's residence."

I exchanged a look with Brodie. A ruse? For what reason?

"After hearing from the Ainsley-Townsends, we received word that Amelia had been found." He paused again, overcome, then gathered himself.

"She was found as you see her there. I contacted our personal physician, and he was able to arrange to have her received at the hospital."

"And you've made the appropriate notification with the authorities?" Brodie inquired.

"I would prefer to keep this matter as discreet as possible for now. A man in my position... You do understand," Sir John explained. "With the hope that you may be able to find whoever has done this."

"If we are to proceed, sir, we will need the name of yer physician," Brodie replied. "As well as any other persons you might have perhaps had a disagreement within the past."

"Surely you're not suggesting that whoever did this might be known to us?"

"If we are to make our inquiries, sir, we must know all the facts," Brodie explained. "Otherwise, there is no reason to continue. It would be a waste of your time."

Bluntly spoken. Of course, Brodie was right, I thought.

Sir John nodded stiffly. "Whatever you need, of course."

"Your daughter had her coming out this spring," I commented. "Lady Mainwaring had shared that her engagement was to be announced."

"A man from a fine family," Sir John replied. "Yes, it was to be announced at Christmas holiday. Surely you're not suggesting anything amiss in that regard."

"It is part of the information we would like to follow," Brodie explained.

"Very well. He will need to be contacted. This will be a shock, you understand?"

"Of course."

"I would like to see your daughter's room, as well," I interjected.

"I've told you that she was not present last evening," Sir John replied. "What could you possibly hope to find?"

"There are often things that might not be considered important at first glance," I explained. "That might very well tell us something about where your daughter was going and who she might have met with instead of meeting with Miss Ainsley-Townsend."

"That would be extremely upsetting for Lady Mainwaring..." Sir John started to protest. "Surely you understand?"

"Nevertheless," I insisted.

"Of course," he stiffly replied then had the head butler summon the housekeeper.

"You will please remember to be discreet, and keep me informed regarding anything you learn," Sir John added, with a look at both of us as his housekeeper, Mrs. Gray, arrived and he made my request.

I thought Mrs. Gray's name most appropriate as the woman was a vision in shades of that same color— gray hair pulled tightly into a bun at the top of her head, gray gown with just a hint of white at the collar, her expression also quite gray.

Dour was the word that came to mind, as she nodded at my introduction with a frown then inclined her head in the direction of the stairs just beyond the formal drawing room.

The stairs, along with the second-floor landing and the hallway just beyond again, reminded me of Sir John's position, with thick carpet underfoot and opulent fixtures on the walls and overhead.

The doors to the rooms on the second floor were all closed. A maid appeared with a silver tray from one of those rooms— presumably that of Lady Mainwaring. There was a brief nodded exchange from Mrs. Gray and the maid continued to the stairs.

Amelia Mainwaring's rooms were across the way and farther down the hall, the door also closed.

"Miss Amelia's rooms," Mrs. Gray announced.

To her credit it did appear that her expression changed. A touch of sadness perhaps? Then her gray lips thinned once more, and I wondered if she practiced disapproval in the mirror each morning after donning her stiff white collar. I appreciated my own housekeeper, Mrs. Ryan, with her boisterous Irish humor not to mention her lemon sponge cake, all the more.

I was forced to begin my visit to Amelia Mainwaring's rooms under that beady gaze. As if I was some sort of criminal rather than having just been appointed with Brodie to make our inquiries on behalf of the Mainwaring family. I ignored Mrs. Gray as I slowly made my way about the sitting room.

There were the usual things to be found in the rooms of a young woman. Her sitting room was elegantly furnished, no doubt at the direction of her mother.

A bit over the top for someone of Amelia's age, I thought. The furnishings and drapes were of the sort that might be found in a royal sitting room, as well as quite dark and impersonal as I attempted to learn something about the young woman.

I ventured next into the bedroom, Mrs. Gray hovering at my elbow with an occasional sniff of disapproval. Here I had a better sense of the young woman who had an obvious penchant for porcelain in the almost whimsical collection of animal statues on a side table.

The door to her wardrobe was slightly ajar. Upon opening the wardrobe I discovered something peculiar. Her formal dressing gown and nightgown were both still there. Most interesting for someone who was supposedly planning a stay-over with a friend.

When I would have searched through the other items there, Mrs. Gray reached around me and promptly shut the wardrobe door.

A look in her direction and she backed away, but the disapproval was there. My gaze then fastened on something else in the far corner of the room—a racquet.

It was finely made and had seen quite a bit of use. It seemed that Miss Amelia enjoyed the sport of lawn tennis. It gave me additional insight into the young woman. I set the racquet back in the corner.

Amelia Mainwaring collected porcelain statues of rabbits and birds, but also played lawn tennis— whimsical and yet competitive, characteristics quite different one from the other. And it appeared that she was an avid reader. There were books on the Louis XV nightstand beside the bed.

What might that those books tell me about Amelia Mainwaring?

Three books by Jane Austen had been set to one side of the table, while another book with a bookmark lay on the table.

I picked up the one she had apparently been reading as indicated by that bookmark. It was my novel about my main character Emma Fortescue's latest adventure!

The novel was a thinly disguised fictional account about my sister's disappearance, with all the names changed of course to protect the real persons involved.

Although I had to admit I had wanted very much to use my former brother-in-law's real name. My way of *twisting the knife* as they say. Not in a murderous way, although I had been tempted out of desire to punish the man for what he had put my sister through, not to mention the risk to her life.

Most interesting, I thought now, regarding Miss Amelia's preference for books. It seemed that in addition to my other observations, Miss Amelia Mainwaring was very much a romantic, and far from the shy and retiring sort in her choice of books.

I ignored Mrs. Gray as I made a slow inventory of the room and what I had discovered. I went next to the writing desk on the opposite wall across from the wardrobe.

It was in the Queen Anne style and appeared to be made of rosewood with the distinctive curved cabriole legs and pad feet. The fiddle back chair with cushioned seat was in the same style. And there was a framed photograph on the desk.

It was a photograph of a handful of young ladies and young men, dressed in sporting costumes, each with a racquet in hand. A gathering of fellow players it seemed, and Amelia Mainwaring and the other young ladies smiled while the young men variously mocked the camera with stiff, proper poses.

Yet, another insight into Miss Mainwaring.

The chair at the desk sat back instead of neatly tucked into the chair well as one might have expected. Had she been writing something at the desk, and then hastily pushed the chair back? What might that tell me?

As she had from the beginning, Mrs. Gray continued to hover about, as if she thought that I might lift something. I needed a diversion so that I could search through the drawers of the desk.

"Oh dear, is that Lady Mainwaring calling out?" I asked with a concerned expression. My comment had the desired effect.

"I must check on her," Mrs. Gray announced with. "Are you quite finished, miss?"

"It is *Lady Forsythe*," I corrected her. I couldn't resist, although I rarely used the title. There were occasions however when it produced the desired results.

"Yes, of course," Mrs. Gray stammered. "Please wait for me in the hallway," and then as an afterthought. "Milady."

Sour-faced biddy, I thought, and assured her that I would. "Of course."

As soon as she had gone, I immediately returned to the desk.

There were four drawers in the desk, two each side of a center space where a porcelain rose sat in a crystal vase, and once more I had the impression of someone who was quite romantic.

One drawer held a fountain pen, an elegant piece, along with a blotting pad to prevent smearing. Another drawer held a letter opener, the next drawer was empty. I finally found what I was looking for in the last drawer— sheets of Amelia Mainwaring's personalized stationery.

She might have exchanged correspondence with the man she was to be betrothed to at the holiday season, or possibly someone else that might indicate her thoughts before she left.

I didn't dismiss anything as I knew all too well that among the titled, marriages were often arranged and frequently between a young man and woman for benefits of wealth or title. If a young woman was fortunate there were feelings of affection that grew over time.

If not... My sister's marriage was an example.

The match had seemed perfect, then ended in disaster and scandal. Fortunately, Linnie seemed to have recovered from that and was quite ecstatic with her growing *acquaintance* with James Warren.

What secrets, I thought now, might the desk reveal about Miss Amelia Mainwaring?

Quite typical of the young woman I was gradually getting to know from what I had already discovered in the rooms, the thin vellum personalized stationery in the last drawer was embossed at the top with her initials in a design of delicate pink feathers that created the initials A and then M.

However, far more important and upon closer inspection, there were impressions at the blank page on top, no doubt left from a note that Amelia Mainwaring had written. What might it tell us?

I heard a sound in the outer room. It seemed that Mrs. Gray had returned.

I quickly lifted the sheet of stationery and tucked it into my travel bag, then hastily closed the drawer.

"It appears that Lady Mainwaring is still resting," she informed me, glancing about the room then back to me, as if to make certain that everything was in order.

I gave her a cool smile. "Perhaps a sound as she was sleeping," I suggested. "It has been a very difficult last several hours."

With that, I swept past Mrs. Gray. I didn't wait for her as I returned downstairs and joined Brodie.

It appeared that he had finished questioning the head butler.

"I would like to speak with the driver now," he informed Sir John. "Since he was the last person to see yer daughter. It has been my experience that the smallest detail might be important, something he perhaps forgot to mention."

"Yes, very well."

"And any of the staff who might have interacted with Miss Mainwaring before she left to meet her friend," he added.

"Of course," Sir John stiffly replied.

Over the next two hours, Brodie questioned the members of the staff who would have had contact with Miss Mainwaring while I made notes.

That included the coachman, the downstairs butler, as well as the upstairs maid. I added Mrs. Gray to the list, who might well have overheard something said between Lady Mainwaring and Amelia, as she had been most uncooperative with me.

Sir John presided over the questions, all the while conducting business through his personal secretary, sending off messages most efficiently, as if the very difficult situation had not occurred.

It was very near four o'clock of the afternoon when Lady Mainwaring appeared, looking quite pale and drawn. She was acquainted with Brodie through her earlier contact with myself, and formal introductions were made.

Once more I was impressed by his ability to sympathize at the same time he gently inquired if he might ask her a few questions.

There was little she could tell us about the previous day. It had seemed normal in all aspects. Amelia was looking forward to shopping with her friend, an acquaintance through their families, and then the stay-over, to return the following morning.

"She hoped to have Beatrice... Miss Ainsley-Townsend, as part of her wedding party," Lady Mainwaring, then added, "Amelia was to become betrothed at the holiday."

"And the name of the young man?" I inquired, as it seemed that it might be important.

"It is... a family arrangement. Sir Anthony Blackstone."

That took me back a bit, although I suppose that it shouldn't have. I made a note of it.

Though she made a great effort, Lady Mainwaring had broken down in tears at this point in the conversation.

"Please forgive me."

"I understand," Brodie gently told her.

Sir John then insisted that any further questions would have to be asked at a later time as Lady Mainwaring was obviously quite distressed. Mrs. Gray then escorted her once more to her rooms.

When she had gone, Brodie asked Sir John for the name of their private physician.

"That would be Doctor Marcus Fielding..."

"It would be most helpful if ye would contact the good doctor and let him know we would like to speak with him."

"You do understand the need for the utmost discretion," Sir John insisted.

"Of course."

With that, it seemed that our meeting was at an end.

The rain had let up and settled itself into a heavy mist beneath darkened skies as we left Portman Square.

"Ye seemed somewhat surprised at the name of the man Miss Mainwaring was to have been betrothed to," Brodie commented.

"Sir Anthony Blackstone is old enough to be her father," I commented. Not that it was all that unusual among the upper class— alliance of families, possibly an arrangement for other purposes, that sort of thing. Still...

"Ye were surprised at the arrangement," Brodie commented in that way he had of instinctively knowing there was more that I had to say in the matter.

"It's just that I had a certain impression of Amelia Mainwaring as I looked about her rooms."

"What might that be?"

"She was most orderly in the way she kept things— small mementoes, even whimsical things, porcelain figures that I found on a table, and the books she read. There were copies of books by Jane Austen on her night table, and another one that she was obviously reading most recently. And there was a photograph at her writing desk."

"Photograph?"

"It was obviously taken some time ago, a picture of her with friends after a game of lawn tennis."

"And that was unusual?"

"It seemed that she was not the sort to simply accept an arranged marriage."

"Ye have some experience with that?" he remarked.

He knew quite well that I had once been engaged to be married— also an arranged situation; families, wealth, and all that.

And hopelessly boring. It had ended and I had taken myself off on one of my first adventures that had ended on the Isle of Crete...

I chose to ignore his comment.

"There was also a piece of stationery in the writing desk," I went on to explain.

In the darkened shadows inside the cab, I felt the question rather than saw it on his face as he turned slightly toward me.

"It still had impressions from the last note she wrote to someone," I continued. "It might be useful to have Mr. Brimley look at it."

The chemist had become a good friend through our past inquiries. He had expertise that had provided several important clues, along with his medical skills.

"The housekeeper didn't object?" Brodie replied.

I smiled to myself.

"There was a moment when she was called away." I felt that dark gaze on me.

"And the note paper just happened to find its way into yer bag."

A shadow stepped from among other shadows near the gated entrance to the Mainwaring estate, and stared after the departing cab.

Angus Brodie, formerly of the Metropolitan Police, had a reputation for being formidable in his private inquiries. There had been mention in a brief newspaper article that he had been commended by the Prince of Wales over a previous matter.

And the woman with him?

Lady Mikaela Forsythe, according to the dailies, a member of the upper class who had made a name for herself with her novels, and her association with the detective Angus Brodie.

Most interesting...

Three

〜

"I CONFIRMED the appointment with the physician first thing this morning," Brodie commented as I arrived at the office on the Strand.

When he finally looked up, I recognized the frown as I had seen it on numerous occasions in the past, most usually when he was displeased with something. That *something*, this morning, was apparently me.

I had started out early with the best of intentions that rapidly disappeared with my aunt's preparations for the rapidly approaching All Hallows party she was hosting at the Grosvenor Hotel.

She had decided on the location some months before and had been quite excited about the planning and preparations. It was also a location where her guests from beyond London might stay afterward before returning home.

I had stayed over as her seamstress had arrived first thing with the costume she had been working on for my aunt. Everyone who attended the party was to be in full costume. She had decided to attend as Marie Antoinette and had modeled the costume for me.

"I had Madame copy the gown from a painting, and I will have make-up to complete the costume. What do you think?"

I was not particularly acquainted with the French queen, undoubtedly due to the fact that she had been dead for almost one hundred years, and the fact that I was not the art aficionado in the family. That appreciation belonged to my sister.

However, I had complimented her and Madame. The gown was exquisite. Then there were the plans for the forthcoming party that she wanted to discuss with me.

The food would be prepared at the hotel. And then there were the decorations that had been in the planning for weeks, a magician and actors who were to perform throughout the evening, and she had persuaded my friend Templeton to give readings as well as call spirits forth with the Ouija board.

The previous evening I had explained to Brodie that I needed to assist with the holiday preparations my aunt was making. He had seemed most amenable at the time, considering the recent change in our relationship.

Admittedly, I wasn't at all certain what to call our relationship — partners, associates most certainly in the inquiry cases that we had undertaken since that first one when I acquired his services in the matter of my sister's disappearance.

Now, there was the other aspect of our relationship. Of an intimate nature, one might call it, that my sister had pointed out.

"Oh for heaven's sake, Mikaela. I don't know what you're dithering about. It's quite obvious."

When I had demanded to know what she was talking about, she had been uncharacteristically blunt.

"I believe it has to do with 'toe-curling' as our aunt would call it, something quite descriptive don't you think, and something I had never experienced prior to Mr. Warren..." she added, then quickly went on. "And other *things*," she said with a casual wave of her hand.

"Most certainly, Mr. Brodie is quite a stirring man. And as your protagonist in your novels, Emma Fortescue would say, he undoubtedly 'tastes most deliciously.' I believe that is what you wrote in your last book."

I wasn't aware that she had been reading my books as she had once declared them to be somewhat risqué and not the usual literary sort. However, she obviously had read at least one with that particular reference.

"I don't care to discuss it," I had informed her.

The problem was if I were to discuss *it*, I would choose to discuss it with my best friend, someone I trusted. And that was precisely the problem. In the time we had known each other, I could say most definitely that Brodie was my very good friend and that I trusted him, with my life as it turned out on more than one occasion.

And as to the *thing*, it would have to be regarding his proposal of marriage. It had come in one of the rare moments apart from the business of murder, blackmail, and extortion.

It was simply done, just the two of us, not what someone else might have expected, and I was quite undone by it all. And that was the problem, I am not in the habit of being undone.

I have endeavored to be in control of every aspect of my life. I had most certainly not come undone with excitement at a previous proposal of marriage that I had quickly escaped.

In the handful of years since, I had my travels, the success of my novels and the inquiry cases I shared with Brodie. I was fine with that and quite pleased with my life. I didn't need anyone...

Then, there was Brodie.

He could be quite obstinate and at times difficult to deal with. However as my aunt had told me when she recommended him to me— he was the most honorable person she had ever met, and he could be trusted with the most difficult of situations. Most certainly my sister's situation at the time had been very difficult.

There was that other thing, of course, that my sister had most recently described— he made my toes curl. It was a simple as that.

Realistically, it might also be that edge of danger that always seemed to surround him that intrigued me. Or it might be as simple as the soft-spoken way he called me lass.

Ridiculous as that was, I was far from being a lass any longer, as had been pointed out in the dailies more than once about my status as *spinster novelist*, by more than one pundit.

It might have been the way he looked at me with that dark gaze as if he saw me, really saw me with all my faults and at my worst moments, and then with just the touch of his hand...

His proposal was unexpected along with the simple token he had given me, a medallion that had once belonged to his mother.

However, it was what he told me next that no one, not even the man I had once been betrothed to had ever understood, or thought or said— *"I will give ye time..."*

And that was the part that I suppose was terrifying. He knew me, along with my fears and anger, along with the stubbornness and my independent nature, as no one ever had or cared to.

We had parted the previous evening after leaving Marylebone and our meeting with Sir John and Lady Mainwaring.

I had made my usual notes regarding our meeting with Sir John while at Sussex Square, and was most anxious to learn when we might be able to meet with their family physician regarding Miss Mainwaring's death.

I had spoken with Brodie by telephone earlier.

"Is all well with her ladyship?" he now inquired as he was most familiar with my aunt's peculiarities and eccentricities.

"If one considers planning for the event as if the Queen was to be in attendance," I replied. "And she's asked Templeton to participate as well."

He looked up then. "I'm almost afraid to ask."

"She's enlisted Templeton to do card readings for guests." I didn't mention the Ouija board, as he had a dislike for such things.

"Does that include Mr. Shakespeare?" he asked.

With anyone else that might have seemed an odd question, however in our association he had learned a great deal about my friend, Theodora Templeton, well known actress of the London stage and throughout the world who claimed to communicate with the spirit of Sir William.

Not that anything might be proven other than the occasional bit of information she was able to provide in the course of more than one investigation that had proven to be quite accurate.

Brodie was more than doubtful of her ability in that regard while I left the possibility open. Still, he was tolerant of her eccentricities, perhaps out of his friendship with Munro, a fellow Scot, who seemed to have fallen under Templeton's spell. Or quite possibly it was the other way around.

Our meeting with Dr. Fielding was to be at ten o'clock that morning at the morgue at St. Thomas hospital where Amelia's body had been taken.

"What about meeting with Mr. Brimley regarding the note paper?" I asked. "It might be able to tell us something about Miss Mainwaring's whereabouts before she was found in the park."

"When we've concluded our meeting with the physician," Brodie replied.

The bell at the landing sounded most insistently then, a device installed by Mr. Cavendish to let us know when a coachman or cab had arrived.

"I'll make my notes on the board when we return."

"Aye," was the only response from Brodie as he seized his umbrella from the stand and followed me from the office.

Mr. Cavendish greeted us with a smile. "Good day, Miss Forsythe, Mr. Brodie."

He looked quite dapper, much like a doorman at a hotel in a top hat and red wool coat with gold epaulettes, coattails tucked under on the platform where he sat. I could only wonder where he might have acquired the garments. His usual costume was cast-off pants and shirt, woolen scarf and patched jacket, with a cap. Rupert the hound sat beside him, tail thumping on the sidewalk in greeting.

"Mind you now," Mr. Cavendish added. "There's a chance of an encounter with all sorts of ghosts and goblins out and about this time o' the year."

~

The morgue where Dr. Fielding had arranged for Amelia Mainwaring's body to be taken was across the Thames from Westminster, St. Thomas Hospital in Lambeth, where he was also a professor of medicine.

He had agreed to meet Brodie at the Lambeth Road entrance located at the back of the hospital.

Brodie announced our arrival to a clerk and Dr. Fielding promptly arrived.

"Yes, I was informed that a lady might accompany you," he commented, his gaze meeting mine briefly. Did I see a vague annoyance there?

"Not what one usually expects in such circumstances. If you would prefer to wait here, Miss Forsythe?" he suggested.

"Not at all," I replied. It was not the first time I had encountered that sort of response.

"Very well," he stiffly replied and then escorted us to the private room.

The business of death is never pleasant, most particularly when murder is involved. There was a cold, brutal aspect that was impossible to ignore, the complete disregard for human life, the taking of something often in a most brutal way. And sadness, most particularly when it was a child or a young woman, both too often victims.

Even though I had viewed dead bodies before, I was reminded that one could never be fully prepared for it. It seemed there was always some startling aspect to viewing a body.

I had discovered that during my very first inquiry case with Brodie. At the time, the body was that of my sister's maid, Mary Ryan, who had disappeared with her.

I experienced that initial reaction all over again now as the doctor turned on the electric and then proceeded to the table where Amelia Mainwaring's body lay.

Perhaps it was the sight of her, so young, a reminder of my

sister's maid and the fear then that I might find my sister the same way along with the sadness I felt at a life so young, and cruelly ended.

For his part, there was that professional detachment as Brodie slowly circled the table, making his own observations as he asked questions of Dr. Fielding.

"What have ye determined as to the manner of death?" he asked as I took out my notebook and fountain pen.

"It appears that strangulation was the cause," Dr. Fielding announced. "There is obvious bruising about the neck. Some hours had obviously passed afterward. Rigor mortis had fully set in." Dr. Fielding looked over at me at the scratching of my pen across paper.

"Rigor mortis is..." he started to explain, no doubt for my benefit.

"The stiffening of muscles and joints after death due to chemical changes in the body. It is said to occur between one and four days after death," I replied, citing what Mr. Brimley had once explained about the condition of a body.

"And since Miss Mainwaring disappeared day before last, and was alive at the time, it would seem that the body was discovered no more than twelve hours after death." I caught the amused expression on Brodie's face.

"Quite so," Dr. Fielding commented with obvious surprise.

"What about the fact that she had obviously been positioned in that particular manner, much like in death photos," I asked. "Is it possible she was attacked at another location and then placed there?"

"Residue on the clothing might suggest where the incident occurred," Brodie said, more to himself and I made a note of it.

Unless of course, she was in the habit of wearing black when out and about. I had noticed it immediately when the lights were turned on. It seemed that the Mainwaring family had provided clothes appropriate to the situation.

"The garments she was found in were removed upon arrival

of the body," Dr. Fielding stiffly replied. "The family has provided these garments for the period of formal mourning."

"It would be helpful to have the other items," I tactfully commented. "In the interest of providing Sir John and Lady Mainwaring with answers in such a dreadful situation," I added.

"It's possible they are still within the hospital, although clothing is usually disposed of to avoid the spreading of disease," he replied.

That hardly seemed likely of the present situation, I thought, but didn't say it.

"I'm certain Sir John would appreciate yer assistance in the matter," Brodie said then, quite direct.

"I will ask the attendant," I interjected.

"That won't be necessary," Dr. Fielding informed me. "I will make the request. If there is anything you need in my absence, please make note of it."

With that he left the room.

"What is it?" I immediately asked Brodie, having recognized a sudden change in his expression as he carefully moved the collar of the young woman's gown to better inspect her neck.

"There are faint bruises, however nothing to indicate that she struggled when she was attacked," he commented.

I remembered the bruising that I had seen about Mary Ryan's neck when she was found. It had been substantial. However, there were very few bruises present in this case.

"The natural instinct would be to fight back when a person is attacked," he commented. He then gently turned the young woman's head in the opposite direction to inspect the other side of her neck.

"The bruising would be far more as she struggled and there would be other indications."

"Her fingernails?" I suggested.

"Precisely," Brodie replied as he then lifted one hand and then the other and inspected the nails on the fingers.

Dr. Fielding abruptly returned. "An attendant is making

inquiries into the state of the victim's garments, whether or not they have been disposed of," he assured Brodie, ignoring me as if I was nothing more than a spot on the wall.

"Was there any residue beneath the nails when the body arrived?" Brodie asked. "Or any indication of assault of a personal nature?"

"Out of respect for the family, there didn't seem to be any call for that sort of information that would only cause more distress and grief..." Dr. Fielding started to protest.

"With all due respect, sir," Brodie replied. "There are things that all manner of injury might tell us about the person who did this. I understand that it is a most delicate matter, however quite necessary," he insisted.

"No other... injuries were found," Sir Fielding said quite emphatically. "There were no other marks, or residue under the fingernails."

Brodie nodded. "Thank ye for yer expertise, sir. It is most important to the inquiry."

"Will that be all then? As you might well imagine, the family is most anxious to have Miss Mainwaring's body returned to them for the appropriate mourning."

"Of course," Brodie replied, with a look across at me, and then not to be put off. "And the items we requested, sir?"

"The attendant will provide them. I'm certain that you understand, I have other matters I must attend to, a class awaiting my arrival for a lecture I am to give."

By all means, I thought, a lecture was most important as compared to the grief of a family who had just lost someone in a most dreadful manner.

I reminded myself that if I was ever in a critical situation from injury that I might be better left to my own devices rather than seek the attention of Dr. Fielding. Lecture indeed! And with that, it seemed that our meeting was at an end.

We left the holding room and waited in the receiving area.

The attendant we had first encountered upon arrival eventually appeared with a bundle wrapped in brown paper.

"We will need a signature, sir," he reminded us.

Brodie made an impatient scrawl across the form at the young man's note board, then took the bundle and thanked him.

"No residue under her nails, no other signs of assault, and only the faintest marks on her neck," I commented as we left the hospital and found a cab.

"It would seem that was not the reason for the attack," I added. "Then it had to be for some other reason."

"Ye are the only woman I know who would find all of it curious, instead of fainting away at the sight of a dead body."

"I don't faint," I reminded him. After all it wasn't my first body.

We called next on Mr. Brimley, the chemist very near the office on the Strand, who had assisted us in previous investigations and had provided information that had been most helpful in solving those crimes.

He might have been a physician after studying at King's College, however life or rather the streets of the East End, had taken him in a different direction.

He saw to the needs of the poor, dispensing medications, assisting women who had either attempted to rid themselves of an unwanted pregnancy in a place where poverty and starvation was rampant, or assisting in the delivery of the child. And then there was his treatment of all sorts of complaints and wounds, including bullet wounds. I could personally attest to his skill in that regard.

Mr. Brimley was also known to have a curiosity in the occasional body part that he came across— a severed hand or foot, and his most recent acquisition —a human eyeball.

All were meticulously preserved in jars with the appropriate solution for him to analyze and study. Most fascinating, as he put it.

However, we now had little to go on— no residue that might

have told us something about Amelia Mainwaring's attacker, and the lack of any significant marks that led to her death.

"Mornin', sir. Miss." We were greeted by his assistant, Abby. She couldn't have been more than fourteen or fifteen years old, however wise beyond her years.

She had lived on the streets, making her way as best she could, which meant prostitution. She was exceedingly bright, with a worldly way about her that was almost heartbreaking, except for the fact that she didn't see it that way at all.

Mr. Brimley had taken her in to assist in his shop when she showed a fascination for the profession as well as his research. She earned a small income— the most he could afford to pay. Still she seemed quite satisfied with the arrangement.

"Mr. Brimley says I could be a right fine chemist one day, or a physician! He even said that he would introduce me to a good friend at college," she had excitedly explained not long ago.

"He's even showing me how to read and write!"

"*Teaching* you how to read and write," he had corrected her at the time.

Actually, I could imagine it. More and more it seemed that women were taking places in professions once dominated by men. It was slow progress, but progress nevertheless, along with acceptance of women authors. After all, the ruler of Britain was a woman!

As usual, Mr. Brimley was in the back of the shop that he called his laboratory, with those jars of specimens, chemicals and powders, a pill making machine, along with microscopes along the counter at the wall, and photographic equipment— a recent addition as he studied those specimens that he gathered.

He looked up, with a slightly myopic gaze behind glasses with unusually thick lenses that he'd had specially made with magnifying lenses. They gave him the appearance of an enormous bug, slightly balding with the few hairs that were askew, and wearing his usual apron.

All about him were jars of powders and potions as he sat

before the pill making machine. A smile greeted us as he swung around on the stool.

"Mr. Brodie, Miss Mikaela, it is a pleasure to see you, as always. What brings you here? A new inquiry case, perhaps?"

"Your assistance is needed," Brodie replied.

"Is it disappearance or murder this time?" he asked with enthusiasm.

It occurred to me that amidst his working with body parts in jars along with all sorts of those who sought his services, our inquiry cases appeared to provide a welcome diversion.

Brodie explained the facts of the case, few as they were.

"And you have the young woman's clothes?" Mr. Brimley gestured to the wrapped bundle.

"Aye," Brodie nodded. "To see what ye might be able to tell us."

Mr. Brimley gestured to the countertop that contained those microscopes. "Let's have a look, then."

He unwrapped the bundle, then spread the garments out on the counter.

"A young woman of some means," he observed. "The small bunch of cloth flowers at the waist not usually something found on those in the East End, and the size of the garment is quite slender which suggest someone of a younger age, and it is finely made by a personal seamstress, no doubt.

"There are no obvious stains about the gown— blood or that sort of thing," he added as he continued his inspection.

"No signs that the garment was torn, nor the other garments." He looked up. "I would say that the young woman was not harmed in the usual way we see all too often."

He continued to mumble comments, more to himself as he continued with his inspection. Then, "What is this?"

He peered closer at the bodice of the gown. "Some sort of residue. Yes, yes, quite; crystals or powder of some sort on the fabric."

He set aside the magnifying glass, opened a drawer under the counter, and retrieved what appeared to be a surgical instrument. Considering the man's expertise that I had experienced in the past, I was not surprised.

He also pulled a piece of paper from another drawer then returned to the garment on the counter and proceeded to scrape the front of the gown where he had found that residue.

"This might tell us something," he announced.

He then moved down the counter to one of the microscopes and deposited some of the residue onto a glass slide which he then placed under the microscope lens. He turned on the attached electric light and proceeded to examine the residue.

"Yes," he commented. "It's possible. But to what purpose?" he said more to himself, like a scientist with his observations and questions.

"What does it tell ye?" Brodie asked.

Mr. Brimley looked up. "Oh yes, quite. Forgive me. I went off a bit there. Tell me, was there any sweet smell about the corpse?"

"The girl had been dead for some time when she was found," Brodie replied. "There was no mention of a particular smell by those who had examined her."

"Well, then, there are always ways," the chemist announced. "Do you have a match, Mr. Brodie?"

A match?

Brodie and I exchanged a glance. That seemed an unusual request.

"Aye," Brodie replied. Reaching into his pocket, he retrieved the tin of matches he usually carried. He handed it to Mr. Brimley.

"You might want to stand away," the chemist cautioned. "If I'm correct, this could be most exciting."

I might have chosen another word for what he was about to do as Brodie gently pulled me back a distance from the counter.

Mr. Brimley deposited the residue that he'd scraped from the front of the Amelia Mainwaring's gown into a metal bowl.

Brodie pulled me farther back as Mr. Brimley struck a match and dropped it into the bowl.

The explosion burned brightly and sent a cloud of pungent fumes into the air. Mr. Brimley smiled with satisfaction.

"Just as I suspected— ether."

"Ether?" I remarked with more than a little surprise.

The chemist nodded. "That might explain the minimal bruising about the neck that you mentioned, Mr. Brodie."

"Aye, it didna seem that the marks were severe enough to overcome the young woman," Brodie replied. "Even though the physician stated that her neck was broken, that being the cause of death."

"Most interesting," Mr. Brimley replied as he washed his hands. "My guess would be that ether was used to drug the young woman and render her unconscious..."

"And the marks we saw might then have been enough to complete the act," Brodie added.

Mr. Brimley nodded. "There would undoubtedly have been no resistance from the victim."

"How much strength would it have taken then?" I asked.

Mr. Brimley shook his head as he dried his hands. "From what you tell me about the young woman, she was fairly small," he shrugged.

"It would have taken very little force. A strong lad would have no difficulty and could easily see the matter done."

But to what purpose? Drug her and then strangle her? To say that we now had more questions than answers was an understatement.

"There is another matter," I replied as I recovered from that bit of information. I retrieved the note paper I had taken from Amelia Mainwaring's desk.

"I thought there might be," Mr. Brimley said with a smile that now gave him the appearance of a kindly grandfather, and I was reminded that appearances could be most deceiving.

Not that Mr. Brimley was unkind, quite the opposite.

However, no grandfather I knew from my aunt's circle of friends went about making diagrams of eyeballs in jars or dropping matches onto deadly substances with the delight of a child.

"Is there some way to see what was written on the note that left these impressions?" I asked, handing him the piece of Amelia Mainwaring's stationery.

He put on his glasses that gave him that bug-like appearance and studied the note paper.

"I believe I may be of assistance."

He crossed the work area and retrieved a jar from among several on a shelf, then returned. It appeared to contain some sort of black powder.

"Potassium nitrate, coal dust, and sulfur," he revealed. "Sticks to the hands, and paper. It can be quite useful, but one must take care when using it."

I looked at Brodie, most curious.

"Gunpowder," he translated as Mr. Brimley laid the note paper on the counter then opened the jar and sprinkled some of the mixture on it.

"There is just enough residue of oil," he continued to explain and winked at me, then grinned. "Ah, yes, there it is. You can see the letters quite clearly."

I stared at the message that emerged.

I cannot do this. You understand. If you are my friend, you must tell no one.

I looked up at Brodie. "Cannot do what?"

"It would seem that the young woman was of a different mind about something," he replied.

I read the message again. *If you are my friend...*

"According to Sir John, she was to have met Beatrice Ainsley-Townsend at Harrods for shopping, then a stay-over was planned."

Brodie nodded. "It might be useful to speak with Miss Ainsley-Townsend."

Four

WITH THE NECESSITY of timeliness in the case we had now undertaken, I sent round a message to the Ainsley-Townsend residence as soon as we returned to the office on the Strand.

Brodie had suggested that it might be better received if the message came from me and although I was not personally acquainted with the family, I used my formal title as it was very likely to be acknowledged rather than a request from a former inspector with the Metropolitan Police.

It was a method we had used in the past, and within the hour we had a response from Lady Ainsley-Townsend that she and her daughter were available after luncheon.

We arrived promptly at two o'clock of the afternoon at the townhouse at Waverly Square, the residence of the Ainsley-Townsend family through the holiday season before they left for their country home north of London for the rest of the winter.

I introduced Brodie as a longtime acquaintance of the family; not precisely a lie as he had been acquainted with my aunt ever since the matter of my Greek adventure. I spared them the details which might have been a bit off-putting for members of polite society.

"Your request seemed most urgent, Lady Forsythe," Beatrice's mother commented as we awaited the serving of tea that she had requested.

Tea was one of those strange thoroughly English afflictions as Brodie put it. For myself, I much preferred coffee and he was of the same habit. Unless of course there was some of my aunt's Old Lodge whisky to be added. As a bit of refreshment, of course. However, we both graciously accepted tea in the matter of moving the meeting along to the reason we were there.

During the ride from the Strand I had thought how best to begin the conversation. Death was never easy no matter the circumstances, and by the information we did have, Lady Ainsley-Townsend's daughter was a very close acquaintance of Amelia Mainwaring. Close enough that it appeared the two may have conspired in some adventure with the cancelled stay-over and that note sent round.

Beatrice had joined us as well. She favored her mother with her dark hair, her features almost an exact copy and most attractive with hazel eyes, no doubt from her father who was not present.

Having thought of several ways to approach the topic, I decided to keep the matter as simple as possible. Tea had been served and I waited until the maid had left the room. I directed our inquiry to Lady Ainsley-Townsend.

"We are here on behalf of Sir John and Lady Mainwaring," I began. "And their daughter, Amelia." I caught the slight flicker of response in Beatrice's eyes.

"It seems that the two young ladies had planned an afternoon of shopping and then a stay-over."

"That is correct," Lady Ainsley-Townsend replied. "It was cancelled at the last minute. What has that to do with your request to meet with Beatrice?"

"There has been an... accident," I explained. It seemed the gentlest way to inform them what had happened.

"What sort of accident?" Beatrice replied.

I thought the meeting might be ended as I explained the few details I had decided to share.

"There has to be some mistake," Beatrice replied, her face suddenly pale. "I spoke with her only the day before. I cannot believe it. This is impossible."

Brodie gently assured her there was no mistake. There were quite naturally tears, and her mother, equally upset, immediately insisted that we leave.

"No," Beatrice spoke up. "If I can help in any way... For Amelia."

Her voice trembled, but there was a strength there that I much admired.

"She sent you a message, asking that you tell no one. It seems that she had perhaps made other plans," I suggested.

She looked at me with more than a little surprise.

"What note? What other plans?" Lady Ainsley-Townsend asked. She turned to her daughter. "You said nothing of this."

"Amelia asked that I not tell anyone..." Beatrice replied. "You must understand, she was my friend. I wanted to help her, as I knew she would help me."

"You knew of her plans."

"She was so very happy..."

Difficult as it was, Beatrice told us the reason Amelia Mainwaring had cancelled their planned shopping and stay-over, a ruse for Amelia to leave her parents' home without suspicion.

Then, the hastily written note Amelia had sent round afterward that Mr. Brimley had been able to retrieve from Amelia's stationery, and the reason, explained by Beatrice— Captain William Mathison of the Royal Fusiliers.

They had met some months before at a charity event for war wounded who had returned from India. After Captain Mathison was released from medical, he had contacted Amelia and they had discreetly met several times even as arrangements were made for Amelia to marry someone else.

It was complicated and not all that unusual. As the second

son from a prominent family, Captain Mathison had chosen a military career, an honorable enough choice but hardly one that was acceptable to Sir John Mainwaring for his daughter.

Still, Amelia and Captain Mathison continued to meet, and he had proposed. With the formal announcement of her betrothal to another to be made at the holiday season and Captain Mathison soon to return to India, they planned to wed in secret and then leave together. Amelia was to meet him the night she disappeared.

"I have the original note..." Beatrice explained.

I accompanied her to her rooms where she gave me the note in question. There I noticed a photograph very similar to the one in Amelia Mainwaring's room.

"We belonged to the same club," she explained. "That photograph was taken the year before. I had a nasty cold at the time and couldn't attend.

"It was taken by Mr. Paul Laughton, photographer to the Queen. Amelia had it made for me. I didn't know that it would be the last photograph of her," she added through more tears.

We took our leave shortly after. Beatrice reached out and took my hand.

"You will find who did this?"

I had assured her that we would.

~

"We need to meet with Captain Mathison," Brodie said, breaking the somber silence inside the coach upon leaving. "He must be told. And he may be able to provide information that could be useful."

I could only imagine the man must be quite beside himself since Amelia had not met him as arranged, and now to learn that she was dead?

"Of course," I replied.

It would be far too cruel to learn what had happened from the newspapers. And there were questions Brodie wanted to ask with a natural suspicion of everyone until a case was finally resolved.

It was not often that I had second thoughts about the inquiries we made. Most often the outcome far outweighed any difficulty— a child found, a murder solved that brought solace to a grieving family, a criminal at last made to account for what he had done. But that was not the present situation.

I could only feel a deep sadness for the news we would take to Captain Mathison, that he would carry back with him to India as he returned to his duties there.

"I can call on him alone if ye want to remain at the office," Brodie said then, his hand covering mine.

He seemed to sense my thoughts. It wasn't the first time.

With anyone else I would have replied that they were being ridiculous and then told them to sod off. But this was Brodie.

I curled my hand into his warm one, and shook my head.

The Mathison family lived in Hampstead. However in making several inquiries, Brodie was able to learn that after leaving medical care, Captain Mathison had taken up temporary lodging at the private residence of an old schoolmate near Park Lane before returning to India.

Now, Captain Mathison leaned heavily on his cane as he stared out at the street beyond the windows of the formal parlor. He had been formally released from Netley Hospital a few weeks earlier, the site where military wounded were treated.

He was tall, slender, with neatly trimmed brown hair and a brown mustache, and dressed in the formal uniform of the Royal Fusiliers. He cut a dashing figure in spite of the pallor on his face, no doubt from the prolonged hospital stay. I could see how a young woman might be taken with him.

His manner upon our arrival had been curious at first, as Brodie had not gone into details in the note he sent round. Then there was shock and disbelief. I had feared the man might suffer a relapse of some sort, but as they say, he had *soldiered on*.

"I made inquiries every place I could think where she might have gone, except with the family, of course, not wanting to alarm them or betray anything if..." he explained haltingly, then continued, "if she perhaps had a change of heart.

"I was aware of her parents' choice for a match," he added. "Certainly not a soldier or a military posting to some place far away. However, she was excited and most determined to set off and live our own life together. I admired that about her.

"When there was no word, I had determined to send round a note. If she had changed her mind, she might at least respond." He took a deep breath, as if gathering himself.

"She was so looking forward to traveling to India..."

He paused again. "I could never imagine something like this, and that perhaps I am to blame for agreeing to meet her alone that afternoon. If I had not, she might..."

I heard the unspoken, that she might still be alive. It was natural to blame himself.

His voice had gone very quiet. "I purchased her ring two days ago."

"Ye could not have known what would happen," Brodie told him. "But ye may be able to help us now."

Captain Mathison turned then. He forced back the emotions that briefly appeared on his face. He nodded.

Brodie had questions, of course.

Had Amelia spoken of any recent difficulty with her family? Had they perhaps learned of their relationship? Was there a threat of some kind, or the mention of someone following her when she was out and about? And then, was there any concern or misgivings on her part as she planned to join him?

The answer was the same to each one. There was nothing to indicate either by word or manner that she was upset by anything. Point of fact, she was excited and had made the arrangements for them to meet that last time before leaving London together.

"Was there any reason for her to go to Hyde Park?" I asked.

He shook his head. "Is that where she was... When it happened?"

I nodded. There was no reason, I thought, to mention the photograph or show it to him.

"We were to meet at St. James Square, and then continue on to the Grosvenor," he said then. "She spoke of having a family— she thought four children was a good number. If only..." he paused, leaning heavily once more on his cane.

"I am to report soon to the Port of Southampton for my return to India. I cannot leave without knowing... I will pay for your services, sir." He continued in spite of the emotion in his voice. "Whatever it may take to find the person responsible for this."

It was well into the evening when we left Captain Mathison. We were nearest to Mayfair and Brodie directed the driver there.

He had been there before, but not since we had returned from the north.

Prior to that he had stayed over at the townhouse for one reason or another. But that had changed since our return. I told myself that it was undoubtedly my imagination that something seemed changed about Brodie as well.

We had not discussed his unexpected proposal at the conclusion of that previous case. He had simply said that he would give me time.

Did I have misgivings?

After living on my own the past few years, with my travels and now the success of my writing career, why did I hesitate?

Was I afraid that marriage would prevent me from those things? That he might object to my travels, or the time I needed to write my next novel? An endeavor that required what I referred to as my *alone time*, where the ideas simmered and then bubbled to the surface as my character Emma Fortescue encountered her different adventures?

Those did not seem to be obstacles. Brodie had always fully supported my novel writing endeavors and even inquired from time-to-time what *Miss Emma* was up to at the present with what seemed to be genuine interest.

As for my travels, I had admittedly seen most of the places that I had an interest in with the exception of Australia, which would have required several months absence.

I had to admit that with my participation in our inquiry cases I had far less interest in traveling.

I found the cases fascinating and exciting, not to mention challenging. It was most satisfying to help solve a crime. And if I was completely honest about it, the dangerous part of it all was thrilling as well. Not to mention that they provided new challenges for the protagonist of my novels which seemed to appeal to my readers.

Of course, Brodie had commented more than once that I had to be completely deranged to have such interest. He'd never known a woman with a penchant for solving crime, and warned there would come a time when a case might be too difficult or the business of murder might become overwhelming.

Then there was the fact that we were from completely different backgrounds. Yet, there had never been anyone who understood me the way Brodie did, in spite of his grousing and occasional explosions of temper over something I had done. Most usually that involved some risk on my part.

I knew that he valued my ideas and thoughts as no one ever had, even as he challenged me. He made me think beyond the obvious for some deeper hidden clue or motive. And then... There was that other part of our relationship.

"Scandal!" Those of proper society undoubtedly whispered and lectured their virginal daughters against such things— such things being an affair with a man not of their class. I didn't give a fig what they thought, or said.

Our arrangement— relationship, association, or whatever one chose to call it, I thought suited us both very well. At least it had seemed to.

What then had changed? What had possessed Brodie to propose? And the way he had proposed? What was the reason that I had hesitated?

However, I knew the reason he had proposed. He had told me that day at Old Lodge.

"I want more..."

And, the truth was, when I chose to admit it, *I* wanted more. What then was the reason that I hesitated?

I knew the answer if I was completely honest with myself. It was there in the memory of finding my father dead in the stables as a child. Then, the aftermath of the scandal, the lies, his infidelity, and my determination even at that young age that I would never let such a man into my life. Even as I knew that Brodie was not the same.

There was more, of course. More that I had mentioned before, the things that I knew were important and that a man obviously wanted— family. Most particularly, I was certain it was important for a man who had lost the only family he knew when he was just a young boy.

Why couldn't things remain as they had been?

With a parting word, Brodie paid the driver after we arrived in Mayfair.

Mrs. Ryan, my housekeeper, had supper waiting, one of her specialties— traditional Irish stew that she had often made for my aunt. It was her own version that included a good amount of dark beer, perfect on a crisp autumn evening with the threat of rain.

She had prepared it in the past and Brodie had complimented her by consuming two servings at the time. That, in spite of the fact he had teased her it was an Irish concoction after all, but he assured her that he would forgive her for that.

To say that she was quite taken with him was an understatement. I was certain it had everything to do with the fact that she rarely had anyone else to cook for. When I was working on one of my novels, meals were often quite simple and taken in the front parlor as I worked.

"It has been a while since you were here last, Mr. Brodie," she greeted him now as we entered the foyer just as the rain set in.

"Aye, well, there have been other matters that needed my attention," he replied, and left it at that as he gave her his hat and coat.

"I knew you would be here tonight, of course," she continued in that faint Irish brogue. "We Irish have our ways, you know— the wee-folk out and about, particularly this time of the year. Knew it was going to rain, as well."

"It's never wise to doubt the *wee folk*," he replied, humoring her.

Not that it would have been difficult to determine that it might rain, I thought, as their conversation went right around me as if I was not there. A look out the window would have certainly revealed that.

"And I've made my cherry chip cake for dessert," she added as she turned toward the kitchen. "Though you must save a portion to take back with you for Mr. Cavendish. And there was a telegram received today, miss," she added. "Sent round from the messenger office. I put it on the desk, along with other mail."

Her Irish stew was a success, although neither of us seemed to have much appetite. Brodie was thoughtful, barely touching his bowl while I idly pushed around the food in mine, contemplating what we'd learned earlier that day.

"Amelia and Captain Mathison didn't know each other very long," I pointed out, in an attempt at conversation. "Only a few months as he recovered from his injuries.

"It is possible that there was some disagreement between them," I continued. "Perhaps all was not as well as he or her friend, Beatrice, would have us believe. An argument that he chose not to tell us about that might cast suspicion?"

"Perhaps," Brodie replied as he sat back in the chair.

One word over the last hour. It was like trying to take a bone away from the hound. However, I supposed it was progress.

"They were to have met alone," I added what we had been told. "It would have been easy enough, I suppose. A disagreement that got out of hand, tempers flared and all that."

I realized that it was all conjecture of course. "And then in a fit of rage when she rejected him... Motive, means and opportunity?" I reminded him.

"Perhaps."

There was that *bone* again.

I laid my napkin aside and rose from the table. Brodie did as well and followed me into the front parlor where I usually did my writing when working on one of my novels.

"What about the photographs that were sent?" I asked as I reached for the bottle of Old Lodge whisky and poured us each a dram. "Captain Mathison certainly had the opportunity and the means," I pointed out, the tension at the back of my neck turning into a full-blown headache. "And he knew where she would be."

"They were to have met at St. James Square," Brodie pointed out. "What reason would he have had then to go to Hyde Park, a man in his condition with the injuries he has? And the motive?" Brodie inquired.

He was right of course as far as their arrangement to meet at St. James Park and then continue on to the Grosvenor Hotel, quite near to the rail station that would take them to the Port of Southampton or some other location where they might have married.

"A crime of passion?" I suggested. "What if she decided against the marriage for some reason?"

"She had made plans to leave London," Brodie pointed out. "By her friend's words, she seemed verra happy. And there is the second photograph. What would be the reason to send it to the family?"

He did have a way of seeing every aspect of a situation. It was one of the things I admired, the way his thoughts worked. Of course, I realized it no doubt came from his early life on the streets and his work with some of the worst criminals.

"A man scorned? Or perhaps blackmail?" I suggested. "He may have intended to demand money from her family."

"Blackmail perhaps if she had only been abducted. However, she was obviously already dead in the second photograph," he replied.

"Then you're certain he didn't kill her?"

"He had purchased the ring just two days prior," he reminded me what Captain Mathison had shared with us. "That is not the act of a man who has changed his mind," he added.

That dark gaze met mine. For a moment it seemed we were no longer speaking of the case. I went to the side table and refilled his glass.

"What then would be the purpose for someone to murder her? And what about the photographs?"

"The first one might have been a warning," he replied.

"And the second photograph?" I asked. "What reason would someone have to take it and send it to the family? A warning? How could it be a warning when the young woman was already dead?"

"You're forgetting the note that was sent with it," he reminded me.

And then there were three...

I hadn't forgotten. "You believe there will be more."

"The girl's murder was not the act of a spurned lover. And by that note, it was not random," Brodie replied.

A sudden chill ran down my spine with thoughts of the Whitechapel murders. As much as the police had been able to determine, they were thought to be the acts of some deranged person against prostitutes in the East End. No one had as yet been arrested according to the daily newspapers.

But this, a murder of a young woman in a far different part of London? And that note that had been sent with that second photograph that there might be more?

It most certainly did seem that Amelia Mainwaring's death was not due to a broken affair, but something far more ominous.

The conversation ended as Mrs. Ryan appeared at the entrance to the parlor.

"Excuse me. The driver you requested has arrived, Mr. Brodie" she announced.

Requested?

I tried to ignore the disappointment as Brodie tossed back the contents of the tumbler and set it on the table.

"Thank ye kindly, Mrs. Ryan, and for supper as well," he replied.

"Good evening, then, Mr. Brodie. And this for Mr. Cavendish," she added, handing him a small paperboard box of the sort used in the bakery shops.

He thanked her once more as he went to the entrance and retrieved his coat. He tucked the slender box that undoubtedly held some of her cherry chip cake inside the large pocket of his coat.

"The constables on the watch that serve Hyde Park might have seen something that night that could be useful," he commented. "I will have Dooley make inquiries."

Mr. Dooley had served with Brodie when they were both with the MP and had assisted in our inquiries in the past.

It was a place start.

At a glance through the entry windows, I saw the rain that had threatened earlier had set in and was now coming down quite heavily. The driver with his rig on the curb huddled atop the coach.

"The photographs might reveal something as well," he continued in that logical, very circumspect way as he pulled on his gloves. "It's important to find out who took them."

"Of course." I had accompanied him to the entryway. "The weather is dreadful, the streets may very well be impassable," I pointed out, as they often were due to flooding when the winter weather set in. "You might stay the night and return to the office in the morning," I suggested in an attempt to ignore the persistent feeling that something had very definitely changed between us.

It certainly wasn't as if he hadn't stayed over before. That dark gaze met mine again.

"I thank ye, but it would not be proper." He angled a look in the direction of the kitchen where Mrs. Ryan had disappeared after delivering the cake.

Proper? It wasn't as if she wasn't aware of our *arrangement*. There had only been one comment that had quite surprised me at the time.

"It's about time you had a man in your life," she had announced. "Even if he is a Scot. He is a fine figure of a man."

But it was more than that, and I knew it.

"Wait..."

He shook his head. It was there in that dark gaze, what he had told me at Old Lodge, and I knew it— he wanted more.

"Good night, Mikaela."

He left without a backwards glance and climbed into the coach, the lanterns atop barely visible, then disappearing altogether as the driver made the turn at the end of the street.

Bloody hell!

I returned to the front parlor and poured myself another dram. Bloody stubborn Scot, I thought. He wanted more and had made that perfectly clear.

What did I want?

If I was completely honest with myself, I knew the answer.

Impossible, I argued as I crossed the parlor to my desk. The stack of mail was there with that telegram on top.

At a glance at the envelope, it was marked the evening before from Edinburgh. It had been sent from the telegraph office at the Waverley Hotel, and it was from Munro.

He had returned to Edinburgh at the conclusion of our last case after I had made arrangements for Lily, the girl who had assisted us, to come to London.

She was intelligent, brave, and resilient, and I liked her very much. In some ways, she reminded me of myself at that age. And no minor part of it all, she had been instrumental in getting us both out of a very difficult situation.

After all was said and done, I had made a proposition— no pun intended in spite of the fact that she was employed as a maid to the ladies at a brothel at the time.

The brothel had been forced to relocate after a fire and it seemed that the *ladies* employed there might also be forced to relocate. Lily was between prospects as it were, with Madame sadly informing that she could not afford to continue to pay her until business resumed.

I had discussed my proposal with Brodie— something unusual for me. I usually made a decision on my own and then set out to make it happen. I wasn't in the habit of discussing something with anyone else before setting off.

However, I valued his opinion and his thoughts on the matter. He had reminded me that taking on a fourteen-year-old girl might have its challenges, especially one set in her ways and quite accustomed to surviving on her own. I assured him that I was well aware of that.

I thought on balance that the positive aspects outweighed the negative ones. And the truth was that I cared very much what happened to her. Most particularly as a result of my acquaintance with Brodie.

Not that I hadn't been aware of the poverty in certain parts of London before our association. However, the past many months had exposed me to those harsh truths, not to mention Brodie's own background.

Quite simply, I cared about the girl and couldn't bear to see Lily left to that same fate, perhaps forced to work in a brothel with the other *ladies* in order to survive. But for how long before some misfortune befell her— disease, the brutality of such a profession, or the crime that seemed to be part of it?

What would her fate be?

And so, I had made that proposal— that she come to

London, put an honest effort into her education, all the while she would be paid a monthly stipend that would be put into an account and held for her once she had completed that education.

Of course, there were details to be worked out— where she would live, who would be responsible for her, how to be accountable for seeing that she received that education. However, my proposal had been met with less than enthusiasm.

"I know how to read and write," she had protested before we left Edinburgh.

That is if her version of writing could even be deciphered. As for reading, that was limited to messages the ladies at the brothel had sent back and forth with one request or another. Not precisely a formal education that might open doors in the future, other than the doors of a whorehouse.

And she had not been in favor of funds kept for her, instead of paid directly to her.

"What if I need something? How am I to pay for it?" she had asked.

I had explained that anything she needed would be provided if the request was reasonable.

"Sounds more like being sent off to prison," she had replied.

I had then explained what the future might look like with her previous work versus the opportunities that might be available to her if she agreed to my proposal.

"Ye have to remember, livin' as she has with what she sees daily on the streets, it's hard to put her trust in a stranger's word," Brodie had reminded me.

He knew something about that.

I had been disappointed but realized that it had to be her choice. Then, the week before, she had sent a telegram all on her own— resourceful girl that she was.

She was willing to try my proposal, as long as I agreed that she could leave at any time if she chose to do so.

Negotiations— resourceful indeed.

I had agreed and Munro had agreed to return to Edinburgh to

make the arrangements and return with her— if she had not changed her mind again.

It appeared that she had not. They were to arrive in London that next afternoon!

I thought then of Brodie, with his warnings and no small amount of caution about taking the girl on.

"She reminds me of yerself," he said. "A bit headstrong. Ye might think on that."

At the time I preferred to think that somewhat strong-willed, even prickly manner was a result of what she had been through, with no family, forced to survive by her own wits. Very much like someone else I knew.

I had to admit that I was very much excited for her and this new beginning.

Five

"YOU'RE A MITE PREOCCUPIED THIS MORNING," Mrs. Ryan commented with a glance at the contents of the coffee carafe on my desk. "And that's three cups of coffee already. Bad night, was it?" she added.

I knew well enough from being raised in my aunt's household with her army of servants, there was little that went unnoticed. And that seemed very much the case this morning.

"And you've not touched your breakfast either," she added.

It was a bit like being scolded by one's mother I imagined, or nanny as it were. She was right of course, and that made it all the more aggravating.

"Will you be going out then? Perhaps to Mr. Brodie's office?"

As I said, very little went unnoticed.

"We have that new case. I need to make some inquiries." And there was now the matter of Lily who was to arrive with Munro on the afternoon train.

Brodie was to contact Mr. Dooley regarding anyone else who might have been seen in Hyde Park the night Amelia Mainwaring was murdered, while I would undertake the task of trying to find who might have taken those photographs.

"I have a telephone call I need to make," I added. My sister might be a place to start.

Linnie was well connected into the London art scene with her own pieces being shown since returning to her work with Mr. Warren's encouragement. She was also at present quite involved in the preparations for our aunt's All Hallows party.

The important question was— who had taken those photographs? The actual murderer? Or someone else?

Was it a professional photographer? The same man who had taken the photograph of the four women? What then was the motive? Some slight on the part of the Mainwaring family? Perhaps against Sir John for some reason? But that did not explain the note that was sent with that second photograph.

While it seemed unlikely that the murder was linked to something involving Sir John, it was not a possibility to be ignored.

The photographs had been of a very high quality, much like what one would see in a photographer's studio or on display in a gallery.

There was someone else who might be able to assist regarding those photographs— Lucy Penworth, who had once worked for the London Times and was now employed with Alex Sinclair of the Special Services— part of a group that operated beyond the usual boundaries of the police or the military in particularly sensitive matters on behalf of the Crown.

Lucy might very well have some thoughts regarding those photographs and those who provided photographs for the newspaper.

It would take a good portion of the day, and it would be hours before I would have a chance to go to the office on the Strand.

For now, the case was most important, particularly considering that note.

My call to my sister's residence revealed that she was not there. She had already departed for the Grosvenor Hotel and the party that was planned at week's end.

However, I was able to speak with Lucy Penworth at the offices of the Special Services. The matter was too serious for a lengthy telephone conversation, and we made arrangements to meet in an hour.

I pushed away from my desk.

"We will be having a guest." I thought I might as well prepare Mrs. Ryan for Lily's arrival.

"Mr. Brodie?" she inquired.

Apparently not, considering his departure the evening before.

"A young lady from Edinburgh." How best to explain this as far as was needed? "An acquaintance from our last inquiry case, I've invited here. She will be arriving this afternoon. She'll be staying for a while."

Mrs. Ryan's eyebrows had disappeared into her hairline. I rarely had guests, other than Brodie, due to my need for privacy when working on my novels.

In truth, it was a surprise to both Lily and myself as she had seemed most insistent that education and the prospect of a better life seemed boring, and *not for her*, having to say yessir and yes ma'am all the time.

As she had explained it, the ladies treated her nice— most of the time, and whenever the brothel might re-open, Madame could pay her again, and she might have the opportunity to meet a *nice fella*. As if nice, available *fellas* appeared all the time among the clientele at a brothel.

Mrs. Ryan's eyebrows were still among the missing.

"A young lady, miss?"

Even as she said it, I realized that might be a bit of a stretch of the imagination. However, if Lily had chosen to take up my offer, then I was going to do my part. Once I figured out what that was going to be.

I would be seeing my aunt no doubt when I went to Sussex Square. I would inquire about tutors and private school, along with other things that went along with sponsoring a young girl.

"The second bedroom will need to be prepared," I replied as I put my notebook in my bag for my meeting with Lucy Penworth.

I dearly loved Mrs. Ryan. Other than my great aunt, she was undoubtedly as close to a mother as anyone might be to me. More particularly after the loss of her own daughter.

"Of course, miss."

Her eyebrows still hadn't made an appearance.

Lucy had agreed to meet me for luncheon at a tavern near the Tower where the offices of the Special Services were located. I had explained that I needed her assistance with a matter regarding a new inquiry case.

As she had described it, it was almost impossible to have a private conversation at the offices at the Tower.

"Everything is very hush, hush, with others listening all the time," she had explained in that brief telephone conversation earlier.

She had arrived ahead at the Anchor and Bell, and waved from the table nearest the back as I entered.

I received the usual round of stares from the mostly male customers— not unusual as most pubs and taverns rarely saw a woman beyond the hired help. However, Lucy seemed quite comfortable and greeted me with a smile.

"I thought it best to meet here. They know me well enough," she explained. "The cook's wife is from Warsaw, and they serve a devilish good piroshky with soured cream."

I had first experienced the meat turnovers on my travel to Budapest. As the saying goes when in Budapest... or the Anchor and Bell tavern in London.

The piroshky was marvelous.

"So," I began. "How are you getting on with everyone at the Special Services Agency?"

She had not been working there long, having first worked at

the London Times. And of course there was Alex Sinclair, also with the agency. She lit up like a Christmas tree on Christmas Day each time she spoke of him.

"He really is quite brilliant, you know. What with his computing machines and other inventions for the agency."

I fully expected additional glowing comments.

"Quite well actually," she said. "I'm given information-gathering tasks. Many of them are boring facts much like working for the newspaper. But on occasion there is something important." She was thoughtful.

"Did you know that the Tower is haunted?" she asked.

In fact, I did, or at least knew of the rumors of haunting— that of Anne Boleyn, Catherine Howard, and other unfortunate souls who had their heads lopped off or were drawn and quartered over the centuries.

"The guards at the Tower swear they've seen them when on night duty; headless spirits wandering about the place, and no one will go into the White Tower at night."

Templeton would have loved it. I could imagine her and Wills searching for those ghosts— a somewhat eccentric actress accompanied by her own ghost or spirit, as it were, in the form of the bard himself, William Shakespeare. At least to hear her tell it.

I was not particularly a believer in such things, although my aunt claimed that one of our ancestors had a habit of wandering about Sussex Square which was almost four hundred years old. She had never actually seen the spirit however there were often things missing that then reappeared in a different place.

Not that it might have been forgetfulness on my aunt's part. It was not something I was about to suggest. In other things she was sharp as a blade. However, on a past visit, Templeton had been quite intrigued after a supper party one night.

She had taken herself off into the older part of the manor that included a garret and tower— nothing on the order of the Tower of London, but a tower nonetheless. One that I had always been quite intrigued by.

Templeton had returned quite excited after an absence of some time.

"I've seen him!" she declared. "Just as I was leaving the Tower. He's quite tall. He approached me and appeared to be speaking about something. Then..." The next part had my aunt most interested.

"I would swear that if the man was alive, he was about to seduce me! Most insistent. I barely escaped..."

"Oh my," my aunt exclaimed. "He did have quite the reputation with the ladies. There was more than one duel fought over the matter. William de Lancey as I recall."

Which of course might have explained his demise.

"Not at all," my aunt had informed us. "He fell in love with a young lady, they wed, and had eight children."

I had been quite surprised by that.

"According to family stories he was absolutely besotted with the young lady. It had to do with curling of the toes. No woman had ever refused his advances or excited him so. He was my two times great grandfather."

That explained a great deal, not to mention the toe curling. Not that I shared all of that with Lucy Penworth. I supposed everyone was entitled to their family stories, and ghosts.

"Tell me about this new inquiry," Lucy asked now, eyes sparkling with interest. As a former writer for the Times, she loved a good story.

However, in the interest of our clients, Sir John and Lady Mainwaring, I was careful not to reveal any details of this most dreadful case.

I explained that I needed to know about photographers the newspaper used for their articles and profiles, including the crime section of the daily.

"If you're in need of a photographer, I would imagine that one of the portrait photographers might be a better choice. Surely you know of several," she replied.

This was a portrait of a different sort considering the two photographs the Mainwaring's had received.

"However, if you need someone for the usual sort found in the dailies, there are a handful who provide photographs from time to time for the newspaper."

She proceeded to give me the names of two of the most frequent providers of photographs.

"Jefferson Talbot provides most of the photographs for the Metropolitan Police and their crime sheet in the dailies. He's a bit of an odd duck. According to Mr. Lowry at the Times, Talbot was the one who took photographs of the women who were murdered over in Whitechapel.

"As I said," she continued. "He's very odd. Can you imagine wanting to take such photographs?"

Most interesting, I thought. And according to the newspapers, the murderer had never been caught.

"And the other photographer?" I asked.

"That would be Davey Morris. He's a young chap, more of a street photographer. However he's quite good and he happened to take the photograph of that poor woman over at Covent Garden not too long ago who was crushed to death under that toff's coach.

"The only way the police would have known who did it was because of that photograph. Not that it was any consolation to her family. There wasn't anyone going to speak up about someone of the upper class running someone over, if you know what I mean— no offense intended, Miss Forsythe."

"None taken," I assured her.

However, I understood perfectly well. It was something I was frequently reminded of, that class division that I found to be quite disgusting after all my travels, not to mention something that had been an obstacle more than once in past inquiries— things that a *lady* shouldn't be part of, or trouble herself with.

"Do you know where both of them might be found?" I asked.

"Talbot has a studio. I can get the location from the clerk at the Times. As for Davey, he can usually be found on the street, at Piccadilly Circus. He takes a lot of photographs and sells street scenes for the photo viewers that everyone has now— a lot of monuments and the royal palace; fancies himself a crime photographer."

I appreciated the information and wrote it down in my notebook. Most interesting about Mr. Talbot, I thought. Not that it meant anything, yet. Still it was a place to start.

Lucy promised to send round the address for Talbot's studio as soon as she received it.

I was familiar with street photographers who might be found on any street corner out and about London. Box cameras were increasingly popular. Along with the modern invention of film, the fascination for stereopticons and public photo viewers at two pence for things people might never see, the fascination had only grown.

My friend, Theodora Templeton, quite famous on the stage, regularly had photographs taken in costume for her latest play. She had heard there was a time in the not-too-distant future when plays might be put on film and then shown to a larger audience.

But for now, a young woman had been murdered and then posed in a most hideous and horrifying way, then had a photograph taken of her. Not the first time in my association with Brodie I wondered what sort of cruel or insane person might do that.

Lucy and I parted with just enough time for me to hire a cab for King's Cross Station where Munro was to arrive with Lily on the afternoon train from Edinburgh.

The station with those arched entrances filled several blocks of London that all lead into the main station, its enormous dome overhead covered in glass and metal panels.

Shops, restaurants, and the ticket hall dominated one side of the imposing structure while overhead boards announced arrivals and departures of the trains.

King's Cross Station was once the largest station in London, with more than fourteen tracks and a series of tunnels that connected various parts of England and beyond. They much reminded me of a basket of snakes I had once seen in India slithering all about in a dozen different directions.

This time of the afternoon the station was filled with arriving and departing passengers who crowded the platforms. I found the platform that Munro and I had departed from some weeks earlier in time for the arrival of the train from Edinburgh.

Mr. Munro is easily recognized as he stands a great deal taller than many men, most usually wearing black trousers, with a black coat over, his gaze always watchful in that same way as Brodie, an instinct that came from living on the streets.

He managed my aunt's estates and occasionally assisted in our inquiry cases, as he had in our previous one.

He had strong if handsome features, a piercing blue gaze, with hair as black as a raven's wing, and he was particularly skillful with a knife for protection— also acquired on the streets of their youth.

He had taught me the skill that might be useful for a young woman on her own before I departed for my first adventure, and had presented me with a blade that I still carried inside my boot. As he told me then, one could never be certain about other people. I had certainly learned that in my partnership with Brodie. I was most grateful.

"Miss Forsythe!"

I turned and spotted Munro among the sea of passengers that streamed toward me, an unusual expression on his face that was most usually void of any discernible expression at all.

However, it was not Munro who had called out but the person he wrestled and kept a firm hold on beside him.

Lily finally managed to free herself and dashed forward. When she reached me, she flung her arms around me, cheeks flushed, dark eyes sparkling with excitement, her hat was askew, and her hair had come undone.

"Oh, pardon!" she said then, looking up at me. "I didn't mean to..."

"It's quite all right," I replied as she was obviously very excited about arriving in London.

"Lord, I never seen anything like this..." she exclaimed in a voice that drew the attention of others as they passed by.

"I mean, I seen parts of Edinburgh but nothin' like this. And the train!" She leaned in close as if to share a secret. "It has leather seats and velvet on the walls. I ain't never seen..."

"Ye have never seen anything like it!" Munro corrected her quite to my surprise.

"That's right. I never seen anything like it."

Munro's gaze rolled skyward. It seemed that it might have been a most interesting journey from Edinburgh.

"And there was food. Can ye imagine, Miss Forsythe? I never seen such..." She corrected herself. "I have never seen such."

Actually, I could imagine as I had the opportunity with Brodie to experience dining aboard the train on our recent return from the North to London.

When I had asked Munro if he would return to Edinburgh to escort Lily to London I had included funds for train fare, his stay at the Waverley Hotel, and more than enough to see that Lily had clothes to wear for the journey other than the maid's uniform from the brothel or the threadbare clothes she was wearing when last I saw her.

He had come up to the mark somewhat in that she now wore a young lady's traveling costume of skirt, shirtwaist and jacket that almost fit her.

I was reminded that at fourteen years, as best Lily could remember, she was at that between age; between child and young woman.

"And there was so much food!" she continued excitedly. "I tried to put some biscuits in this," she held up a lady's reticule. "But Mr. Munro said as how there was plenty of food where I was goin', that I didna need to pinch none."

I looked over at Munro who appeared as if he might be about to have apoplexy, and suggested that we find a coach.

We reached the carriage queue as another party had just arrived. I gave the driver the location for my aunt's residence at Sussex Square as I wanted to speak with my sister regarding gallery photographers she might know of as the two photographs were of excellent quality not usually found in street photographs.

That of course raised all of my questions all over again. Most importantly, for what reason was Amelia Mainwaring killed and then posed in that horrible way? What was the purpose?

Motive, means, and opportunity, I kept turning them over in my mind as I listened to Lily's excited chatter about the trip from Edinburgh.

"Sussex Square?" Munro repeated.

"My sister is there assisting with the planning for the All Hallows party. I need to speak with her about a matter in the new inquiry we've undertaken."

And it seemed as good a time as any to introduce Lily to both Linnie and my aunt.

She chatted on about her adventure traveling from Edinburgh. She had never been on a train before, and most of the other passengers were *quite respectable.*

"They even have a small room if ye need to relieve yerself," she continued. "Mr. Munro explained how everything worked."

She grinned at him. He mumbled something and fixed his gaze out the side window of the coach.

Oh, my. This was certainly going to be an adventure.

Lily grew quieter the closer we came to Sussex Square, her eyes wide as she leaned out of the coach and stared at the estates and manor houses we passed. Her eyes widened even further as the driver turned the coach in through the front gates.

"Crivvens," she exclaimed in thick Scots Gaelic. "Is this the Queen's palace?"

I had never thought of it as such. For my sister and myself, it was our great aunt's home where she took us to live after the death of both our parents. My travels to foreign places had given me a new perspective on how other people lived.

However, I supposed that having lived as Lily had, much the same as Brodie and Munro, and now seeing Sussex Square for the first time, it might seem like a palace.

To be certain it was a several hundred years old *palace* that had only recently— I used the term liberally as it was actually within the last few decades — acquired inside plumbing, electric, and the cursed telephone as my aunt referred to it. And then there was the new addition she was planning. Progress to be certain.

"This is where my aunt lives," I explained as the coach rolled to a stop before the main entrance at Sussex Square. "My sister and I lived here at one time."

"Is yer aunt a duchess?"

I had never really thought of her as that. She had always been our aunt, someone who loved us, cared for us, tolerated our differences, and saw to it that we were educated.

However the title was there. We had been reminded of it at royal affairs even though she waved it off.

"Rubbish and poppycock," as she said on more than one occasion, and once as a foreign dignitary bowed to her, "I do hope that he doesn't split out his pants."

To say that our upbringing was somewhat unusual was an understatement. All in all however, I didn't consider that we turned out badly. I hoped for as much for Lily.

My aunt's head butler greeted us at the entrance. "Good day, Miss Mikaela. As always, it is good to see you."

Beside me, Lily gave him a long look. "He looks like Hoskins at Madame's house."

To which his eyebrows shot upward. "Beg pardon, miss?"

It did seem as if there were to be a great many raised brows when it came to this adventure I had undertaken.

I inquired as to my aunt's whereabouts. However, she called out before he could respond and then appeared from the parlor in what could only be described as full costume considering the rapidly approaching All Hallows party.

"Mikaela! So good to see you, my dear!"

And marvelous to see her as well... If I could actually see her beneath the costume she wore including full make-up and elaborate head piece.

"What do you think?" Aunt Antonia asked, cutting a pirouette in the entrance hall. "Templeton was good enough to send over Mrs. Finch to do my make-up. I think it's quite marvelous."

Elvira Finch was my friend Templeton's dresser and make-up expert for her roles on the stage.

I had one thought— Oh, my!

I should be quite accustomed to such scenes as Linnie and I had grown up with our aunt's... shall we call them, eccentricities which had made everything quite exciting.

After all, this was a woman who had been planning a safari to Africa at the age of eighty-three until she had the misfortune of injuring her ankle— only a temporary delay, she had insisted until she recovered.

Then, found standing on her head afterward to improve circulation and healing of said ankle. Not to mention sneaking into men's private clubs out of curiosity, and attending theater for a play for men only— dressed as a man.

"Most entertaining," she had declared at the time.

I had to agree.

My sister had said more than once that our somewhat unusual childhood had undoubtedly contributed to my desire for adventure.

"You are just like her," Linnie had declared no few number of times.

Now, in addition to the party at the Grosvenor, our aunt was in the midst of planning an addition to Sussex Square manor with the assistance of her architect. My sister had suggested there was more going on there than merely going over the man's drawings.

My thoughts on the matter?

Jolly good! And more power to our aunt if it was true. At her age she should be able to choose her adventures. Africa, of course, and other things...

"Mr. Munro," Aunt Antonia greeted him now. "So good to have you back with us. But you are looking a bit peaked. I hope the trip north was not too strenuous."

"Not at all, ma'am," he replied, which considering his demeanor upon arrival, I considered to be a polite lie. He excused himself and rapidly fled— it was the only word for it, to another part of the house.

"And who might this young lady be?" my aunt inquired.

To say that Lily was equally curious was another understatement as she boldly stared back at my aunt.

It might have been the costume— an elaborate recreation of an 18th century fashion that Marie Antoinette, former unfortunate Queen of France, might have worn including the elaborate powdered headdress —that impressed Lily.

Or it might have been the make-up my aunt wore, complete with a deathly pallor about the eyes and what appeared to be sunken cheeks. Of course no costume of the dead French queen would be complete without the ghastly slash mark about her neck that had been recreated where the guillotine's blade had fallen.

"What are you staring at, child?" my aunt demanded.

"Are ye dead then and still just walkin' about?" Lily boldly asked.

"Oh, marvelous!" my aunt exclaimed, clapping her hands together with obvious delight.

"Just as I planned."

Six

"**YOU ARE MAD, ABSOLUTELY MAD!**" my sister declared as we sat in my aunt's small informal parlor where she had recently had a jungle installed for *practice* as she put it before departing for her African safari— the one that had to be postponed. It had been complete with a monkey that had since been returned to the London Zoo.

"What do you know about raising a child?"

To say that Linnie was quite outspoken in her opinion on the matter was another understatement.

"Experience at having once been one?" I suggested over a glass of the port wine she preferred while our aunt was presently conducting a tour of the house with Lily, who had shown particular interest in the Sword Room.

It contained battle regalia, armor, shields and no small amount of swords of past ancestors. I had loved exploring it as a child.

"Pish tosh!" Linnie replied quite colorfully. "Do you honestly believe that qualifies you to raise a child? And she is hardly a child, but a half-grown young woman!"

"What," I countered, "qualifies anyone to raise child? Most

certainly Aunt Antonia had no practical experience and see how she succeeded." I pointed out.

"Precisely," Linnie replied with a direct look at me.

She took another sip of port while I looked about for a bottle of Old Lodge. We had taken supper with our aunt, that also included Lily.

A memorable experience as our aunt was quite amused by Lily's somewhat lack of table manners and had taken to pointing out the various pieces of silver dinnerware along with the array of China pieces as if it was a grand adventure.

Lily had been quite taken with the education in the finer points of dining.

"Crivvens," she had remarked again. "I was lucky to get a spoon at Madame's," to which Linnie looked as if she might faint.

"Oh, my, how like you," she had commented with a look down the table at me.

And with that validation, I now told my sister, "Precisely!"

"It is possibly not exactly the same," Linnie continued her argument as I found the bottle of Old Lodge and poured a two-finger measurement. I had the feeling I was going to need it.

"We had a governess from the earliest age who instructed us in manners and etiquette... Or attempted to when you had not taken yourself off on your horse or gone adventuring in a hedgerow," she continued.

I had to admit, we had approached our lessons from different points of view.

I simply became bored by it all and devised any method to escape our early lessons in deportment and what was expected of children of our station. What poppycock!

And as for my sister? I dearly loved Linnie, however, we were very different in many ways. Still, I had hope for her considering her... affair with my publisher James Warren as an example. Of course, no one was supposed to know about that.

I downed the whisky and poured another, as the subject of our conversation— Lily, appeared with our aunt.

"Do ye know that yer aunt..." she paused and corrected herself, "her ladyship has a sword that is near a thousand years old?" she commented with great excitement. "Crivvens!" There was that word again. "I canna even imagine a thousand years. But it's a right fine sword. She let me hold it!"

A girl after my own heart, I thought. But I supposed for now the knife Munro had given her would have to do, once she was instructed the best way to use it so as not to injure herself. Swords could come later.

"It's all arranged," our aunt announced, crossing the parlor in full costume with that ghastly make-up.

She grabbed a glass and held it out. I poured. No port wine for our aunt as she plunged on ahead in her usual take-charge manner.

"And Lily is in complete agreement. She shall take your former room, Mikaela. I will make arrangements for a tutor— I believe Marion Abercrombie has someone she will recommend since your tutor is quite past it, or possibly no longer with us.

"It will liven everything up around here," she went on. "I do dislike being bored. After all," she added with a look in my direction. "You have your novels and your inquiry cases with Mr. Brodie. You cannot possibly attend to all the needs of a young girl.

"And she is going to need a new wardrobe. There is now a substantial cut in her skirt. I may have been a bit overenthusiastic with the rapier," she added. "I shall have to contact Mademoiselle."

My aunt's seamstress? I emptied my glass.

It was now Linnie's turn to roll her eyes. "When was this decided?" I asked when I had somewhat recovered.

"It was somewhere between William's sword and the rapier you practiced with at about the same age," our aunt replied. "And she was telling me the most exciting story about your escape from the fire at the brothel in Edinburgh."

"Oh, good heavens!" Linnie exclaimed.

I don't usually discuss aspects of the inquiry cases I undertake with Brodie. But there you are. That particular aspect of the case was out now.

Lily nodded excitedly. "And then we were taken and put in the cobbler's shop at the Vaults."

"Vaults?" Linnie's color had faded several shades. "Whatever are the Vaults?"

"It's an old underground part of Edinburgh," our aunt who was quite well informed, chimed in. "There is an entire part of the city down there. There were clandestine activities, smuggling, prostitution. People actually lived there for quite some time. And apparently a cobbler's shop? Most interesting. You must tell us all about it," she added with a look over at me.

And pigs fly, I thought, according to the old Scottish saying. I did need to speak with Lily about keeping things to herself.

In that way that my aunt has of taking charge, it was all decided. Lily was to remain at Sussex Square for the time being. There she would receive tutoring, a new wardrobe, and an additional education in, as my sister put it afterward, our aunt's most unusual adventures.

"You cannot possibly be considering this arrangement," Linnie had commented in an aside afterward. "The poor girl..."

The *poor girl*, whom my sister knew little about save the story about the brothel and the Vaults, was quite capable of taking care of herself. It was one of those things that my dear sister was lacking in— a greater view of the world around her. Still, I had hope for her.

I have frequently stayed over at Sussex Square for one reason or another in the past. However, as it seemed that my room had been confiscated, I returned to the townhouse at Mayfair.

"Ye're not peeved at me for wantin' to stay?" Lily asked as she accompanied me to the entrance at Sussex Square where I waited for my aunt's driver to bring round the brougham.

Peeved? How could I be when I had experienced the same sort of *between* years as she was about to experience, and had somehow managed to emerge unscathed?

And there was another part of this— the excitement of our aunt's planning for all of it. I had not seen her so enthusiastic in...

Well, not since she had planned to go to Africa on safari.

The truth was, she was getting on in years and if she wanted this in spite of my sister's dire predictions, then I was in favor of the arrangement. After all, I had come out of such an unusual upbringing quite successfully. Aside from my sister's opinion in the matter.

It didn't mean that I wouldn't be a presence in Lily's new life. Quite the contrary, I still would, much like a surrogate mother or *spinster* aunt.

There was that word again.

I had spoken only briefly with Brodie about my plans for Lily. Even though those had been somewhat diverted by my aunt, he would undoubtedly learn of it from Munro.

Mrs. Ryan had everything in order in the extra bedroom when I arrived at the townhouse.

"Where is the young miss?" she inquired.

"She has decided to remain at Sussex Square for the time being. My aunt is most excited about it."

She made the sign of the cross for emphasis. "Saints preserve us."

~

The next day...

From my visit the previous evening, I had the name of the photographer my aunt had commissioned to take photographs of her guests for the All Hallows party the coming evening— Paul Laughton.

My sister was familiar with his work that was frequently on display at the National Portrait Gallery.

He had first presented his early photographs at the Exhibition. Our aunt remembered those early daguerreotypes.

"Marvelous man," our aunt had said in a way that seemed... How shall I say it? Almost intimate?

Our aunt had never married, as she insisted she had never met a man worth giving up her single status for. However, there were rumors of several affairs over the years, not to mention the architect who was currently providing drawings for the expansion of Sussex Square.

"Marvelous man," she had said most recently regarding John Waverly Atherton.

Marvelous seemed to have a most interesting meaning.

Before leaving Mayfair I sent round a message to the studio of Paul Laughton. I had questions about the photographic process that was used on the pictures of Amelia Mainwaring, and there would be little opportunity to speak with him at the party that evening.

"Give me thanks to Mrs. Ryan for the cake she sent with Mr. Brodie," Mr. Cavendish commented as I arrived now at the office on the Strand.

"The hound was most appreciative. Almost took me arm off." He grinned. "I can't afford to lose another limb. That would make things a mite difficult."

Indeed, I thought.

"Is he about?" I inquired, referring to Brodie.

"He went out and about earlier and had me send round a message for Mr. Dooley. A new inquiry case, is it then, miss?" he asked.

"So it seems," I replied, and with very little to go on so far, I thought. Still, I felt a deep sadness and obligation for the Mainwarings.

Admittedly, it certainly wasn't the first time we had taken on a case with very little to go on except a dead body. My sister's case came to mind. Still, we had those two photographs and I was hopeful we might learn something from them.

It also seemed there was little that escaped Mr. Cavendish's attention. Most particularly with the errands he ran for Brodie or myself regarding a case. And to be certain, he had an incredible knowledge of the streets of the East End of London as well as other parts of the city that had proven to be most valuable in past inquiries. The streets were a bit like his own information source, gathered here and there from people he knew.

I liked the man, and it was safe to say that he was much like a partner in our inquiries.

I bent down and scratched the hound's ears, a familiar routine, then climbed the stairs to the office.

My chalkboard across from Brodie's desk, where I usually wrote our clues in a pending case, was glaringly barren. Another indication of the scant information we had at present for the inquiry into Amelia Mainwaring's murder.

Brodie was at his desk holding up the telephone earpiece with an expression reserved for a select few— a mixture of anger with a healthy dose of resentment thrown in for good measure.

"Of course," he bluntly replied and then slammed down the earpiece in a way that I was surprised it didn't shatter. He came out from behind the desk and went to the coat rack.

"We've been summoned to police headquarters," he announced, drawing his umbrella from the stand much like a weapon.

"Summoned?"

"Chief Inspector Abberline has requested our immediate presence."

Abberline.

Now there was a despicable piece of human existence if ever there was one.

I had no liking for the man most particularly after his refusal to inquire into my sister's case. However, Brodie's resentment went farther back, to the time he was an inspector with the MP.

There had been some difficulty— and I gathered that was putting it mildly —over some case Brodie was involved with. There had been an accusation made against Brodie of taking a bribe, to *look the other way* as the case involved someone high placed with the MP.

According to Mr. Dooley who had worked with Brodie, it wasn't true.

"Some of the lads might do such a thing, but not Mr. Brodie," he insisted.

It was Brodie's word against those who made the accusation.

Threatened by the chief inspector when he learned of it, Brodie had been prepared to make known Abberline's involvement in the disappearance of evidence in another case that Brodie had learned about that resulted in charges being dismissed. It was a case of quid pro quo— an advantage traded for something else, as it were.

Confronted with the circumstances of that prior case being made known, Abberline offered a proposition. In exchange for Brodie's silence in the matter of the *missing* evidence he would ignore the alleged bribery charge. However, there was one further stipulation.

Abberline wanted the names of those among the MP who had given Brodie the information about the evidence that had gone missing.

Unwilling to sacrifice any of his fellow constables or inspectors and with that stubborn Scots code of honor that had been well-abused by English authority through the years, Brodie had resigned and left the service of the MP without divulging any names.

According to what Mr. Dooley had explained at the time, "He walked away with his head held high and the admiration of the other lads, and holding a bit of a guarantee against Mr. Abberline taking it to others."

That most certainly explained the chief inspector's attitude in the investigation into my sister's disappearance when I had first hired Brodie to make inquiries.

We reached the sidewalk along the street and Brodie asked Mr. Cavendish to secure a cab.

Brodie's every movement, from putting on his gloves, to the posture of his body spoke of anger.

When a driver arrived, he assisted me into the cab, his handsome features a mask of barely controlled fury. He gave the driver the location of the headquarters of the Metropolitan Police.

"It seems there is a situation that Abberline believes we may have an interest in," Brodie explained the call he had received.

"A disturbing photograph has been received by a member of Parliament. It seems that gentleman is a member of Sir John's private club." He looked over at me then.

Oh, dear. So much for Sir John wanting to keep matters private for the time being as we conducted our investigation. And now another photograph received? And the chief inspector had obviously been brought into the matter.

Abberline kept us waiting for more than an hour at police headquarters before finally asking for us to be escorted into his private office. All the while, Brodie displayed remarkable calm.

It was another part of him that I much admired. Given what I knew about his past with Abberline, I was most certain it would have given Brodie great satisfaction to suggest what Abberline might do with his request. But he did not.

"It's all about power," I commented in the small office where we had been asked to wait upon our arrival. "His power over you."

"Some sort of expert in these matters, are ye?" Brodie replied.

"It's simple enough to see. He knows you, and making you wait after he summoned you is meant to undermine you and put you in your place."

It was then the young constable who had first noted our arrival appeared to let us know that the chief inspector would see us then.

"Oh, dear," I said, rising from my chair. "We have been kept waiting so long... I feel quite faint. Might I have some water?" I asked.

"Why yes! Of course, miss. I will get that right away."

I caught the narrowed glance that Brodie gave me. "Ye don't faint," he commented with a suspicious expression.

"I suppose there is always a first time," I suggested.

"Abberline will be havin' a fit and fallin' in the middle of it to be kept waitin'."

"Will he?" I replied with an innocent expression.

Before Brodie could respond the young constable returned with a pitcher and glass.

"I do apologize, miss," he stammered.

I took several sips of water and smiled up at him.

"Thank you so very much. That is much better. You've been most considerate."

"Are you recovered now, miss?" he anxiously asked.

"Yes, quite all right now." I thought Brodie might split something as he passed his hand over his mouth either to smother a curse, or possibly prevent laughing out loud.

"The chief inspector..." the young man reminded us both.

"Yes, of course. We wouldn't want to keep him waiting," I replied.

I stood and took Brodie's arm for support after my supposed *faintness*.

My good friend, Templeton would have been quite proud.

"If ye'er certain that ye've recovered..." Brodie most definitely struggled to keep a straight face.

Mr. Abberline was standing before the window of his office that faced out onto Whitehall Place, his hands clasped behind him. The constable announced our arrival and the chief inspector turned, most agitated it seemed by the expression on his face.

Ah, yes, I thought. Exactly as I remembered him from that first case regarding my sister's disappearance— thin wispy hair over a glistening head that he sought to disguise by combing what little hair he had over to the side.

He had a sharp beady gaze, mutton-chop whiskers in the current fashion with an attempt at a mustache that matched the thin hair combed over on his head. He was quite short but drew himself up as he turned as if that might increase his height. Or to emphasize his position of authority considering his past with Brodie?

"Yes, yes, of course, Whitherspoon," he snapped at the young constable. "You may leave."

It was disappointing, to say the least, that the man had not changed since that first encounter. He was still full of himself, pompous to the point of arrogance. My opinion had not changed as well.

"Brodie and... Lady Forsythe," Abberline barely acknowledged him in a supercilious tone. However I was more than aware of his acknowledgement of my title.

However, there were times when it gave me a certain advantage. This seemed to be one of them as he looked at me.

"Please be seated, Lady Forsythe."

However... it did seem more of a command than invitation. I chose to remain standing with the hope that the meeting would be brief. Brodie remained standing as well.

"Ye sent for us," Brodie reminded him, which caused Abberline to frown.

"If you please," he insisted in a tone that sounded more like an order than a request. Brodie nodded. I then took the chair across from the desk as he also took a seat.

"You are making inquiries in the matter of a certain young woman's death for Sir John Mainwaring," Abberline began.

Brodie and I exchanged a look. We had only begun to make our inquiries and Sir John had insisted on discretion. Most interesting.

Brodie neither confirmed nor denied the comment.

"Yer call seemed most urgent," he reminded Abberline. "How can I help ye?"

I had to smother back a smile as he most efficiently took the moment away from Abberline. The chief inspector was aware of it as well as he went quite white around the mouth— a favorite saying of my aunt.

"You are aware of Sir John's position."

Brodie merely nodded.

"This is a matter that should have been brought to me." Abberline's voice rose in agitation.

"Sir John insisted that the matter be kept in strictest confidence," Brodie replied.

"The death of his daughter under mysterious circumstances is a police matter!" Abberline fairly shouted.

"In consideration of his position," Brodie emphasized.

A position that outranked Abberline, given Sir John's title, and his very close relationship with certain members of the royal family, I thought.

"We were asked to maintain privacy in the matter for the time being," Brodie clarified.

"Nevertheless, I should have been informed!" Abberline had begun to pace the office on the other side of his desk.

"I would prefer to have you arrested for obstructing the matter!" he threatened Brodie. "However, I have another problem that exceeds what I would very much like and my hands are tied."

I glanced over at Brodie for his reaction, his expression calm, not the least perturbed as he waited for the moment.

"I have been instructed to leave the matter of investigating the case in your hands."

I didn't bother to hide my surprise. Sir Avery Stanton, the head of the Special Services, perhaps? He seemed to know things that others— obviously Abberline —were not privy to.

The chief inspector had returned to the desk. He pushed a portfolio across the desktop toward us.

Brodie opened the folder. Inside was a photograph not unlike the second photograph that Sir John and Lady Mainwaring had received. Except it was not a photograph of Amelia Mainwaring.

It was a photograph of another young woman and she was

posed in the same manner that Amelia Mainwaring had been after she was murdered! And there was a note as well— *And then there were two...*

Abberline appeared as if he might have apoplexy.

"The young woman is Miss Catherine Abbington-Thorpe," he continued. "She is the daughter of—"

"Sir William Abbington-Thorpe," I suggested. I was well aware who her father was from connections through my aunt. "He is counsel to her majesty, the Queen."

"Yes, quite," Abberline replied. "That was delivered to the family last night. Perhaps you can understand the gravity of this matter." This directed at Brodie.

"God knows the reason..." the chief inspector started to say, then appeared to decide against it. "You are to conduct the investigation with all possible haste. Do you understand, Mr. Brodie? And you will keep me informed of everything in the matter."

"Of course," Brodie replied. Considering his history with Abberline, I thought it highly unlikely that he would send daily dispatches to the chief inspector.

Abberline had been told that Brodie was to have charge of the investigation. Considering the two families this now affected, the reasons seemed obvious— no publicity, no scandal, but find the person responsible.

To say that the arrangement rankled was another understatement. However, Abberline was no fool. Those now involved knew other people in high places. If he objected or thwarted Brodie in any way, it appeared that the chief inspector's ambitions might disappear into air.

Oh, my, wouldn't that be dreadful, I thought, as we left Whitehall Place with that new photograph in hand.

"Sir Avery?" I questioned as we found a driver and made the return to the office on the Strand.

"That would be a safe assumption," Brodie replied as he stared out the window of the coach.

Seven

I WAS NOT surprised that Sir Avery agreed to meet with us straight away. It did seem that he was expecting it.

Alex Sinclair joined the meeting, his expression most somber as the head of the Special Services stood and greeted us.

On the whole, I liked Sir Avery. Brodie's opinion, most particularly after our previous case, continued to be... reticent.

"He knows a great many people," I had pointed out on the ride over from the Strand. "He's not full of himself like Abberline, and it's understandable that someone is needed who isn't encumbered by those like Abberline."

"Aye."

And that summed up the total of the conversation to the Tower where the Service had their offices under that stone fortress that had stood over London since the time of William the Conqueror. It somehow seemed appropriate, I thought.

"Good afternoon, Lady Forsythe," Sir Avery greeted me, most congenially. "Brodie."

Oh good heavens! I thought. It was as if the two men were about to square off with each other— or in the very least in Brodie's case —when we now had two clients who had suffered greatly and were very much in need of our services.

"Sir Avery," I took the moment and the conversation. "We met with Chief Inspector Abberline. You were contacted in the matter by Sir William Abbington-Thorpe, and perhaps Sir John Mainwaring?" I suggested.

He nodded. "Please, sit down," he replied. "I will explain."

It was a simple matter in the beginning. Lady Mainwaring had contacted him, a longtime friend of the family— a fact that she had not disclosed to us, about the first photograph the family had received.

Sir Avery had recommended that she contact Brodie and myself. He assured her that we could be trusted to use complete discretion in looking into the matter.

More recently there had been a serious argument between mother and daughter in the matter of the young woman's choice to marry another, which I had already discovered.

As we now were aware, Amelia Mainwaring had taken herself off to meet Captain Mathison but had never arrived at the appointed time and place. The Mainwarings then received that second photograph and the horrifying certainty that their daughter had been murdered.

And now it appeared there was a second, similar murder. Sir Avery studied the photograph that Sir Abbington-Thorpe had received.

Sir William had immediately contacted him in the matter. In the case of his missing daughter, two constables had found her body, positioned much the same as Amelia Mainwaring's body.

"I'm well aware of your... dislike for Abberline," he told Brodie now. "Not unwarranted, I grant you."

"How long have ye known of Miss Thorpe's? Ye should have made us aware of this from the beginning." Brodie snapped.

"Yes, I'm aware of that. Be that as it may, I want you to continue in the matter. I trust your discretion and your ability to see this most delicate matter through."

And not Abberline? Most interesting. I looked over at Brodie.

He said nothing at first and it occurred to me that he might well refuse under the circumstances that involved Abberline.

"I have conditions," he finally said.

"I thought you might," Sir Avery replied.

I listened, fascinated by this verbal sparring of two men who obviously respected each other— to a point, however wanted something from each other.

"I want full authority over Abberline. I will not have him interfering or expecting me to inform him on the progress of the case."

"Granted."

"I want to bring in someone else since it seems we have a most complicated case. I am to have full authority over that person with no interference from anyone, including yerself."

There was one person I thought of that he trusted beyond all others in such matters— Munro.

Sir Avery nodded.

"And I will not have any of yer *other people,* whom I know full well ye employ— spying on me or my associates."

Brodie had suspected that Sholto McQueen from a prior case was spying— as he called it —and then reporting back to Sir Avery regarding Brodie's inquiries in what was a very private matter at the time.

The man's involvement might very well have jeopardized the outcome of the case. Not to mention the lives it might have endangered. And it had gotten him killed in that previous case.

"And the full cooperation of the agency if need be, and without question. If ye canna agree, then we will take our leave," Brodie added.

In the silence that followed, I was fairly certain that Sir Avery wouldn't agree. Brodie gathered his umbrella and abruptly stood.

"Agreed, to all your demands," Sir Avery replied. "With one of my own. You are to keep me apprised of each development in the case."

Brodie nodded.

Sir Avery rose and held out his hand. Brodie did not take it.

"If a man's word canna be trusted, his handshake is nothing more than an insult," he told Sir Avery. "I trust yer word, that ye willna break it."

There was more behind the comment that had me looking over at Sir Avery. "Agreed upon as well, Mr. Brodie."

"What was that about?" I asked as we left the Tower offices of the Special Services Agency.

"That was about giving fair warning to the man."

"You were quite determined. For a moment I thought you might walk away," I commented. That dark gaze met mine.

"There are things that ye must be prepared to walk away from," he admitted.

"But Sir Avery is a man of some influence..." I thought of Brodie's present work in private inquiries and the possibility of advancement with a man like Sir Avery.

He had been appointed directly by the Queen after certain situations and dangerous incidents in the past. It appeared that he answered only to a handful of people very high up, perhaps only to the Queen herself after some nasty business that included an assassination attempt.

I glanced over at the man next to me in the coach. Stubborn to be certain, but the most honorable man I had ever known.

"What is the next step in our case, Mr. Brodie?" I asked.

It was late afternoon when we returned to the office on the Strand with that new photograph and instructions from Sir Avery to find the person or persons responsible.

"We need to speak with the second girl's family as soon as possible," he commented as we entered the office. He set his umbrella in the stand. "And I will ask to see the files the MP has on the Whitechapel murders. I left the MP before that case was opened."

"You believe there may be a connection?"

"It canna hurt to see any evidence they had in the cases along with possible suspects. No stone unturned," he added.

And I wanted very much to speak with Jefferson Talbot, who provided crime scene photos for the crime pages of the Times. An odd duck, Lucy had described him.

Uncertain how he might be contacted, I turned over another stone and sent round a note by messenger to his studio in Stepney.

~

"I've been thinking..."

Actually, I had been doing a great deal of thinking regarding the situation between us. But everything had been quite hectic since returning from Scotland, what with the new case, my aunt's pending party, and now with Lily's arrival.

He had said that he would give me time. What did that mean? A week? A month? Longer?

I did feel that I owed him an answer. There just never seemed to be the right moment...

He looked up with that dark gaze that I found so intriguing and quite stirring, and now with his thoughts obviously on the case before us.

I had rehearsed it several times. "It's just that..."

The telephone rang, that jarring, jangling sound that my great aunt hated after having one installed at Sussex Square. As much as I supported new inventions as they came along, at present I was inclined to agree.

Brodie picked up the earpiece. "Aye, of course." He glanced at the clock on the wall behind me that had been installed after the fire some months before in the course of another case.

"I understand, and thank ye." He set the earpiece back in the cradle.

"Sir William Abbington-Thorpe's representative," he explained. "We have an appointment in one hour with the gentleman and his wife." He abruptly rose from behind the desk and went to the coat rack.

"There was something ye wished to say?" he reminded me.

Now was not the time, I could hardly tell him in the process of going out the door to question a family that had just learned their daughter had been murdered.

I went to the rack and seized my long coat and gathered up my travel bag.

"There will be time later," I replied. I brushed past him and that delicious scent of cinnamon— his alone, that I had become accustomed to, but not without noticing the frown as his dark brows came together.

Coward, that little voice whispered.

The ride across London was most silent.

Sir William and Lady Abbington-Thorpe lived in Kensington, the letters A and T mounted on gates at the entrance to the circular driveway.

"Abbington-Thorpe," Brodie commented. "One would think that one name would be sufficient."

"Usually to make notice of the alliance of two families through marriage," I explained.

"Her ladyship," he added. "Lady Antonia Montgomery-Fraser and yerself as well, Lady Mikaela... Montgomery-Forsythe."

Of course, my aunt had long ago dropped that affectation. I had as well. However, he had me there for just a moment as he hesitated at my name, and for just that moment I wondered what he would say in consideration of that question that loomed between us.

"Another coach," I hastily announced as our driver pulled the team in behind another one.

"Sir William's representative did say that he would attend as well," Brodie explained as we stepped down and made our way to the front entrance where we were promptly greeted by the head butler.

We were shown into the library and introductions were made with Stephen Thorpe, Sir William's legal representative and brother.

"Sir Avery Stanton has recommended you most highly," he commented to Brodie.

"And you as well, Miss Forsythe," he added with obvious curiosity.

"Miss Forsythe is an associate," Brodie explained. "There are often aspects of an inquiry case that require a more refined perspective."

"Yes, of course. I quite understand. Sir William will be joining us momentarily. As you must understand this is a very difficult time. I have spoken extensively with Sir Avery and I'm here merely to give support in the matter."

It was then that Sir William arrived. He was quite stout, short of stature with gray streaked hair and an equally gray face which under the circumstances was to be expected.

"Lady Abbington-Thorpe is indisposed, as I am certain you will understand," Sir William explained.

The questions Brodie asked were much the same as those asked of Amelia Mainwaring's parents:

When had they last seen her? Was there anything different in her demeanor, or something that was bothering her? Was there any communication received with that photograph? Or afterward?

Brodie then asked if there had been any disagreements with Sir William's acquaintances or associates.

"Are you suggesting that it might be someone I know? Retaliation against me for some reason?"

"It is necessary to look at all possibilities," Brodie explained.

"Preposterous!" Sir William explained. Then, "No, of course not!"

To his credit and as I had seen in the past, Brodie remained calm. There was nothing in his manner that suggested otherwise.

"It is imperative William that we all remain as calm as possible in order to find out who is responsible," Stephen Thorpe told his brother.

"What about Lady Abbington-Thorpe?" Brodie then continued. "Would there be anyone she might have encountered, someone who might have a complaint against her family?"

It was obvious that Sir William struggled to maintain his composure. But rather than anger he simply shook his head and replied in a quiet voice, "Not that we're aware of. Her family as well as mine is well respected."

"What about a romantic connection?" Brodie then asked.

"That is most personal. I hardly think that is appropriate..." Sir William started to reply.

I thought of Amelia Mainwaring and the reason she had left her family residence with the excuse of visiting a friend, that had ended quite badly.

Young ladies had been known to object to suitors chosen for them by their families, as I knew only too well. An alliance of names as well as fortunes?

"We realize this is very difficult," I added. "However there may be situations that are perhaps thought to be most agreeable but somehow prove difficult or against one's wishes," I suggested. "A broken engagement, or some slight to a young man or his family."

Sir William shook his head, a calm manner somewhat returned. "Catherine was not betrothed as yet. There had been discussion with another family and she seemed most amenable. I can think of nothing that would cause someone to do this dreadful thing."

Discussions. Oh my, how very thoughtful and caring for a young woman.

"May we know where the young lady's body has been taken?" Brodie then asked, a perfectly natural question and important to our inquiry. However, it had the expected reaction.

"Good heavens, man!" Sir William responded. "What reason...?"

I exchanged a look with Brodie and returned to the conversation.

"There may very well be some clue that could be useful to our investigation. I am certain that you would not want something overlooked, Sir William. And I assure you that all consideration and care will be taken."

He looked very much like a balloon that had suddenly deflated. He looked over at his brother who nodded.

"Yes, of course, I see your point. Are we quite through?"

Brodie thanked him for his time and Sir William excused himself to see to his wife.

His brother provided the name of the family physician who had been called in when the young woman's body was found. Her body had been taken to the physician's private office out of consideration of the family.

I frowned.

In our past inquiry cases and encounters with victims, the class distinction was not lost on me. The poor were taken to a police holding facility and from there most often to a pauper's grave, while those of the upper classes were treated distinctly different with the family notified and private arrangements then made.

I thought of my own choice for such *arrangements*, a flaming Viking send-off much as my aunt had stipulated. No muss, no fuss, ashes and all that.

"Some additional garments will be necessary," I commented thinking of what we had discovered on Amelia Mainwaring's clothing.

"There may be something in the clothing she was wearing at the time, that might provide a clue," Brodie explained. "If ye will be so good as to acquire additional items. Miss Forsythe will provide them to the physician."

"Yes, I understand. Let me speak with my brother. I'm certain that something can be arranged. The family will of course wish to have the necessary funeral garments provided for the laying in period."

Oh, of course, I thought, without saying so. By all means, lay Catherine Abbington-Thorpe out where everyone can parade by, hang black bunting around the mirrors and the front gates. The Vikings had it quite right I thought, but didn't say that aloud either.

Stephen Thorpe excused himself to return quite promptly with Lady Thorpe's personal maid and a wrapped bundle.

"Lady Anne personally selected the garments," the maid announced with reddened eyes, and handed the bundle to me.

"Miss Catherine was such a bright, lively young lady," she said through what was obviously a new round of tears.

We had the physician's name and the location of his private office. Stephen Thorpe had sent along a letter of permission for us to view Catherine Thorpe's body.

I thought the weather quite appropriate as our coach left the Abbington-Thorpe manor in Kensington— ominous with the threat of more rain and an icy cold that had set in. Perfect for viewing dead bodies.

"Did you ever get accustomed to it— the sight of a dead body?" I asked from the gloomy shadows inside the coach.

"Does it become just part of the routine when making inquiries? Facts and details entered into a report? A name, description, all of it then filed away?"

I couldn't see Brodie for the shadows, only the outline of his shoulders and the silhouette of that mane of dark hair. But I could feel that dark gaze.

"Her death was not the first body I ever saw," he eventually replied. I knew who he spoke of— his mother.

"When ye must go about on the streets in places like Edinburgh and London, ye see things; a body in an alley, a lad not much older than meself lyin' in a gutter, starved to death. And things since. It is easy to look away or simply tell yerself that its part of the job."

He paused. "But when it is someone ye care about, ye canna look away. Ye remember that they meant somethin' to ye, or someone else. Whether it's a poor lad lyin' in the gutter for want of a piece of bread or someone with a title, they need for ye to see them and remember."

Perhaps that was the reason for a family to lay out a loved one, so that others would remember.

However, I was still in favor of the Viking ritual. The thought of my bones lying in a casket for the next few hundred years, possibly vandalized by grave robbers as was quite common, was not an appealing thought. Who would remember me two hundred years from now?

"What about a murderer?" I asked.

"There is a reason for them as well," he replied.

Brodie had never seemed particularly religious and as my aunt had once pointed out, he was no saint. But I was not prepared for the answer he gave.

"Aye, there's a reason not to look away from them as well."

"What would that be?"

"In case the Devil needs help identifying them when he comes for their soul."

I did not specifically believe in Heaven or Hell. My spiritual education was somewhat lacking due to the circumstances of my youth and more along the lines of séances and card readings that my aunt had at Sussex Square to broaden our education.

Then of course, there was the occasional visitation by a three-hundred-year-old playwright, courtesy of my friend Templeton, that I was still inclined not to believe.

However, I was not one to leave anything to chance. I was very aware, with all my travels, there was far more that we did not know about our existence, than we did know.

Sir William's physician was cooperative with our examination of the body of Catherine Abbington-Thorpe, most particularly after Brodie mentioned that if the good doctor had any objections he might want to discuss those with Sir Avery Stanton.

The physician's initial hesitation immediately disappeared, if not the look he gave both of us as we stepped into his private examination room.

He provided the cause of death— strangulation, the same manner as Amelia Mainwaring, and informed that he found no other injuries.

In consideration of his somewhat reticent attitude after conducting our own examination of the body, Brodie requested the victim's garments.

"I assure you that my examination was thorough," the good doctor replied, quite offended I thought.

"I am certain that ye have. The request is for other reasons," Brodie responded with a look in my direction.

"The family has agreed and provided additional clothing."

I produced the wrapped garments at which time Dr. Higgins stepped to the door of an adjacent room and summoned an assistant, a dour woman he referred to as Miss Proctor.

She looked at both of us with an owlish expression, then nodded when the doctor informed her of our request.

Polite even in the face of disapproval or outright antagonism, Brodie thanked both Miss Proctor and the doctor for their assistance when the garments Catherine Abbington-Thorpe had worn when she was abducted and then murdered were given to us.

"How do you do it?" I asked as a driver arrived and we set off for Mr. Brimley's shop with the clothes neatly wrapped and deposited into my travel bag.

I had seen it before on several occasions as we made our inquiries in a case. There were undoubtedly more instances that I was not aware of— the disdain of those of a certain class even in a situation where Brodie was called in to assist them in a most difficult situation.

"What is that?" he asked now as we traversed London to the East End and the chemist's shop.

"The way he treated you. The questions he asked even after

he'd been told by Sir William to cooperate with you, and the woman... As if you were some sort of criminal. I wanted to slap her in the face!"

That dark gaze found me in the gathering gloom of the late afternoon inside the coach.

"It's not the first time," he replied. "And, most definitely not the last."

"I know, but you are only trying to help the family and after Sir William had made the request, the doctor still acted as if it the questions you asked were insulting."

"That bothered ye?" Brodie asked.

"Yes!" I replied most adamantly.

"It's because they're afraid."

"Good heavens!" I exclaimed. "Afraid of what?"

"Look about ye," he gestured to the street through the open window of the coach.

"They believe that where they work and live is safe. They need to believe it. When something like the two murders happen, they simply want it all to go away wrapped up in a tidy little package so that they can go on with their lives.

"When we come along and ask questions, it's a reminder that their world is not safe and perhaps they have failed in some way."

I had never thought of it that way. It was a reminder how very different our two worlds were.

"Why do you do it?" I then asked a question I had never asked before.

He didn't reply right away, that dark gaze fastened on some distant point beyond the coach window. Then he turned and looked at me through the growing darkness inside the coach.

"A long time ago, no one cared about a young woman left for dead in a rented room with little food or heat," he eventually replied and I knew it was about his mother.

A ghost of the past, as I'd once heard it called, the things one carries with them.

"And because I can," he added. "Even in this part of London.

I can be a voice for those who canna speak. Why do ye do it, Mikaela Forsythe? For the adventure of it? The excitement? Something for yer next book perhaps?"

There was no criticism in his voice or by his expression, merely a simple question.

My sister had asked that same question more than once. While it was true that I had used some of our cases as the basis for Emma Fortescue's adventures in my books, I knew that it was more than that.

Certainly being shot, held at knifepoint, and very nearly attacked by a pack of dogs was most dangerous. But it wasn't the danger, or the adventure of it.

It was the memory of a young woman's body pulled from the Thames, a young boy from the streets, his body thrown aside like so much garbage, and exposing someone who felt safe and privileged, and committed the most horrible of crimes.

I had not written about any of those. There had been justice for them and it was enough. I hadn't known the reason until this moment, only that it was there inside me.

"Because I can." It was a simple as that.

I caught a glimpse of that dark gaze that softened as Brodie looked at me across the interior of the coach.

"Ye're a rare one, Mikaela Forsythe."

Eight

IT WAS WELL into the evening when we finally returned to the office on the Strand.

There was only a trace of powder that Mr. Brimley was able to find on Catherine Abbington-Thorpe's jacket, no doubt from the way the garments were handled before they were given to us. However, that small trace was enough for the chemist to identify it.

It was a residue of ether, the same that had been found on Amelia Mainwaring's clothes.

But what did it mean? That both young women had been drugged before they were murdered? How was the murderer able to do that without someone seeing something or being aware of it?

I stood before the chalkboard where I had added the information we had in both instances. I had made two columns, one for each murder, and then added the respective clues to each, scant as they were.

I had also taped the photographs that we now had to the board, courtesy of the surgical tape Mr. Brimley had provided.

It really was a most impressive invention, now used in most surgeries, rather than tying one up in layers of bandages. And it was most useful now as I stared at the photographs.

There was something that we were missing, something about those photographs.

The first one I had received some weeks earlier. It showed Amelia Mainwaring in a garden setting, which had seemed some-what strange at the time I received it considering the time of year.

The second photograph received by Sir John and Lady Main-waring had been that ghastly death photo with Amelia posed on a park bench. I had thought it almost arrogant at the time, as if someone— the murderer —was boasting about what he'd done.

We now had two more photographs to add to the board. The first photo of Catherine the family had given me was much the same as the first one received by the Mainwarings, very definitely a garden scene. The second one was another death photograph, taken in an empty coach at some point in time after Catherine Abbington-Thorpe had left the dressmaker's shop.

She had been posed much the same way as Amelia Mainwar-ing, as if she was merely out and about taking a ride in a coach. The Abbington-Thorpes had received that ghastly photograph only hours before they were contacted by the Metropolitan Police.

She had been found by the hapless driver who had returned for his rig and found her body.

Brodie had his name from Abberline. He had been ques-tioned by the chief inspector's people, but Brodie wanted to speak with him again. As I knew only too well, there was often a resent-ment against the Metropolitan Police.

People most often responded to Brodie's inquiries about a certain matter where there was a suspicion against the Metropolitan Police. Through our past inquiries I had learned that it was frequently with good reason.

Brodie and I had shared supper from the Public House across the Strand along with a dram of whisky to warm the chill that seemed to have set in, one that I suspected had more to do with the sad details of the case.

Now Brodie had a fire going in the coal stove and had poured us both another dram as I stood before the chalkboard and stared at the photographs. Most particularly the photographs that had been taken earlier of each young woman.

"What is it?" Brodie asked.

It was amazing how perceptive he was, somehow sensing that I was mulling over some matter. However, I reminded myself it was one of the reasons he was most successful in our inquiry cases. There was another reason that poked its head up at me— that it might just be for other reasons as well, that had to do with our personal relationship. I chose to ignore that for the moment.

"These photographs of Amelia Mainwaring and Catherine Thorpe..."

I chose to shorten her name much of the same opinion as Brodie that two last names were quite aggravating.

"What about them?"

"They're part of the same photograph," I announced what I had suspected and now looked again to make certain of it.

"Yes, most definitely."

Brodie joined me in front of the chalkboard, that gaze narrowed as he, too, stared at the photographs.

"A garden setting with trees in the background," I recounted what Lady Mainwaring had insisted when she first sent me the photograph.

"Here and here," I pointed out the second photograph taken of Catherine Thorpe.

"I thought it somewhat odd that the first one seemed to have been taken during the summer months, and then this one as well," I explained. "I might never have realized it if I hadn't seen the photograph in Amelia Mainwaring's room!" I excitedly announced.

"The two photographs were originally part of one photograph," I added. "You can see by the bushes here and the entrance to the small house." I pointed out the edge of the one photograph. "And then in the background of the photograph taken of Catherine Thorpe!"

"Bushes and a house?" Brodie replied skeptically.

"There's more," I announced.

He looked at me with keen interest, curiosity to be certain, and something else that I liked. Some might have called it approval, but I knew that it was more.

"If you look very closely in the photograph with Catherine Thorpe you can see small flags on poles in the distance," I explained.

"Go on," he replied.

"If you look here you can just see the edge of a racquet in Catherine Thorpe's hand."

"A racquet...?" he looked at me skeptically.

"Lady Mainwaring had been certain the first photograph was taken in their private garden. However, it was now obvious that the photograph was taken in the gardens at Wimbledon, undoubtedly when the two young women were there either about to begin a game of lawn tennis or possibly had just concluded one!"

"Tennis?"

Never let it be said that Brodie used more words, when one word would do.

He did not go on and on about something as some men were wont to do, endlessly bragging or boasting about something or another— something that women were accused of. That bit of wisdom no doubt promoted by a man impressed with himself.

"That would explain the reason the first photographs seemed to have been taken in an earlier part of the year— summer perhaps as neither young woman was wearing a coat with sleeves rolled back."

"I suppose that ye've been to Wimbledon?" he replied then, a full sentence.

"My sister and I were both invited to join a ladies' club that frequently played there. She was never the athletic sort, and I could never see the purpose in chasing around fuzzy little balls."

"Fuzzy little balls?" There was a look in that dark gaze, something very near laughter. I realized then how that sounded.

"I see yer point," he replied.

He burst out laughing then and I thought he might *have a fit and fall in the middle of it*, as I had heard him say on more than one occasion.

He grabbed me and kissed me.

It was not the sort of kiss that usually led to other things, but the sort that barely contained his laughter. I say not usually... "I..." I whispered, his mouth gently brushing mine. I did very much want more.

"Aye?"

He waited and I saw something in that dark gaze, that question that needed to be answered. I hesitated. I was not in the habit of sharing my thoughts about such things—intimate things.

"It's late," he finally said, stepping away. "I'll have the Mudger signal for a cab, and then see ye home."

Late. It most certainly was, in more than one way. I silently cursed myself as he stepped out of the office.

What was wrong with me? Why couldn't I simply accept his proposal? But I knew...

When he returned, I had put on my long coat against the rain and cold of the evening. He seized his coat and then escorted me down the stairs.

"The driver was just heading back to the barn," Mr. Cavendish informed us with a long look at me. "He agreed for one more fare, especially practically across the whole of London."

"Let's be off then," Brodie told him and assisted me into the coach. When he went to give the driver the location of the townhouse, I decided that I really should go to my aunt's residence.

"Sussex Square it is," the driver nodded as Brodie settled himself on the seat across in the coach.

"I suppose I should see how everyone is surviving the arrangement," I commented, pushing back my anger at myself.

Brodie was aware of Lily's arrival and now the slight change of plans for her to reside with my aunt, at least temporarily.

When we had first spoken of bringing her to London he had been most supportive.

"Not every day a young one gets the opportunity to escape the poverty and danger on the streets. As yer ward she will have a chance at life."

As he knew only too well, it was an opportunity that could make an enormous difference in one's life. For certain it was going to be a new adventure for both Lily and myself.

The light from a nearby street lamp fell across the floor of the coach, and the man sitting across from me. His expression, usually something I was quite familiar with, was unreadable. Then a bemused smile.

"I would place a bet that her ladyship has the matter well in hand."

Well in hand— words to remember the next morning as I rose from the bed in what had once been my sister's rooms to the sound of chaos in the hallway beyond. Sounds that included laughter, a string of very colorful curses, and other sounds I hadn't heard in a very long time.

I quickly donned my skirt and shirtwaist— the only clothes I had at present, having slept in my underthings when I returned the night before. Then I opened the door of the outer sitting room that still contained some of my sister's early artistic efforts.

It was as far as I got as I stared at the sight in the hallway.

There was more laughter, another round of curses, then one in particular as the *sight before me*, realized she was not alone.

"Oh, bloody hell!" Lily exclaimed. "I didna know ye was here, miss!"

Indeed.

I had two choices— the first one was to return to the bedroom and attempt to convince myself that it was all a bad dream given the absurd time of the morning with first light just appearing around the edge of the windows.

Or two— face the situation. The situation being, Lily in chain mail armor, dragging an enormous sword behind her.

There was now in the sword room a half suit of body armor with a sword appropriated from the stand beside it. My friend Templeton with her belief in spirits from the beyond would undoubtedly have declared that one of my ancestors was now wandering about in search of his garment and sword.

If one believed in that sort of thing.

"Her ladyship said as how I could wear it for the party, if I could get the damned chain mail on and carry the sword."

Lily was somewhere behind the helm that ancestor had once worn.

"Apologies, miss, for the curses. Her ladyship says as how I need to learn to speak proper. Although, she does curse a bit herself."

I seriously reconsidered choice number one. Then decided it was probably best to assist her as she dragged the sword, before she managed to slice the carpet to shreds.

I grabbed the sword before she managed further damage.

"How do ye do that?" Lily asked as I wielded the sword a safe distance away from her.

"Practice," I replied. Although it was much heavier than I remembered. A pistol was far more efficient, I thought.

"Oh, excellent!" Came from the opposite end of the hall. "Mr. Symons mentioned there was some sort of commotion."

My aunt appeared, having stepped from the lift that she'd had installed and had been using since injuring her ankle some months earlier.

"I see that you managed quite well." This obviously was

meant for Lily as we stood in the hall, the sword now propped before me.

"Good morning, dear," my aunt greeted me.

"Chain mail and a sword for a costume?" I replied, quite taken aback that she would allow such a thing.

"Yes, well it is short notice of course," my aunt replied. "But the child must have something to wear, and the damned things are only gathering dust."

Somewhere in the spirit world, if it existed, our ancestor was either rolling with laughter or plotting revenge. I sincerely hoped it was the former.

"Isn't it a bit over the top?" I suggested. "Lily has only just arrived." Although admittedly I wasn't certain what that had to do with it.

"Over the top?" my aunt replied.

This from a woman who was going to appear at her All Hallows party dressed as Marie Antoinette complete with make-up to give the appearance that she had been beheaded. Quite grisly.

"Good heavens, no, not at all," she replied. "And it does bring back fond memories, don't you think?"

"Did ye wear the armor?" Lily turned to me, eyes sparkling with mischief.

"Briefly." I thought it best to avoid any further details.

"Full armor," my aunt explained. "There are still marks on the wall in the sword room where she practiced with the sword."

"It's only very minor," I attempted to move the conversation past that subject as I noticed Lily's keen interest.

My aunt smiled as she congratulated Lily on having been successful, for the most part, in donning the chain mail and hefting the sword from the mounting stand.

"Do come along, young lady. We'll use the lift— marvelous thing. You would have a devil of a time on the stairs with that sword." She leaned toward me with a mischievous smile as she turned to escort Lily to the lift.

"A bit like the rabbits come home to roost, wouldn't you say?"

"Chickens," I corrected the deliberate reference to some of my earlier exploits.

"Yes, of course dear," she said with a wave of her hand. "Rabbits, chickens— this is going to be such fun. Oh, do remove that frown from your face, Mikaela. It will give you wrinkles."

This from an eighty-five-year-old woman. Perhaps eccentric was a better description.

I had the beginning of a headache.

Needless to say, I arrived back at the office on the Strand quite early after a brief visit to the townhouse for a change of clothes and Mrs. Ryan's sponge cake.

"What are you looking at?" I asked the hound as I arrived, as if I expected a response. He cocked his head and nudged my hand with his nose.

"I do appreciate the sympathy," I told the beast as Brodie referred to him.

Of course it was the smell of the sponge cake that had caught his attention.

"Ye're right early, miss," Mr. Cavendish commented, rolling out from the alcove under the stairs.

"It seemed far safer to come here." I commented.

"A bit of difficulty at Sussex Square?"

Difficulty. Now there was a word. I thought of rabbits and chickens.

"He has a visitor," Mr. Cavendish informed me. "Arrived well before first light. An odd one, I say, going about in the shadows and enough to set the hound off. Talbot was the name as I recall. The hound didn't like 'im and tried to take off a leg before I could call 'im off. But Mr. Brodie has the bloke well in hand."

Jefferson Talbot! The photographer Lucy Penworth said worked for the Times from time to time, and had taken photographs of at least three of the Whitechapel victims.

I wanted very much to speak with him about how the

photographs of Amelia Mainwaring and Catherine Thorpe had been taken. Equally important, I wanted to know his thoughts on who might have done it.

Jefferson Talbot sat in the chair across the desk from Brodie. He was long and lanky and whenever he did stand I was certain that he would very nearly rival Brodie for height. And most interesting, he was dressed in full formal attire including a long-tailed coat. His features were quite thin. Sunken cheeks gave him a gaunt appearance, his prominent jaw covered with a sparse beard.

However, the gaze he turned on me as I entered the office was sharp as a blade, narrowed slightly. But that might have been from the smoke curling about his head from a cigarette in an ivory cigarette holder that he held aloft much like a composer's baton.

Quite a presentation, I thought. And all before nine o'clock of the morning.

Brodie looked up, his eyes narrowed as well, but hardly from cigarette smoke.

"Mr. Talbot has arrived in response to yer inquiry."

I set my umbrella in the stand and removed my coat and neck scarf as Mr. Talbot stood, unfolding himself from the chair. He made a theatrical bow, waving the cigarette before him much like that orchestra leader I had first imagined.

"Good day to you, Miss Forsythe."

We exchanged greetings.

"I was most curious about the note you sent," he then explained.

"It's in the matter of an inquiry case that we've taken," I explained. "I have questions regarding how photographs were taken, most particularly at night and outside of a studio, on the street, or in a park."

"And you thought that I might be able to assist you in some way," he concluded. "Most... ladies," he emphasized. "Are not usually concerned with such things."

"Nevertheless," I replied as Brodie sat at the desk, chin propped on one hand, listening to our exchange with what appeared to be an amused expression.

"You have been recommended as someone with some knowledge in the matter," I continued. "You have provided photographs for the Times newspaper in the past, taken at the scene of crimes.

"Your skill with the camera might provide us with valuable information."

"I would be happy to assist in any way that I can," he replied with a grand flourish of his cigarette.

I took out my notebook, then asked him to explain just how photographs were made. He smiled with another flourish.

"There are two common types, both made with glass plates," he began. "A wet plate negative and a gelatin dry plate. Both are created by a light sensitive chemical fixed to the plate then exposed to light through the camera."

Both glass plate methods could be quite time consuming, according to his description. And quite expensive, he added. He usually reserved that process for families of the upper class, in his studio, or occasionally with a special project.

I thought of the Whitechapel victims and the fact that it appeared those photographs had been taken with minimal light.

"What about photographs taken at night?" I asked.

I saw some vague response in the expression on his face. It might have been amusement, or...?

"You are certainly curious, Miss Forsythe."

"I am merely attempting to understand how it all works."

Again there was that faint almost-not-quite-smile that made me wonder what the man's thoughts might be.

"How might you compensate for the lack of light?" I then asked. "For a photograph taken at night?"

He clenched the ivory cigarette holder between his teeth and spoke around it, his gaze on me quite keen.

"I have used a flash lamp from time to time as warranted."

He then explained how it worked. "A gentleman in Germany

has invented a flash lamp that is merely a narrow trough filled with a chemical mixture. When ignited by the photographer or an assistant there is a small explosion of light. It can be a bit dangerous if the chemicals are not mixed correctly."

"What about box cameras and the use of photographic film?" I then asked.

"You seem to be quite well informed as to the latest processes, Miss Forsythe."

"Merely curious," I replied. "It does seem quite marvelous that most people can now take the most casual of photographs."

He merely nodded. "The work produced is not of the quality that it is with a glass plate. The rolled film must then be processed."

"Would film be suitable for photographs taken at night?"

"It might be done, but there would be a loss of clarity and definition of the subject."

"Where might the film be processed?"

"Most of my brethren in photography have their own place for such things— a dark room if you will, for extracting the glass plates then transferring the image onto photographic paper. It takes some time for the photo to develop.

"Amateurs might develop their own rolled film, however most of them take their work to someone who might be able to assist— a chemist or someone who dabbles in such things."

This last bit of information with noticeable disdain, I thought.

"Do you consider your photographs to be art?" I then asked. He was thoughtful before replying.

"There are times when an opportunity presents itself with a subject that could be considered quite artistic. Some of my colleagues have a small niche in a gallery or a museum where they are allowed to display their work."

"Have you had your work displayed, sir?" I then asked, most curious since he seemed to consider himself quite the artist.

Once again there was that very odd expression.

"I display my own work, Miss Forsythe."

It might have been my imagination, but it seemed that he chose his words most carefully. I wondered what that might mean.

"You have been quite successful," I commented.

He shrugged. "It is not so much a profession as an art. However, if the opportunity is there..."

I showed him the first photograph of Amelia Mainwaring. Did I see a faint reaction?

"A typical photograph that a family might have taken. Most definitely taken with a glass plate camera. See the clarity and definition of the subject? Pleasant looking young woman."

I then showed him the second, additional photograph of Catherine Thorpe.

"Is it possible to make copies of photographs?" I asked.

He picked up that photograph.

"It can be done with a glass plate," he replied. "One simply washes the plate with the solution for the additional copies, blocking out the other subjects." He looked at me then.

"What reason would they want additional copies— that is the question."

Indeed, I thought. I then handed him the second photograph of Amelia Mainwaring received by her parents, posed in that dreadful death pose.

"Ah, a commemorative photograph," he replied.

That was putting a gloss on the situation. But to each his own, I supposed.

"It appears to have been taken at night, the features quite clear with very little light. And no shadows, possibly with a flash lamp. Quite well done. Almost as if..." He smiled as he studied the photograph.

"You were saying?" I prompted him. I could have sworn that he saw something that caught his interest.

"The angle, the tones have been captured in spite of the nature of the photograph," he explained.

I was most curious. "Such as?"

"It was obviously taken straight on the subject, rather than at a downward angle that would have created shadows even with a flash lamp.

"The person taking the photograph would either have to lower the camera and hold it— quite an accomplishment given the weight of a glass plate camera —or to have taken the time to shorten the frame it sits on.

"She's actually quite lovely— the subject," he continued. "Almost as if she was posing."

That was an unsettling observation, since it was obvious the sort of photograph it was.

"Someone you know, perhaps?" he then asked.

"A client."

"Ah, yes, an unexpected death perhaps? A last photograph for the family. And you have been asked to inquire about the circumstances. Nasty business, murder."

That was straight to the point.

"You've taken photographs of victims in the past," I commented, while Brodie continued to sit behind the desk with that quiet demeanor that I knew quite well was anything but quiet, his thoughts churning.

"Three of the victims of the Whitechapel murders."

"Hmmm, yes. An opportunity presented itself. As I said, nasty business, murder. But the subjects were most intriguing." He smiled again, that gaze watching me.

"And it appears the police are no closer to finding the one responsible now as they were then."

Did I detect a hint of amusement at that comment? A glance over at Brodie revealed no reaction whatsoever to that.

I thought of something my sister had once said as we toured the Louvre in Paris several years earlier.

"I've been told that a photographer's work is often recognizable, much like an artist's paintings, very much like a signature," I added. "Do you recognize who might have taken that photograph?"

That smile again. "You are an inquisitive creature, Miss Forsythe. Just so, most of those of my profession have a certain style to their work."

"And yourself, as well," I presumed.

He stood quite suddenly, reached across the desk and snubbed out what was left of his cigarette in the ashtray.

Brodie and I stood as well. It seemed quite obvious that our meeting was at an end.

Talbot placed the ivory holder in the pocket of his coat, then turned to me and seized my hand. He bent low over it and brushed a kiss across the back of my fingers.

"Most... enlightening, Miss Forsythe. You must come to my studio and allow me to take your portrait, to remember you by."

I wasn't at all certain that was how I wanted to be remembered, if at all; propped up in a stand like an umbrella, or sitting quite stiff as rigor mortis set in. I did wonder how they laid out a body for burial that was quite stiff in that position. Another point in favor of my choice for a Viking send off.

He bid us both good day then, and left through the rain that had set in. I couldn't prevent the impression, dressed as he was in most unusual attire for day wear. The formal evening attire with tails reminded me of an undertaker or the characters in Gothic novels that had become quite popular recently.

I looked over at Brodie after Talbot had departed. His experience, on the street with past cases and with the MP, had made him an excellent judge of character.

He often observed details that others missed. And while I had also become a student of human nature on my travels, my abilities were nowhere near his.

"What do you think of Mr. Talbot?" I asked.

"The man seems quite taken with ye."

A bit of Scottish humor there by the expression on his face. I ignored that as I went to the water closet to wash my hands.

"The man is quite... different," Brodie commented after I returned.

Different— now there was a word. I might have used a different one to describe Talbot.

"Do you believe he could have been the photographer who took the photos of Amelia Mainwaring and Catherine Thorpe?" I asked.

"He did seem to have a great deal of knowledge how the photographs might have been taken."

"And what would be the motive?" Brodie asked.

He did have a habit of pointing out a very critical point in the matter.

"Perhaps some sort of animosity toward those of the upper classes?" I suggested.

"He does consider himself to be an artist, one who has been forced to take crime photos," I added. "Something that he perhaps considers beneath him. Much like the speculation about the Whitechapel murderer— that the man who has killed those women has a resentment of women of the lower class."

I came away from the chalkboard where I had made notes from our conversation with Jefferson Talbot.

"I suppose there is always the possibility that he is quite insane." And not someone I would want to meet on a dark and stormy night.

I had visions again of scenes from one of those gothic novels about vampires and creatures of the night lurking about.

That described Jefferson Talbot quite perfectly, someone who appeared to prefer to go out at night and with a penchant for photographing dead bodies...

Nine

THE BELL RANG at the landing, followed by the appearance of Mr. Dooley of the Metropolitan Police.

He was in full uniform and doffed his hat in greeting as he saw me. As opposed to when he worked privately for Brodie, he looked quite official all polished and buttoned up in his uniform.

"Mornin', miss. Mister Brodie. In answer to yer request the chief inspector said as how the records are available in the police docket file at Whitehall Station."

He stretched the collar of his uniform as if uncomfortable.

"I'm to escort ye there and oversee any request ye might have." There was a look that passed between the two men.

The fact that we were to be given access was obviously at Sir Avery Stanton's orders in spite of Abberline's previous obstruction in our inquiry cases.

"Any difficulty with Abberline?" Brodie asked.

"You know the man as well as any," Dooley replied. "There's to be two other constables present at all times as well."

"In case I might lift any evidence from the docket?"

Mr. Dooley relaxed with a shrug of his shoulders. "He would like to see this new case solved. He sees it as his ticket to the Commissioner's office. It's a sore subject, and best watch yer back while ye're there, sir. Just a word of caution. As I said, ye know the man better than most."

Brodie nodded.

It wasn't the first time that he had been thwarted in an investigation— my sister's case came to mind.

He looked over at me. "It might be best that ye not go, if any difficulty should arise," he suggested.

I went to the coat rack and retrieved my long coat against the usual morning rain this time of year.

"You will need someone to take notes, of course," I pointed out.

I made certain that I had my notebook and pen for any information we might find that could be useful to our case.

"I thought that might be your answer. Ye're to behave yerself," he added. "Given yer dislike for Abberline."

"And you as well, Mr. Brodie," I reminded him.

The chief inspector did not disappoint.

He appeared from his office as we arrived at Whitehall Station of the Great Scotland Yard, pompous with that air of superiority toward Brodie.

In consideration of their past association and what I now knew about the difficulties between the two men, I was not surprised.

Amelia Mainwaring's body had been discovered by two constables on the watch. Catherine Thorpe's body had been discovered by the driver of her coach when he returned to his rig after waiting for her to arrive.

Brodie had asked for the driver's name so that he might be questioned. In the meantime, he wanted to speak with the two constables who had found Amelia Mainwaring's body at Hyde Park.

"My office has provided the pertinent information in the

matter," Abberline snapped.

"Nevertheless, yer assistance now for the requested information is most appreciated," Brodie commented quite formally. "As ye well know from experience, there might be some small detail that could be of importance from the constables who were on the watch and discovered the body."

Flattery, and this from a man who detested Abberline, however put the interest of the client and the solution of the crime above that. It seemed to have the desired effect.

"Of course, and Lady Forsythe if I'm not mistaken," Abberline acknowledged me with that supercilious demeanor that I remembered so well. "Still pursuing adventures in crime solving?" he added.

The moment was simply too good to pass up. "Someone has to." I replied.

Abberline's face went from his usual pasty disapproval to white, then flushed red.

"You must be careful, interfering in matters that do not concern you," he finally managed to say.

How was it that in the space of a few hours in the same day, I felt the need to wash.

"A client's need does concern me."

"As I said, Lady Forsythe, you must be careful. You wouldn't want to find yourself in a dangerous situation with no one to assist you."

I have learned several things about Brodie in our association. There are occasions when there is no way of knowing how he might react or what he might say. And most assuredly, the present situation was not where one might want to rock the boat.

As I say, no way of knowing.

"A threat, Mr. Abberline?" he asked in a quiet voice so that only the chief inspector and I heard, Mr. Dooley and the constable at the desk some distance apart.

For his part, Abberline had the audacity, or ignorance, to smile. "Not at all, merely a... concern."

Brodie nodded with incredible calm that much reminded me of Rupert, the hound, before he methodically began to separate a limb from some carcass he had dragged back to the alcove under the office on the Strand.

"There is no need for yer concern," Brodie told him. "Miss Forsythe has no need of protection."

I did appreciate the compliment.

"However, in the event that she should, the person would have to answer to me."

I had never felt that I needed Brodie's assistance or his protection. However, the situation at the Crystal Palace some months previous came to mind after I had been shot. Then, when I took myself off in search of a missing boy and found myself being hunted by men and hounds. More recently I had been trapped in an underground vault. And each time, Brodie was there...

Not that I couldn't have handled each of the situations myself, I thought. And then there was Abberline— obnoxious in the least, arrogant and much like a bug that I would have liked very much to squash.

"Yes, well, I'm certain that your vigilance is very reassuring, Brodie," the chief inspector replied as a clerk arrived to inform him that the room he had requested was available along with the docket files as well as the two constables who had found Amelia Mainwaring's body.

Brodie nodded. "And if I should have an additional request?"

I sensed more that passed between the two men and thought of the costume Lily wanted to wear to my aunt's All Hallows party— chain mail and swords, combatants squared off at each other. An amusing thought, but not far off the mark.

"You have only to ask, of course."

To which a most colorful comment sprang into my mind. Translation? When pigs fly.

"Mr. Timmons will assist in whatever way you need."

With that we were escorted by Mr. Timmons down a hallway adjacent to the front desk and into a small office where the docket file with the report the two constables had made after finding Amelia Mainwaring's body had been laid out.

Along with that were our two guards that were mentioned— the young constable, Mr. Timmons, and another constable who positioned himself just outside the office door. Mr. Timmons nodded sheepishly.

"Most interesting conversation," I commented.

I removed my coat and hat and set both aside then took out my notebook and pen. I looked over as Brodie did the same.

In the past I would have either argued or ignored a comment that anyone would have to answer to him for me. I was not in the habit of needing anyone to fight my battles for me.

Most certainly there had never been anyone, not even my father the short time he was part of mine and Linnie's lives. And the truth was that if anyone tried to hurt her, they had to answer to *me*.

This was something quite new for me. Oddly enough I didn't feel the need to argue the point with him.

"If you don't mind, sir," Constable Timmons said somewhat hesitantly as he approached the desk.

"The chief inspector said I was to remain if you should need anything more."

"I would like to speak to the constables who found her body," Brodie informed him.

"Mr. Abberline said this was all we were to provide sir. Beggin' yer pardon."

I looked over at Brodie.

"Thank ye, Timmons. I'll be certain to let ye know if there is anything else," he replied.

The constable leaned in close. "You should know that I don't agree with some of the chief inspector's ways... Mr. Handley neither." He angled a look through the door at the constable there, our second guard if we should become unruly or break any laws.

"He said as how he worked with you before and respected you. We're just followin' orders."

"Quite all right, Timmons," Brodie replied. "I understand."

Timmons then took up his post inside the door to make certain that we didn't pinch any of the files.

We spent the next hour, going over the docket that contained the report turned in by the two constables who had discovered Amelia Mainwaring's body in Hyde Park.

"Constables McElroy and Browne made their usual rounds," Brodie read from the docket.

"At four o'clock of the afternoon there was the usual carriageway and foot traffic in the park. Then again two hours later with nothing unusual or suspicious noted; a good many people had already left. At a quarter past eight of the evening, on their next pass by, they discovered a young woman sitting on the park bench."

"Amelia Mainwaring."

"Aye. They stated that it seemed odd that time of the night, especially considering the way she was dressed, in fine clothes but no coat even though it was quite cold. Not what one usually sees, a woman out by herself that time of the evening unless it's for another purpose."

Another purpose— as in prostitution, I thought.

He continued to read the report the constables had turned in after finding her body.

"The young woman made no response when they approached her. Upon speaking with her, it was determined that she was in fact dead. A van was called for and the body was transported to the police holding facility. That was just after ten o'clock of the evening. The report ends there."

Brodie fanned through additional pages. "There is a statement from the person at the holding facility where the body was received. Upon their observation it was noted that she was young, and identification determined by a card on her person with information then passed to the supervisor of the night."

"Is that all?" I asked. "The daughter of a person of Sir John's position is found dead and there is only a brief report?"

"The men are instructed to keep to the facts," he pointed out. "They're not encouraged to make any additional statements. That is for the inspector making his investigation. It is noted that the case was turned over to Inspector Mayhew."

"Do you know him?" It seemed a logical question considering his time with the MP, and even young Mr. Timmons knew of Brodie's past association.

He closed the file and pushed it across the desk top, obviously frustrated that there was nothing revealed in the report that might provide us with more information.

"It might help to speak with Mr. Mayhew and the two constables who found her body," I suggested. "Could there be something they might have forgotten to put in the report? Something that didn't seem unusual at the time? Possibly Mr. Mayhew may have some thoughts in the matter."

"It's possible. Things get overlooked in the moment— the usual sort of things a man sees on his watch." He looked past me to Timmons and our other *guard*.

"That could be tricky, since our 'friend' is less than accommodating."

By his comment it was obvious that he spoke of the chief inspector.

"Perhaps Sir Avery can assist," I commented.

Brodie nodded. "Aye."

I had my notes, including the names of the two constables who were on the watch along with the name of Inspector Mayhew who had been assigned the case, even though it was obvious that the chief inspector had been informed that Brodie was to be in charge of the investigation. The man really was quite despicable.

We prepared to leave. Brodie handed the docket file to Timmons.

"Ye might want to make certain nothing is missing from the file," he suggested.

"I trust you, Mr. Brodie," Timmons replied.

"Inspect it nonetheless, for yer own protection and that of the other man as well."

"I see your point, sir," Timmons stammered.

On the street outside the Great Scotland Yard building at Whitehall Place, Brodie summoned a cab.

"Inspector Mayhew?" I asked, knowing how his thoughts worked. "Do you know where he might be found?"

"There are places the men frequent even this time of the day."

"So speaks a man of experience?" I replied.

"I might find him there and it would be more advantageous to question him away from here," Brodie replied. He hesitated. "Not the sort of places where ye should go."

In the past I might have objected to that. However, there were things I needed to do as well. And by each going about our way we might accomplish a great deal more efficiently in the interest of solving the two murders.

"I'll return to the office," I replied. "Not that I'm hesitant about 'those sorts of places,'" I added to make a point. "I need to add the information to the chalkboard, and there is someone I would like to question as well."

I thought of Davey Morris, the street photographer Lucy Penworth had mentioned. He might be able to provide some information about those photographs that could be helpful.

"And then I do need to see how Lily is doing at Sussex Square."

Brodie smiled. "Knowin' the girl, I would be willing to wager that she has the situation well in hand," he replied.

That was what I was concerned about, two equally strong-willed people— my aunt and a young girl from the street with a penchant for chain mail armor and swords.

"A bit like yerself?" he suggested.

"I have no idea what you're talking about," I replied.

. . .

There were no new messages upon my return to the office on the Strand, nor had there been any telephone calls according to Mr. Cavendish who seemed to have excellent hearing.

I had stopped and purchased luncheon at the Public House, then shared my meal with both the hound and Mr. Cavendish. I then set about adding the latest notes to the chalkboard from our visit to Great Scotland Yard.

When I had entered the last of the new information, I stood back and inspected the board and the bits and pieces of information I'd written there. It was like an enormous puzzle where the pieces were scattered about and made no sense.

Odd as he was, the information Jefferson Talbot had provided was useful in helping me to understand how the two photographs of Amelia Mainwaring and Catherine Thorpe might have been taken— a long and laborious process with a glass plate camera.

I had seen them before, monstrous in size, and couldn't imagine how one might have been used to make those photographs. That took me back to the notion of a box camera, or at least one that was more easily moved about. There was something we were missing.

Mr. Cavendish signaled for a cab as I returned to the street after tucking those two photographs into my bag. A driver promptly arrived, and I gave him the location of Piccadilly Circus that Lucy had mentioned.

We arrived at the Circus in good time as the late afternoon traffic congestion had not yet set in. I stepped down from the cab and paid the driver.

I was quite familiar with the Circus that wasn't a circus in the usual sense but a central London thoroughfare in Westminster, that connected Piccadilly leading from the Haymarket and Regent Street, west to Hyde Park that was now sadly part of our investigation.

I had become quite familiar with the "Circus," as it was referred to by longtime London residents during the inquiry case involving my sister. According to city officials there were plans in the making for a tube rail station underground that would supposedly alleviate surface street congestion. The wonders of the modern world.

It also linked the theater district with overhead signage announcing the latest plays at the Empire and Drury Lane featuring my friend, actress Theodora Templeton, and musicals in the British Music Hall.

At the center of the junction of busy streets is a square encircled by street lamps at night. By day the Circus was filled with placards and street signs with a variety of advertising, industrious hawkers, and both aspiring and amateur photographers who set up kiosks eager to take the photographs of those on the street.

And it was here that an ambitious young photographer on the street might be able to take the photograph of some man or woman that would launch his career past selling stereopticon prints for a few pence each.

I eventually found Davey Morris with his camera in the process of taking a photograph of two women who were taking advantage of the break in the weather. One was holding a small dog that was in the process of nipping at her as Davey patiently waited to take the photograph.

He also had a wheeled cart that displayed photographs he had apparently taken previously of street performers, including a mime. There were also photographs that he'd been able to take of actors from the local theaters out and about that included my friend, Templeton.

Not a classic beauty in the sense of some of the other actresses, she had a magnetic personality, as described in the theater section of the newspapers. An intoxicating sensuality even when in a death scene, that drew the attention and adoration of her fans.

Most particularly the men, except perhaps for Mr. Munro, my aunt's manager of her estates, who assisted in our inquiries from time to time and had just returned from Scotland in our previous inquiry.

The fact that they were lovers was one of those well-kept secrets that everyone knew. For herself, Templeton was completely besotted with him. As for Munro? Not quite.

In true Scot's character that I was quite familiar with, it was impossible to know precisely what Munro's depth of feeling might be other than his frequent declarations regarding *that damned woman who speaks to ghosts!*

Of course there was the mural Brodie and I had discovered at Templeton's country home— most revealing, and the first time I had ever known Brodie to be completely speechless. Even myself, quite accustomed to Templeton's eccentricities and affairs— or I should say rumored affairs —had been taken aback. However, I had to admit that the mural was quite an impressive piece of artwork.

"That will be a shilling," Davey told the two women. "And yer photographs will be ready tomorrow, here. Or I can drop off to a delivery service for an additional four pence."

One of the young ladies handed him the coin for the photograph then wrote down her address for the delivery. As they concluded the transaction Davey tipped his hat, then turned to me.

"Good day, miss," he greeted me. "A photograph for yer young man, or husband perhaps?"

Husband. There was that topic again.

He was a pleasant looking young man, somewhat thin, with dark hair that he was constantly pushing back when it fell over his eyes. When he smiled he had the most adorable dimple on one cheek and a direct way of looking at one as if he was already taking the next photograph.

"Some information, if you please," I explained. "I will be happy to pay for your time. I would like very much to know how the photographs are made." I saw the natural hesitance that I often encounter when obtaining information. I introduced myself.

"Lucy Penworth mentioned that you had submitted some

photographs to the Times newspaper and thought you might be able to provide some assistance."

That of course, required the explanation that Lucy was no longer with the Times but was now working for another organization. I didn't go into detail on that one as it was quite obvious that the work of the Agency was kept quite *low profile*, as Sir Avery had explained it.

As the day grew later in the afternoon, Davey's customers were fewer, and he was more than happy to explain the process.

"The film is on a spool inside the camera, rather than using glass plates for one image at a time," he began. "It's quite the innovation that allows me to take several photographs before the film is developed. That usually requires sending the camera to the factory, however I develop my own film," he continued.

He had his own location for that, in the back room of his sister's flat to develop the film and produce the photographs.

"The emulsion on the film produces a negative image. My sister says it stinks the place up like rotten eggs." He laughed at that. "Then when light is shown through the negative onto photo paper it creates an image. Ye can't see it until ye wash it through a chemical bath that causes the image to appear, then a second chemical bath fixes the image. Hang it to dry and there's yer photograph. On a good day around holiday, I will have maybe a couple dozen photos hung up to dry and get to the customers."

At the price I had overheard quoted, actually quite reasonable, that might provide a decent income.

And there was someone by the name of Eastman in the United States who was developing a box camera with different apertures. That of course required an additional explanation.

"It would allow me to set the lens for the proper lighting, particularly out here on the street. This camera is limited to strong daytime light."

That caught my attention.

"So, it wouldn't be successful to take nighttime photos?" I asked.

He shook his head. "The image you wanted to photograph

wouldn't show up. It's the light on the person that the film picks up. But if you had a glass plate camera, it could be possible to take photographs at night with just a small amount of light.

As in the photograph taken of Amelia Mainwaring at Hyde Park for instance?

Or the photograph taken of Catherine Thorpe in that coach in the light from a street lamp that had given her such a ghostly appearance.

I then showed him the two photographs that had obviously been taken at night.

"These photographs were definitely made with glass plate; very clear, and the detail is..." he hesitated. "Both young women look as if..."

I tucked them away before he could speculate further. I had the answer I was looking for.

"I've never known a lady to ask how the photographs are made," he commented. "They don't ask questions, they simply want the photo." He looked at me again with that direct blue gaze.

"You said that Lucy Penworth gave you my name?" he said then.

I could see the wheels of thought turning in his head like one of those perpetual motion machines that Alex Sinclair was working with that he hoped might generate information.

Davey grinned. "She wrote an article for the newspaper about a woman who helped solve the murder of the young woman in the glass box!"

I had read that article as well, quite good actually. That same article had also mentioned Brodie and his inquiry business as well has his former association with the MP.

"It also mentioned that you're the author of those adventure novels with that woman...!"

Clever young man.

"Are you on an investigation now?" he asked, quite excited.

126

I thanked him for the information, without specifically replying to his question, quite aware that Brodie thought discretion was advisable when on a case so as not to jeopardize or endanger anyone.

However, I did purchase the photos of Templeton that I thought would amuse her, along with the extra coin for his time and information.

"I knew it!" Davey exclaimed, apparently taking my non-answer as an answer to his question. "You are her!"

As my friend Templeton would have said, it was time to make my exit.

I had learned a great deal in my conversation with Davey Morris. He was quite knowledgeable, one for detail to be certain. And he had confirmed that the photos of both Amelia Mainwaring and Catherine Thorpe had been taken with a glass plate camera.

That certainly explained the detail and clarity of both young woman's features in those death photos.

I wondered what that aspect might tell us. Was the photographer trying to say something beyond some sort of gruesome penchant for death?

I pondered that as I waved down a coach and gave him the location of my aunt's residence at Sussex Square.

I had not intended to abandon my responsibilities toward Lily after bringing her to London.

At her age, my great aunt was hardly in the position of taking on the raising of a young girl, most particularly one that had spent most of her life on the streets, and the past two years in a brothel.

I was concerned that in spite of my aunt's well-placed intentions and previous experience with myself and my sister, that it was simply too much for her to take on.

It was late of the afternoon when I arrived at Sussex Square, most eager to share what I'd learned with Brodie. I paid the driver and climbed the steps to the entrance of the manor.

Mr. Symons met me at the door, quite disheveled and with a

stricken expression.

"Oh, thank heavens you're here, Miss Mikaela."

I was immediately alarmed not only by his appearance but by that greeting as well. I discarded my coat and thrust it at him as shouts and other dreadful sounds came from the ballroom.

With my adventures, travels to foreign places, and more recently with the inquiry cases I had undertaken with Brodie, there was little that frightened or surprised me.

However, it sounded as if someone was being attacked.

Where was Munro? Where were the rest of the staff?

With my umbrella clutched in both hands I ran toward those sounds...

Ten

THE AUBUSSON CARPET had been rolled back on the floor, the air thick with shouts, taunts, and more than one Scottish curse as my aunt and Lily squared off at each other, rapiers held before them in a stance I was familiar with. They were on the attack.

The two duelists with appropriate attire— a tunic and trousers that looked vaguely familiar, with gloves and face masks, sweat gleaming on their brows and fierce expressions.

There was a slash, then a thrust followed by a chop then deflection, quickly followed by another thrust, the blunted tip of the sword finding its mark.

"Do you yield?" Lily demanded with something very near a giggle.

"Never!" my aunt replied as I stood at the entrance to the ballroom, umbrella in hand, staring at the scene before me.

Silence hung in the air along with what remained of what had been an enormous boxed fern, now a shredded fern, that had survived the parlor and the resident monkey in preparation for my aunt's safari. It was now unrecognizable.

"Marvelous!" my aunt exclaimed now, propping her rapier before her quite expertly. It did seem as if her ankle had fully recovered as she removed her face mask and tucked it under her arm.

"In time, with more lessons you may rival Mikaela, although she is considered quite expert with the blade," she informed her opponent who had removed her face mask as well.

"It was months before all the marks and gouges were repaired in the wood paneling when she took lessons, but very much worth it. I've never worried about her since when off on her adventures..."

It was then my aunt caught sight of me.

"Here you are, dear," she announced. "We've been having such fun."

Hair undone that reminded me of myself, face glistening with unladylike sweat, eyes gleaming, Lily bubbled with excitement.

"Where is Mr. Braithwaite?" I asked.

My aunt smiled at me and patted my cheek as she turned to leave the ballroom, rapier propped over one shoulder.

"Don't frown, dear, it causes wrinkles. There's no cause for concern. Mr. Braithwaite is simply not up to the position.

"After all, unless you've forgotten, you went through three tutors before we found the right one for both you and Lenore." She turned to Lily.

"Come along, dear girl. There is just enough time to change before supper. You will stay over, Mikaela?" she said almost as an afterthought.

"Oh, yes!" Lily added to the invitation. "I want to hear all about yer new case!"

I had not thought to stay over as my former bedchamber had been confiscated for Lily's use. Not that I objected.

As much as I was fond of my housekeeper, for some reason the thought of returning alone to the townhouse was not appealing. And I did want to spend time with Lily even though my aunt had more or less taken her under her wing.

"Of course."

Lily grinned from ear to ear. "And Mr. Brodie as well?"

"I will ring him up," I replied as she raced off toward the stairs.

My sister sailed into the room, perfectly groomed, hair neatly twisted and pinned into place.

"I fear Mr. Braithwaite will never be the same," she commented. "In some ways I felt sorry for the poor man. I don't believe he had ever encountered such a challenge before."

Challenge. That was an interesting word vaguely familiar from my own experience with tutors.

"He declared that Lily is too outspoken, speaks like a guttersnipe, and lacks the most basic of manners, as he fled quite white around the mouth, as your Mr. Brodie would say. He doubts that there's anything that can be done with her," Linnie added. She looked up at me as if another thought had just come to her.

"Do not say it," I warned her.

Her smile deepened. "You cannot help but notice the similarity."

"I don't know what you're talking about." But of course, I did.

"I knew there would be... a period of adjustment," I continued. "Things are quite different here compared to how she lived in Edinburgh."

"I am not certain there is that much adjustment in the world," Linnie declared as we left the ballroom with its fresh nicks and cuts on the wainscoting, and went into the parlor.

"She is very clever," I admitted. "She managed quite well before in a very..." I searched for the right description. "A thriving business environment."

"I believe you are referring to the brothel," Linnie pointed out as she crossed the room and went to the sideboard that contained glasses and a bottle of wine.

Lily had obviously shared some of her adventures with my sister.

"You have to admit that she is completely out of her element.

Have you considered that you may have done her a disfavor?" she asked.

"I considered her chances for survival where she was," I replied with my usual bluntness. "What might the next ten years of her life be like there, or on the streets? And in twenty years, if she lived that long? It is certainly more of a chance than our father gave us."

I caught my sister's sudden change of expression, the sadness there.

I had not meant to bring up unpleasant memories in mentioning our precarious beginning before our aunt took us under her wing.

It was only that I had experienced and remembered far more of that sad beginning of our lives than Linnie. She was younger and I had always tried to protect her from the harsh reality of our father's gambling, the debts, and the other women.

However, to be perfectly honest, Lily did remind me of me.

She was adventuresome, curious, more than a little rebellious, and she was a survivor. And if I could help along the way...

"You're right of course," Linnie eventually replied. "And she does seem to have your strength and courage. I always envied that about you. You are not afraid of anything."

Not precisely true, I thought but didn't say it. There was something I was very much afraid of.

"Perhaps you should pour us a dram of whisky," Linnie suggested, uncharacteristic for someone who preferred sherry.

"I think we're all going to need it for this next adventure. By the way, do you have your costume for the All Hallows party tomorrow night? And what of Mr. Brodie? He will be there, of course."

I didn't have a costume and hadn't the slightest idea about Brodie, although I could well imagine his response to that.

After sharing a dram with my sister and toasting our new adventure, I rang up the office on the Strand. However, there was no answer.

It was possible of course that Brodie's plan to speak with the two constables who had found Amelia Mainwaring's body had taken longer... waiting until they went off their latest shift, or meeting with one or the other at a location away from the police station. And then there was the chief inspector.

Lily was disappointed that Brodie would not be joining us for supper, but brightened at the excuse I made regarding our new case.

"Is it dangerous?" she asked, quite dramatic.

Considering our last adventure together I hoped not, however two young women were now dead and all we had was a scattering of information with no clear direction yet on who might have done it.

I left out the specific details of their deaths and simply told her that it was a simple missing person inquiry, somewhat near the truth as both young women had been missing before their bodies were found.

Her expression fell a bit and I had to admit that it sounded quite boring.

"It involves a photograph that was taken of the young woman before she disappeared."

That piqued her curiosity. "Like them signs of naked women in the Old Town?" she asked.

To say that stopped the conversation at the supper table is an understatement. Linnie's fork clattered down onto her plate and our aunt had the most amused expression on her face.

"I believe it is time for dessert," she announced, eyes watering as she then attempted to keep a straight face.

"Signs with naked women?" Linnie whispered as we retired to the parlor after dessert.

"Only half naked," I replied. "Advertising for..."

"I understand."

After supper concluded, our aunt suggested a game. Not the usual game of whist or backgammon that one might find in other parlors after supper, but a rousing game of poker as our aunt called for a deck of cards.

I had mistakenly taught her the game after my friend, Templeton, returned from a tour of the United States where the game was quite popular. I say mistakenly as my aunt proved to be quite competent.

"Absolutely ruthless," my sister declared after losing ten pounds to her. I did not share how much I had lost since introducing her to the card game.

Lily was equally proficient, picking up quite naturally all the nuances of the game, if there were such things.

At the end of the evening, after a half-dozen hands she had accumulated a considerable stack of the wooden chips while Linnie and I had barely survived.

"I cannot afford this," my sister announced, at which Lily begged for just one more hand.

Linnie conceded. "I might as well continue. What would I do with only three chips?"

While I lost again and our aunt threw in her cards, the last hand seemed to be Linnie's good fortune. I gave her the last of my chips.

She proceeded to consume yet another dram of Old Lodge, quite recklessly I thought, and then whooped with unladylike enthusiasm as she beat Lily's hand and cleared the center of the table of the chips she had won.

"That was quite marvelous. All it takes is a little luck," my sister announced. "It's a shame the chips are not real coins."

Lily winked at me from across the table. Luck indeed.

After our game Aunt Antonia met with Munro about the final details of the forthcoming All Hallows celebration the next evening, and Linnie retired for the night.

Not surprising, Munro refused to wear a costume, while Lily chatted on about the party.

"I never been to nothin' like that before," she exclaimed.

"You have never been to anything like that before," I corrected her.

"That's what I said," she replied with a frown.

I ignored that as she chatted on, eventually wearing herself down with another enormous yawn.

It was very near midnight. However, I reminded myself that in her previous life at the brothel that was usually when her workday began.

After the second yawn, I accompanied her upstairs to my former bedchamber and reminded her to wash and brush her teeth. She hardly saw the reason for that.

"The ladies at the house never brushed their teeth and they had a lot of admirers."

Admirers— the paying sort of course.

I impressed upon her that healthy teeth were far better than gums for eating the toffee chews my aunt kept that she seemed to favor.

After washing and brushing, she donned her nightgown then crawled into bed.

"Tell me more about the inquiry case," she insisted.

Instead of going into further details about the murders, I told her what I had learned about glass plate photography versus film photography. It was not long before I heard light snoring.

I returned to the adjacent sitting room, took out my notebook and recorded the information I'd learned that day. Somewhat boring perhaps, but useful in that it confirmed that the photographs of Amelia Mainwaring and Catherine Thorpe had to have been taken with a glass plate camera.

It was past one o'clock of the morning when I finally set my pen aside. I wondered what new information Brodie might have obtained about the case.

I left the single light on at the writing desk and returned to the bedroom. Lily had curled herself into a tight ball at the edge of the bed and I could only wonder what had served as a bed for her before. Very likely some small niche at the top floor of the brothel.

Even now, asleep, with the full size of the bed, she made herself as small as possible, leaving more than enough room for two.

I removed my skirt and shirtwaist, then slipped in at the other side of the bed.

The break in the weather that afternoon had disappeared, as rain pelted the windows. I had not lit a fire in the fireplace in the sitting room and the bedroom had grown quite cold. Without waking, Lily moved closer.

I pulled the down comforter up over the both of us as she snuggled, childlike, against me.

~

I was wakened the following morning by Lily's excited chatter about the party as she dressed.

"Her ladyship is going as some queen wot got her head chopped off. I seen the make-up. It's bloody wonderful!"

Bloody wonderful. I swung my legs over the edge of the bed.

"She said I could go as a swordsman... I think that's wot she said. Only I canna take the sword with me as it might be dangerous," she chatted on.

She had dressed and shoved her feet into a pair of new boots.

My aunt had the skills and the connections of a field commander when she set her mind to something. In addition to new boots, there were a half-dozen dresses in the wardrobe of the sort appropriate for a young girl, along with a walking skirt and several shirtwaists.

"Miss Lenore said somethin' about her costume. I think she said it was a fox or something like that..."

"A fox?" Most unusual, I thought, as her tastes usually ran toward the mundane— a damsel in distress, some ancient medieval maiden. As a matter of fact, I thought I remembered that she had gone as Maid Marian once with her then husband as

Robin of the Hood— not very authentic considering how Andrew had ended in prison.

"She said it's not real fur but something yer friend's costumer came up with. What about yer costume?" she then asked me.

Oh, dear. It seemed by the hopeful expression on her face that I was indeed going.

"Ye'll need a mask so no one knows who ye are," she continued on. "Her ladyship has hundreds of them and wigs."

I was quite familiar with them as my sister and I had played for hours among the relics of our distant family as children.

In truth, I hadn't thought about going. What with having only returned from the north a few weeks earlier, the new inquiry case, and Lily's arrival, there had been no time to plan.

"And Mr. Brodie?"

She was so excited that I hadn't the heart to tell her that he would most likely have preferred to be shot again rather than attend. He was not up for this sort of thing unless it was in the matter of a case.

There were moments when her streetwise facade slipped, and I was reminded that Lily was in fact barely out of childhood in spite of her too worldly experience. Much like wearing a mask, I thought.

It did seem that even though he wasn't aware of it yet, Brodie *was* going to my aunt's party at the Grosvenor. As for a costume? That seemed highly unlikely.

After we had both dressed, we descended the stairs into a different sort of chaos as my aunt's staff scurried about while others who were to be part of the waitstaff at the Grosvenor Hotel had already departed, including Munro.

My aunt stood in the midst of it all, giving instructions much like Wellington, I imagined, at the Battle of Waterloo. But then I had seen all of it before.

My aunt had taken over the Grosvenor Hotel for staff and guests, and had already sent a coach with her costume and other clothes on ahead. Food was to be prepared by the hotel staff with my aunt's servants assisting.

Templeton was to arrive later in the day along with Mrs. Finch who was in charge of make-up, along with the orchestra, and a variety of other entertainments that my aunt had arranged. Munro and others of my aunt's staff were to see to the security of those attending the party with other hotel guests about.

The only other event that might rival the All Hallows celebration was her Christmas event. I reminded myself of the possibility of leaving the country for that one.

"Crivvens!" Lily exclaimed. "I never seen nothin' like this!"

I smiled to myself as we headed for the kitchen. Get used to it, my dear, I thought.

At the servant's table just off the kitchen, where it was much safer, we helped ourselves to breakfast.

Afterward, Lily insisted that we go up to the Sword Room, so that I might find something to wear to the party.

Together we put together pieces from some long-ago ancestor's wardrobe. It was a hodgepodge of a coat here, pants from some 17th century distant cousin there, and topped off with a sweeping tri-corn hat.

"What do you think?" I asked when we had more or less put it together as best we might. The only thing missing was a saber. The grin that spread across Lily's face told me everything I needed to know.

Afterward, she pleaded for another duel, and I showed her some of the moves I had been taught when in France.

"I never knew a lady could do something' like that," she exclaimed. "Madame always carried a knife in case one of the customers got mean-tempered."

I didn't go into the fact that I also carried a knife, courtesy of Munro when I went off on my first adventure.

"How old is her ladyship?" she had asked me then. She seemed most serious, and her eyes widened as I told her. I saw the dark shadows that followed.

"I never knew anyone that old. No one lives that long."

She didn't yet know my aunt that well.

Her expression sobered. "What will happen when she...?" she started to ask.

I knew the rest of it, of course. I had experienced it myself as a much younger child at the time— the fear that everything might be taken away, that my sister and I might find ourselves out on the street, and for Lily now in a strange city where she didn't know anyone.

"It will happen one day, I suppose," I admitted, I would not gloss things over with her. "However, you have Linnie and myself." Much like a family, I thought.

"And Mr. Brodie too," she added.

There was that.

I then explained that prior to her arrival, my aunt had been planning a safari to Africa.

"She intends to live for at least another twenty years," I assured her. "And I am certain she will accomplish it. She bested you in the duel," I reminded her.

"By then you will be a grown woman and off on your own adventures."

The smile returned. "I was just askin'... Just in case."

I understood only too well— that need to belong, to know that there was someone there... when the nightmares came. Someone you could, perhaps, curl up against in the middle of the night.

We put the swords and other weapons away, and I gathered up the pieces of my costume. When we arrived back downstairs, it appeared that we were alone except for the housekeeper and a handful of servants. Linnie and my aunt had departed for the Grosvenor Hotel.

Lily looked at me expectantly. It seemed there was only one thing to do.

We packed up our costumes to take with us, I requested my aunt's cabriolet coach, and we set off for the office on the Strand.

Not unusual for October 31, even at midday, there were several costumed people on the streets as we passed by. Lily was fascinated, leaning out the coach window and announcing each new goblin or scarecrow we passed, along with someone dressed as an undertaker with a skeleton mask.

"I ain't never seen such things," she exclaimed.

I didn't bother to correct her, as we arrived at the office on the Strand.

"Mornin', miss." Mr. Cavendish greeted me as I stepped down from the coach. "And who might this be?" he asked as Lily stepped down beside me.

After I made the introductions, including Rupert the hound, Lily tugged at my sleeve.

"Is that a costume too?" she asked with a look in Mr. Cavendish's direction. "Where's his legs?"

"I don't need a costume, little miss," he informed her with a grin, obviously having overheard her comment. "And as for me legs, a great big whale had them fer supper. A warning to you."

"Did you kill the whale then?"

"I harpooned 'im and he dove to the bottom of the ocean, never to be seen again."

Oh my, nowhere near the truth, but they were both having far too much delight in the moment.

"Will there be one more for midday meal?" Mr. Cavendish then asked as I turned toward the stairs.

It did seem that Lily would be joining us. I nodded. "Is he about?"

"Since early morn, and presently with Mr. Dooley."

I wondered if there was a new development in the case.

I thanked Mr. Cavendish and led the way to the office at the top of the stairs.

Eleven

BRODIE AND MR. DOOLEY both looked up as we entered the office. There was mild surprise in the expression on Brodie's face while Mr. Dooley nodded a greeting.

"Mornin', Miss Forsythe."

I caught the frown on Lily's face, not surprising considering the establishment where she had worked in Edinburgh.

"Mr. Dooley is a longtime associate of Mr. Brodie," I explained. "They once worked together."

Apparently satisfied with that, the frown was replaced with a cautious smile. "Mr. Dooley." She then went to the chalkboard where I had made my earlier and very meager notes.

"Wot might this be?" she asked as she scanned the few entries I had made.

As I watched she seemed to be attempting to figure out what I'd written, and I realized that she had some ability there.

She attempted the Mainwaring name, more or less with some success then looked over at me.

"Wot is that?"

"It's the name of our client."

"And this?" she pointed to a note I'd made just below Amelia Mainwaring's name. "Dead?"

More than a modicum of reading ability, I realized, or at least enough to get her by on the streets of Edinburgh.

I nodded as I settled the bag with our costumes alongside the desk, and then pulled off my gloves. I caught the look Brodie gave me.

"And this word?" she attempted to sound it out. "Mur... der..."

Hmmm. This was going to be a bit more difficult than I originally thought.

"I need to speak with ye," Brodie said then. He glanced toward the adjacent room as Lily began to chatter about the party that night and the costume that my aunt had provided her.

"I need to be on me way," Mr. Dooley said and then added a parting message to Brodie. "Be careful, sir. He's in a bad temper since the second man you questioned told him about it."

By that description, I had no doubt who he was referring to as I accompanied Brodie into the bedroom. He closed the door.

"Do ye think it wise to bring the lass here?"

"It seemed the better of two possibilities as everyone at Sussex Square had departed for the Grosvenor," I explained. "I didn't care for the idea of simply leaving her with the servants. And we did have quite a good time of it with the costumes," I added.

"Costumes?"

"My aunt's party tonight at the Grosvenor," I reminded.

"Party?"

Oh dear. We were down to communicating with one word at a time. I knew what that meant. As I said, I suspected that he would rather take a bullet than attend.

"She is expecting you to attend," I told him.

"Her ladyship."

Two words. "Lily is expecting it."

"I suppose ye promised that I would go."

"Not precisely."

He made one of those familiar sounds and I thought it best to move the conversation along.

"I had a very productive afternoon." It was always best to keep it to the other matter at hand— our client. "What were you able to learn from your conversation with the two constables?"

"I know what ye're doin'," he replied.

"Apparently something interesting that has Abberline in a fit?"

"Ye can be the most aggravatin' woman..."

"I do try," I then proceeded to tell him what I had learned. As I said, moving the conversation away from any objections about attending the party.

"The photographs very definitely were made with a glass plate camera. That is the reason the images are so clear. That narrows down who was there the night at Hyde Park and then again on the street when the photograph was taken of Catherine Thorpe."

"Are ye quite finished?"

"My aunt has arranged for a photographer to be at the party tonight. It could be useful to speak with him as well and then my sister mentioned a photographic exhibit at the museum," I continued on.

"It is obvious that the photographer is the key to finding out who might have murdered both young women."

"Mikaela..."

There was something in the sound of my name, something low that had me leaning much closer.

"Yes?"

And now... there was a faint creak at the door as it was opened.

"Mr. Cavendish rang the bell at the landing," Lily announced with an amused expression on her face as she poked her head through the opening at the door.

"Fancy that, a bell to announce a delivery. He said it was from the Public House. It smells right fine!"

She disappeared back into the outer office.

"*Fancy that*," Brodie repeated, his mouth brushing mine. I could have sworn there was a grin amidst the dark beard.

I was suddenly starving, and it had nothing to do with luncheon from the Public House.

~

I spent the next hour going over what I'd learned from Davey Morris with Brodie, regarding glass plate photographs as opposed to film photographs.

"Photographs?" Lily remarked with interest. "Is that for your new case?"

She had been studying the board where I'd made my earlier notes. Brodie and I exchanged a look.

From our encounter during the case in Edinburgh I was more than aware of her keenness as well as her maturity, something I would have identified with at the same age. I was careful with my explanation.

"This photograph?" she pointed out the one of Amelia Mainwaring with the second one of Catherine Thorpe.

Perhaps it wasn't a good idea to bring her there. However, what was done was done. It was just a matter of not revealing too much and saving it for later when Brodie and I were alone once more.

I frowned at the expression on his face. He was very definitely enjoying all of this far too much.

"Yes, a photograph of... our client." That seemed the best explanation, just a bit of a stretch of the truth.

"Poor thing, looks like she's dead. I seen pictures like this before in the daily, some important blighter wot got himself runned over by a coach and team of horses, a real stramash. Saw the real thing when it happened. Nasty bit, that. Wouldna even recognized him the way they fixed him up, starin' like that as if he was still alive."

Brodie coughed. He was enjoying this far too much!

. . .

144

Late of the afternoon, with the Strand full of ghosts, goblins, a woman— at least I assumed it was a woman, dressed as Little Bo Peep. It seemed there was little more we would accomplish this day in the matter of our case.

I had made my new notes at the chalkboard with Brodie's information, *to be discussed later*.

Now, I gathered up my bag with my costume as Lily's had gone on ahead with my aunt and sister, and prepared to depart.

"Are ye comin' then, Mr. Brodie?" Lily insisted.

"By all means, Mr. Brodie," I added.

He winced. Lily tucked her arm through his.

"Her ladyship said as how there was gonna be all sorts of entertainment, including someone will be tellin' fortunes, everyone wearin' costumes and masks. Her ladyship is gonna be dressed as some dead queen!"

As I said, I suspected that Brodie would rather be shot on the spot.

"Do come along," I told him.

At the landing below, Mr. Cavendish had joined in the celebration on the street with a pumpkin carved with a wicked expression and a scarf tied about his head. Fancy that, I thought. He looked very much like a pirate!

For his part, Rupert the hound had taken himself off into the alcove and lay there with his head on his paws. It appeared that he was much of the same opinion as Brodie regarding the festivities.

Mr. Cavendish shook his head as he waved down a coach. "The hound has been like that all afternoon. He doesn't like the goblins and ghosts. But I assured 'im there would be plenty of bounty on the street come mornin'." He then let out a sound one might expect of a pirate.

"Aaargh!"

Lily was ecstatic as we climbed aboard the coach for the ride to the Grosvenor, with our driver who was very much in the spirit of things.

He had wrapped a cloak about his head and shoulders leaving

just enough room to peer out the front in order to guide the team and made it seem as if he had no head.

It was on the seat beside him! Or at least a very fine replica of one.

The Grosvenor Hotel was decorated for the occasion, with black streamers and thin wisps of cloth at the entrance as if entering a haunted house covered in cobwebs. Carved pumpkins, a scarecrow, and a mechanical figure dressed as some sort of character out of a Gothic novel also all in black swept its hat from a skeletal head and bowed. Lily giggled.

The ballroom was decorated as well with fake spider webs at the entrance, fires that burned brightly in two fireplaces, and an assortment of staff all in costume as they put the finishing touches to the room. And somewhere in there, a gypsy— in the form of my friend, Templeton —would be reading fortunes for those who dared.

Given her profession as an actress and the variety of costumes she wore for her stage performances I could only imagine how she might present herself for the evening.

Munro appeared in the lobby. It seemed that he had been placed in charge of seeing that my aunt's guests were shown to their rooms. His expression, usually a non-expression as befit his position as manager of my aunt's estates and other things, matched Brodie's.

"The place is perfect for pinching valuables from the guests, everyone wearin' masks and costumes."

"Aye," Brodie agreed. "Best keep a watchful eye. I'll speak with the hotel staff. Perhaps Sir Avery can be prevailed upon to assist." And he was off.

Munro escorted us to our rooms, on the same floor with my aunt and sister who had arrived earlier. My aunt was in the ball-room overseeing the last of the details for that evening.

"Miss Lenore is with her. The hotel staff will be fortunate to survive," he announced.

"Miss Templeton arrived earlier," he added, quite formal

considering their relationship. "The Finch woman is with her if ye have need of her particular expertise."

Once situated in our rooms I sent a note to Templeton's suite. I supposed if I was to pull off the costume Lily had insisted that I wear, I would need Mrs. Finch's assistance.

She was my friend's dresser and make-up person and had accompanied her around the world for her stage performances. She had also assisted me with a disguise on a previous occasion. She was most talented.

We ate early supper in our room. Linnie joined us. Then it was time to put on our costumes and join the festivities in the hotel ballroom.

"I never did anythin' like this before," Lily excitedly told me.

"You have never done anything like this..." Linnie corrected her.

"That's what I said."

I smothered a smile behind my dinner napkin.

Linnie was already in full costume as Mrs. Finch arrived. She had just finished with Templeton's make-up and had sent her off to read fortunes as the guests had already begun to arrive.

"Now," the small woman who was no bigger than a flea said, pushing her glasses back up onto her nose.

"What is to be done with you, Miss Forsythe?"

Lily squirmed and fidgeted, constantly going to the window that faced out onto the street below as guests arrived, and describing how they were dressed.

When Mrs. Finch had finished, she stood back like an artist inspecting her latest work of art.

"Aw right!" Lily exclaimed. "All ye need is the wig and yer hat."

Wig, hat, and slippers that were to go along with the rest of the costume. I looked in the full-length mirror.

Oh, my. Elvira Finch had outdone herself. I had to admit it was rather spectacular and could only wonder what Brodie's reaction would be, if he even figured it out.

Together Mrs. Finch and I then helped Lily dress. The chain mail, coif, and gloves had been delivered earlier by my sister. With a few adjustments— Elvira Finch was up to the challenge, Lily emerged as a knight, complete with Montgomery family crest and colors.

She did make quite a stirring sight that would have impressed the first Montgomery ancestor.

Together we navigated our way downstairs to the main ballroom. I could only imagine the sight we created as hotel staff, my aunt's servants and guests made way for a young knight and the pirate who accompanied her.

There were monkeys, witches, ghosts, cats, devils, bats of course, as well as Harlequins, several people draped in black cloaks, and one guest dressed as a skeleton who held out his hand and bowed before the Knight.

Lily bowed her head, as much as she could manage with the weight of the coif and took the offered hand. It immediately came away from the rest of the skeleton and Lily laughed in delight at the disembodied hand she now held.

"He might need it," I suggested with a sound very much like Mr. Cavendish had made. After all, a good pirate always made those sounds, didn't he? "Aaargh!"

The skeleton retrieved his hand and disappeared in the darkened ballroom to seek out another *victim*.

"Oh, Miss Forsythe!" Lily exclaimed. "I never had such a time!"

"Miss Forsythe?" I heard behind us.

I knew that voice. I turned, tipping my head to get a better look through the mask I wore beneath the tricorn pirate's hat.

"Mikaela?" Brodie ventured with just a hint of doubt that was most satisfying.

"Yer fortune or yer life!" I demanded, playing my role to the hilt as Lily wandered off into the crowd.

There was a familiar curse. "I canna leave ye alone for an hour and ye're up to this mischief."

The ballroom was quite dark with only those two roaring fires in the fireplaces, enormous candles in medieval holders spread about the room that gave it an eerie light, jack-o'-lanterns by the dozens, and fake snakes that danced from the heat of the fires and reached out to the guests that passed by.

I took out the dirk that was part of my costume and pressed it against his chest at the same time, I wrapped my other arm around his neck.

"Yer fortune or yer life!" I repeated.

It really was too tempting, with that expression on his face that was half scowl half grin. As if he didn't know whether to curse or burst out laughing. I settled the matter. I kissed him and it was most delicious. A pirate could do that, I thought, as I lingered and took advantage of his surprise.

Oh yes, cinnamon and Brodie. And a pirate with a mustache that came away as he lifted his head.

"Mikaela…?"

I could have sworn there was a curse in there as I stepped back with great fanfare, swept my hat before me, and then placed it once again on my head. I then held out my hand, complete with pirate's jewels— courtesy of my aunt's collection.

"I believe that you have something of mine, sir," I admonished him as I demanded my mustache back.

He handed it to me, and I affixed it once more on my upper lip. He pulled me against him.

"Ye have it wrong way around."

He removed it, kissed me quite thoroughly, then returned the mustache to my upper lip. "At least it's better than the damned mole."

The mole in question, I had worn in a previous disguise and a previous case. I was impressed that he remembered.

I stepped back, bowed once more, when I would have preferred to stay right there.

"Try to stay out of trouble, as difficult as that might be," he said with what appeared very much like a smile as I made another grand flourish and slipped away through the crowd.

I found Templeton in an adjacent room usually set up as a gentleman's smoking room. Tonight it had been transformed into a reading room with heavy velvet drapes on the walls, her table in the middle with three other chairs set around and her cards spread before her. She was appropriately attired as a gypsy fortune teller.

"Please, come, sit at my table. Let me tell your fortune," she said, the act complete with accent, and added, "If you dare."

I sat as she shuffled the cards, then had me choose seven of them. She turned them over one by one until they were all spread before her.

"Ah, yes," she began. "I see a journey to a far place, and a man; a very handsome man, one who will sweep you off your feet." She looked at me then in my make-up and mustache with my wig and hat and full pirate's costume which I was certain hid my identity.

"Good evening, my friend. Have you accepted his proposal?" Templeton smiled. "Your mustache is twitching."

Twitching indeed.

"How do you know?" I demanded.

"I could say that it's in the cards," she replied.

"Bloody hell!" I told her. She gave me that look.

"Wills may have mentioned something about it."

Wills, as in William Shakespeare, her spiritual and theatrical muse. A more than three-hundred-year-old spiritual muse, if one believed in such things. She smiled.

"So it is true."

"I have not accepted, precisely," I replied.

"Coward."

"I beg your pardon?"

"No need to beg, and I won't pardon you."

"You don't know anything..." I stopped.

"You would be a fool to refuse. He is the only man who has ever challenged you, and puts up with your schemes," she eyed my costume on that one. "And most assuredly lights that fire inside you."

"Fire?"

"Or it might have something to do with... I'm getting something." She looked up in triumph.

"Toes!" she exclaimed. "Yes, that's it."

I stood to leave. "Ridiculous."

"As I said... a fool. The man is obviously in love with you."

Or something to that effect, I thought, as I left the *gypsy* to her next client.

Ridiculous! But I knew my friend was right.

There was so much to see and experience; food created especially for the night; an orchestra with goblins and witches swirling about. As the night continued, I caught a glimpse of Sir Knight with a fox— my sister, of course, and a man dressed as a hunter — James Warren. Out to catch the fox?

And then there was my aunt, lovely as Marie Antoinette. Except perhaps for the nasty fake gash across her neck that Elvira Finch had created. She wove her way through her guests sharing a laugh or comment, then eventually arrived beside me.

"Your party is a great success," I complimented her.

"Yes, isn't it. And the dear child does seem to be enjoying herself."

That is if brandishing her wooden sword with much bravado was enjoying herself.

"And you're quite in the spirit, my dear." She laughed at her own little joke.

"You must have your photograph taken and Lily as well. Mr. Laughton is here tonight. He has set up his camera and created a small studio with props, there across the way. He is such a talented man. I had despaired that he might not accept, but there he is."

Marie Antoinette with her severed head patted my arm. "You must take Lily with you. She will be quite excited to have a photograph. Oh, there is my friend Anne. Oh dear, she's worn the same costume as last year."

And she was off in the direction of Anne, who appeared to be the Ghost of Christmas Past, if I remembered correctly from the year before.

I saw Lily once more. The girl was taking great delight in challenging the various ghosts with that fake sword. I crossed the room and hooked my arm through hers.

"My aunt insists on having your photograph taken." I steered her in the direction my aunt had indicated.

It did require navigating through a *grave yard* complete with headstones, and around that mechanical skeleton that seemed to have acquired an admirer.

The sign at the stand outside the alcove draped with a thick curtain announced the photographer, Paul Laughton.

Beyond the curtain there was a flash of light, then a young woman's voice that announced the subject would have their photograph within a matter of days.

The curtain parted and Little Bo Peep along with one of the Harlequins I had seen earlier emerged. Bo Peep giggled as they left, and a young woman appeared.

"You wish to have a photograph taken?" she asked.

Lily looked at me.

"Of course," I replied.

The young woman held the curtain aside and we stepped into the photographer's *studio* that had been set up in the ballroom.

"I never had me picture taken before," Lily excitedly said as the young woman led her to a raised platform with a screen behind it.

"My father stepped away for a few minutes," she explained.

Lily wanted me in the photograph as well, and I joined her with my best imitation of a swashbuckling pirate as I had once read it referred to.

Mr. Laughton had returned by the time his daughter had us positioned for the photograph. He was a slender man with white hair and an equally white complexion— barely any color at all that gave him a bit of a ghostly appearance. He didn't look at all well and coughed several times into his handkerchief.

His daughter approached him. "If you don't feel up to it..."

He shook his head. "I'm quite all right, my dear. After all we have a knight in shining armor," he commented about Lily's costume. "King Arthur, a future king, and a dashing pirate."

It took some time to position us just right. Lily handed me my mustache that had come away.

I fixed it back into place, then there was that flash of powder that had been described to me, the shutter of the camera closed, and we were recorded for all posterity— Lily as King Arthur and myself as a pirate. Two more photographs were taken of Lily as she posed with wooden sword drawn.

I lost my mustache again, somewhere into the darkness of the floor. However, I wasn't about to go crawling about to look for it. Brodie would be pleased, for certain.

When I would have paid for the photographs, the young woman assured me that it was already taken care of by Lady Antonia Montgomery as part of the festivities for the night.

She let us know that the photos would be ready in two days, and they would have them delivered by courier. I provided my aunt's address at Sussex Square.

As we left, a particularly ghastly misshapen character brushed against Lily on his way presumably for a photograph, and I immediately thought of the character in Victor Hugo's novel that I had read while in France. The costume was quite impressive.

The man stared at me. I had to admit it was a bit disconcerting then he pushed past and entered the alcove.

"Jingo!" Lily exclaimed. "Did ye see his costume?"

We stayed the night in rooms provided, after attending the festivities that included *treats* handed out to guests at midnight by hotel staff dressed as ghosts and goblins.

The treats were a variety of candies and fruit in cloth bags that included a half penny to pay the Headless Horseman from the

Legend of Sleepy Hollow. He was lurking at the entrance to the forest tunnel that had been installed on the guest's way to the tables of food that had been set out.

Afterward, as guests began to depart to their rooms or to coaches for those who chose to return home, Brodie escorted us to our room.

Lily was bubbling with excitement over the tunnel, the costumes of the other guests, and the different entertainments that had been provided.

"I ain't never seen nothin' like it," she exclaimed for what had to be the dozenth time as King Arthur led the charge to our room.

To say that my aunt's party was an enormous success was an understatement, particularly for one young lady— King Arthur that is.

Brodie had leaned in close. "Does she ever quiet down?"

I reminded him that my aunt's party was something she had never experienced before.

"I hate to think what her reaction might be if yer aunt was to take her on safari with her. The place might never be the same again."

I smiled at that. It was a thought. It might prove an excellent experience, although I wasn't certain who would be more the child on such a trip— Lily or my aunt.

"I will see ye at the office in the mornin'," Brodie said in parting.

"Is it about the case?" I had asked with the distinct feeling, in that way that I had come to know when he had learned something that he considered important.

He glanced past me through the open doorway where Lily was still chattering about the party even though there was no one else in the room. He simply repeated that he would see me in the morning and left.

Once inside our room, I listened to Lily go on and on about the evening as I recalled my first experience at one of my aunt's parties as a child. She certainly had a lot of catching up to do in that regard.

And then there was Brodie's parting comment.

When I realized that Lily had been silent for some time, I looked over to find that she had fallen asleep, the wooden sword in bed beside her.

I removed the sword and crawled into bed as well. However, it was some time before I fell asleep, Brodie's parting comment poking at me.

Infuriating man.

Twelve

I ARRIVED at the office midmorning after leaving Lily in my sister's care, the pair to make their way from the hotel back to Sussex Square later that day.

I was certain that I must have heard about the party the night before no less than a dozen times. In spite of it, it was most entertaining and more than a little touching as I listened before leaving the Grosvenor.

I had proposed bringing Lily to London as a way of providing her more in life— an education and some means of taking care of herself beyond working as a maid in a brothel. I had not anticipated the rest of it— the genuine pleasure and happiness it gave her. And myself.

After leaving the hotel I returned to the townhouse at Mayfair, washed away what was left of my make-up from the night before, dressed in something more appropriate than a pirate's costume, then called for a cab.

As I waited for the driver, Mrs. Ryan followed me about. She provided breakfast and coffee— a great deal of it considering what little sleep I'd had the night before, with her endless questions about the party.

Now, as I arrived at the Strand, the street had already been swept courtesy of crews whose job was to clear away the refuse. Only a few pumpkins were left, somewhat the worse for wear from revelers the night before.

They sat like disgruntled old men— heads only of course, grumbling amongst themselves in front of the tobacconist's shop below the office on the street.

As I stepped from the coach, the hound emerged from the alcove, stretched, then greeted me with a lick of the hand.

Mr. Cavendish paddled out behind him on his platform. I provided cakes Mrs. Ryan had sent along with the complaint that she was not going to continue baking for just one person who rarely showed up. I reminded her that Mr. Cavendish was most fond of her cakes and biscuits.

"At least someone appreciates my hard work," she had remarked as she handed over the cakes, then added, "and there's enough for the hound as well."

They did very much appreciate Mrs. Ryan's efforts while I was most anxious to hear what Brodie had learned from his conversations with the two constables who had been on duty the night Amelia Mainwaring's body was found.

My sister had made a comment that morning before I left the hotel, about photographs being considered art. There was a display at the London Museum that she had noticed when she and James Warren had spent an afternoon there a few weeks earlier before taking supper at his apartment. An evening and perhaps the entire night spent together? It did seem as if their *acquaintance* had progressed.

"Oh, for heaven's sake," Linnie had reacted somewhat strongly at my surprise. "The weather had set in, and James didn't want me to catch a chill."

Hmmm. A chill. Of course.

I added a visit to the museum to my list before leaving the townhouse.

Now, I removed my coat, and set my umbrella in the stand.

Brodie had a fire going in the firebox. Mr. Dooley sat across from him. He looked at Brodie with a thoughtful expression.

"The man came to me last night after me shift and spoke of it. I hope it helps."

Brodie nodded. "I appreciate it, and it is helpful."

Dooley stood then, nodded a greeting at me and tipped his cap. He wasn't presently in uniform. Perhaps a day off, I thought.

When he had gone, I sat across from the desk and took my notebook from my bag. Brodie told me of his meeting with Constables McElroy and Browne.

It seemed that he was correct that they were hesitant to tell him anything other than the most routine information that we already knew from the reports.

They had made their last circle of the area they patrolled at half past eight of the evening. Prior to that they hadn't noticed anything unusual. However, on this circle of the area, they encountered a young woman on the bench near the fountain...

The conversation continued from there, almost word-for-word from the report. They had obviously been ordered to say nothing more than the barest of details which we already knew.

And then Mr. Dooley's visit just before I arrived.

It seems that Constable Browne had contacted him away from the police station. There was more that he and Constable McElroy had seen, however the chief inspector had ordered them to say nothing of it as he had his own *people* making inquiries.

"Who are his people?" I asked Brodie.

"Ye're to say nothing of this, it could mean trouble for a good many people who are simply trying to do their job. For his part, Constable Browne is young and hasn't learned that not everyone — not even the man ye share the watch with, can be trusted."

There had been rumors of course. Alex Sinclair of the Agency had mentioned that Sir Avery was determined to clean things up, and I knew well enough from our prior inquiries that there had been the suggestion of corruption within the ranks of the MP.

I nodded, and assured him I would say nothing until he was prepared to.

"There was someone else in the park that evening, encountered by McElroy and Browne just before finding Miss Mainwaring," Brodie explained. The man had just finished shooting some photographs in another area, and was packing up his equipment to leave."

The *someone else* was Jefferson Talbot.

I recalled our meeting at the office only a few days earlier. Talbot had come by somewhat unexpectedly in response to the note I had sent round to his studio asking him to meet with us. To say the meeting was most unusual is another understatement.

He had been congenial and quite forthcoming about his craft, punctuating his remarks with the cigarette in that ivory holder.

He had answered questions about particular aspects of the photographic process and had freely explained flash powder and development processes, including the reasons that many people still preferred glass plate photographs over the new box cameras with film for capturing images.

I had shown him the photos we had of Amelia Mainwaring and Catherine Thorpe, including the one of Amelia posed on the park bench.

He had immediately recognized it as a death photo, from experience it seemed as he had taken photographs of three of the Whitechapel victims for the police that were included in the crime section of the Times according to Lucy Penworth. One of which — the third victim —had appeared on the front page of the newspaper.

I found him to be quite strange, an *odd duck* Lucy had called him. I had to agree.

Limited as my experience was, I did have a keen sense of people. It was something I attributed to my travels, watching people I encountered, and in writing about a variety of characters in my novels.

However, odd as Talbot had been with his quirks, the

cigarette holder, and those moments when I was certain he perhaps knew more than he was telling us— case in point, that he had been in the park the evening Amelia Mainwaring was murdered —I did not have that sense that he might be the murderer.

"What are ye thinkin'?" Brodie asked.

"I don't believe that he's the murderer."

"And this is due to yer vast experience with such things? Or are ye picking up on some message from the other side like yer friend Templeton."

"I do have some experience," I reminded him. "And you must admit that she has been right on at least three occasions with the information she has provided us."

"Two occasions," Brodie replied. "And each could have been no more than a good guess. And the woman claims to talk to a dead man. It's the reason Munro is no longer keeping company with her."

I didn't know that. I simply thought they had perhaps decided on some time apart. After all she had a very busy stage schedule and Munro had the demands of his work for my aunt.

"Ye didna know?"

"How do you know? Perhaps it is simply a mistake or due to her schedule," I replied. However, I could tell from the expression on Brodie's face that neither one was the case.

"He said it was due to never bein' certain who was in her bed... himself or the fellow, Shakespeare."

"That is preposterous! It isn't as if she doesn't know the difference between a man and..."

One that had been dead for over three hundred years? Even as I said it, I did wonder if my friend had taken a step away as they say.

"Preposterous!" I said again. "She is quite taken with Munro, and we both saw that mural at her home in Surrey."

I made a mental note to speak with her as there had been no opportunity the previous evening as she was telling fortunes for my aunt's guests. Just as soon as I had spoken again with Mr. Talbot.

I did wonder what he might say if he knew that he had been seen at Hyde Park.

"I'll have yer word," Brodie insisted, bringing me back to the moment. "That ye'll not go off to Talbot's studio by yerself."

What was this, I thought? Some sort of domineering male attitude?

"It isn't as if I cannot take care of myself," I pointed out. "The man is rail thin and cannot weigh more than Lily."

"I know ye well enough, Mikaela Forsythe. I'll not have ye goin' off and endangerin' yerself as before."

As before...?

Before what, his proposal? Was that what this was? Some sort of medieval attitude about what a woman could or could not do?

"Yer word on it," he insisted.

"Very well."

"Say it."

"I give you my word."

"All of it."

Oh for heaven's sake. "I will not endanger myself."

It was obvious by the expression in that dark gaze that I had not fooled him with my choice of words. It was also obvious that at least for now, he knew that was all he was going to get in the way of a compromise.

"How is Miss Lily?" he asked, changing the direction of the conversation.

"She is... marvelous. I have never seen anyone so excited as she was last night. I doubt she has ever experienced anything like that."

"Ye're quite taken with her," he replied.

"I believe that we all are. My aunt indulges her pitifully, Linnie imagines her to be like me, and the entire household at Sussex Square seems most pleased to have her there."

Except perhaps for Mr. Symons, my aunt's head butler. He

had been exactly like that when I was Lily's age. He would eventually come around, however I wasn't at all certain that what little hair he had left would survive.

"It will take some adjustment, but yes I am quite taken with her as well."

"It would be a shame to risk her future if anything should happen to ye on one of our inquiry cases," he pointed out.

Clever, irritating man. He had very skillfully brought the conversation back round to make his point.

"What of Mr. Mayhew? Do you know him?" I inquired of the man the chief inspector had put in charge of investigating the murders. "Might he have information that could be useful to us?" Two could play this game.

That dark gaze sharpened on me. "I know him." He shook his head.

"He is Abberline's man. He will hardly be willing to share any information. Most particularly in anything that involves me."

Ah, so there was a history there. Possibly from the circumstances surrounding Brodie's departure from the service of the MP?

I studied the chalkboard. We had additional information now after his conversation with the two constables who were on the watch the night Amelia Mainwaring's body was found at Hyde Park, most particularly from Constable Browne. I also added my notes from my conversation with Davey Morris.

It did seem that Jefferson Talbot was the most likely suspect...

"What would be the motive?" I asked Brodie, thinking aloud as we often did.

"Motive?"

"Jefferson Talbot would seem to have had the opportunity," I pointed out. "But what would be the motive to kill Amelia Mainwaring? An opportunity for a photograph that he might sell to the newspapers? And then Catherine Thorpe as well?"

That hardly seemed plausible since neither photograph had appeared in the dailies.

"A bit of notoriety? Perhaps some disappointment after he photographed the three Whitechapel victims?" I made additional notes in that regard.

I turned from the chalkboard when there was no immediate response to my questions. That dark gaze met mine.

"Has anyone ever told ye that ye have a most unusual mind, most particularly for murder?"

"There is someone who has mentioned that on more than one occasion," I reminded him with a faint smile. "However, it is entirely *his* fault," I added. "*He* has taught me quite well."

"Aye, a mistake to be certain. The poor *mon* should be careful of such a woman. She might take it in her head to do him in."

I did like these moments, when that dark gaze softened and there was the beginning of that smile at one corner of his mouth.

"Or perhaps..." he added. "She has already done *him* in."

How was it that he could *do me in*, as he put it with just a look and the way his voice lowered in just that way.

I was an independent, well-traveled woman accustomed to making her own decisions, taking responsibility for myself, answering to no one. And yet...

I wiggled my toes in my boots and turned back to the chalkboard.

"The London Museum," I announced. "My sister mentioned there is a photographic exhibit there. It's possible the curator of the museum might be able to tell me something about the photographs we have."

"Aye. There is someone else I want to speak with," he replied. "Someone the Mudger— Mr. Cavendish, mentioned. He knows a woman who frequents the area around the seamstress shop where Miss Thorpe was to have been the afternoon she disappeared."

A woman? I could only imagine the sort of woman that might be in consideration of several I had met since my first encounter with Brodie.

He had a history, of course, before we met, as did I. Although my encounters could hardly be called a history— my very brief engagement which I ended before I made that dreadful mistake, and then there was the even more brief encounter on the Isle of Crete...

In Brodie's case, it appeared to be quite different, as I remembered the woman I first encountered on the stairway quite *en flagrante* at our first meeting. And he had assured me prior to our more *intimate* relationship that he was not in the habit of associating with *working* women.

He had been most forthcoming in that regard. And after our last inquiry case and what I had learned about his mother and how they had lived, I understood far more.

"Aye, he's always been that way," Munro had commented when he accompanied me to Edinburgh in the beginning of that inquiry case.

"Even as lads fighting to survive on the streets, he had a way about him. He wouldna harm another unless they started it, and never the girls who worked the streets. He would slip them a few coins or a loaf of bread we'd pinched when we had little ourselves, and expectin' nothin' in return.

"It's not that he wouldna set someone right if they needed it," Munro had gone on to explain. "He set me right a time or two. It's as if he didna want to disappoint his mother, even though she was gone. If ye get my meanin'."

I did understand. I had seen that quality in Brodie and on the streets in the inquiry cases we had taken on. Mr. Cavendish came to mind. One of those whom Brodie trusted and took care of.

Honor among thieves? I had never thought of it that way.

It is officially known as the British Museum, established over one hundred years earlier and considered the oldest museum in the world.

It was enormous, the colonnaded buildings surrounded by iron fence work with a gated entrance that filled two city blocks.

Inside it contained exhibits and artifacts from around the world collected over the last hundred years from different parts of the Empire.

I had spent hundreds of hours there, my imagination and sense of adventure fueled by the ancient sarcophagus from the last pharaoh of Egypt, the 3200-year-old statue of Ramses II, and the Rosetta Stone inscribed with text in three scripts, artifacts acquired by British explorers and through the political machinations of foreign agreements.

I had little understanding of those things then, a much better one now having traveled extensively, my appetite piqued by those early museum explorations. I had visited many of the places where those artifacts were found.

While it was exciting to see those places, at the same time there was something almost poignant that a sarcophagus or statue had been carted off by a team of explorers and shipped hundreds of miles away.

Of course, those explorers argued that it was in the name of art and discovery so that others might appreciate these ancient artifacts.

I did wonder if Nectanebo II, who was supposedly the last true pharaoh of Egypt, might feel about having his sarcophagus paraded about London and then placed in the museum for all to look at including sticky-fingered young children I had seen once who had no appreciation or reverence for such things.

Further proof that supported my preference for a Viking funeral upon my own demise. No sticky-fingered children, if you please, or others gawking at my body laid out in some parlor.

There were at least a dozen galleries at the museum spread throughout the massive buildings. Upon my arrival, I was directed to the art gallery which now included an extensive display of photographs.

The museum had added additional exhibits and galleries since my earlier explorations there and it was a very good thing that I had worn my walking skirt and boots as I set off for the art exhibit room.

I could have easily wandered into other buildings and explored as I had on several occasions, my appetite for adventure fed by what I had discovered there. However, now was not the time. I promised myself to return as I eventually reached the art gallery.

I found the display of photographs at the back of the gallery, dozens of photographs mounted on easels and along the walls, much like works of art from artists of the past.

While I had never before thought of photographs as art, there were some surprising and stunning images on display that included a scene of the Thames and London Bridge at last light, the street lamps across the bridge glowing through growing darkness, one of the Queen's horse guard, and another of Buckingham Palace.

There were also daguerreotypes of notable persons, with their bronze tones as a progression of the photography was noted in cards displayed on those earlier forms, including an early one of prime minister Benjamin Disraeli.

I had to admit that he looked very much like an overstuffed toad, as my aunt had once referred to him.

"He's Italian for heaven's sake!" She declared and not in a complimentary way. "They're much better at wine than politics. Although, their food is quite acceptable."

Never let it be said that she didn't have her opinions. And this from a woman whose great ancestor was an immigrant from Normandy in France.

Then there were common street scenes, some that I had seen myself— Hyde Park with couples exchanging greetings, a cyclist with his bicycle as he stopped to chat with a young lady.

And then one photograph, perhaps, was the most poignant and compelling. That of a little girl who couldn't have been more than three or four years old with a basket of flowers on her arm with Covent Garden in the background.

It was in stark contrast to the others taken about London, that included the Houses of Parliament, London Bridge, and monuments.

In the photograph, the little girl wore a patched dress with oversized boots that looked as if they might have been handed down from someone.

She was looking up at the camera, a hopeful expression on her face. Not, I thought, in anticipation of the photograph which she might not understand, but in anticipation of a coin for some flowers.

I wondered if the photographer who took the picture had purchased any that day. That might have made a small difference in her life— a loaf of bread, a biscuit from the bake shop, or an apple.

There were other visitors about here who gathered around the paintings by well-known artists and those not yet well-known as the curator explained the use of light and perspective in the subjects the artists had chosen.

"You seem quite taken with our little girl."

I turned as the curator, Mr. Whitby according to his name tag, smiled at me, his audience having moved on to another part of the museum.

"The photographer has captured just the right expression and tone," he said.

I agreed. It was obvious that it was late of the afternoon in the photograph, the light slanting across her features and that sweet sad smile.

The curator was average height, dark hair that had gone to gray at the temples and his side-whiskers, and a studious, intelligent gaze in his hazel eyes.

"You seem to know a great deal about techniques of photography," I complimented him. He actually blushed.

"I'm a bit of an enthusiast myself." He leaned in close as if sharing a secret. "After seeing some of these pieces and speaking with the photographers, I invested in a camera. Not one of the box cameras, but a glass plate one with three lenses. When I'm not here, I'm out and about taking photographs.

"My next step is to set up my own dark room in the extra bedroom of my mother's house." He looked past me to the little girl.

"This is a favorite of mine. Posed portraits or the landscape photos are quite nice and all that. However, one such as this evokes so much emotion. It is quite honest, don't you think? A moment captured for all to see and share."

I had never thought of paintings or photographs in that way, but thinking of the photographs in my bag I understood his meaning. It was something my sister once said about capturing a moment on canvas.

Of course, she was speaking of Old Lodge, our aunt's home in the Highlands, a rustic stone and timber lodging with that ancient tower that was supposedly a watchtower for raiders intent on thieving cattle or sheep a couple of centuries past. My sister thought it quite picturesque and romantic with all the legends attached.

I had reminded her that according to local history some of those legends were quite bloody. She had not appreciated my input and declared me to be an artistic novice.

We did have much different interests. While she was dabbling away with her canvas and paints, I was off exploring the surrounding forest. Possibly early training for my sleuthing about. Diverse in the least.

"The photographer's work is easily recognizable, as you can see in this other photo as well. I always thought that was nonsense until a friend pointed out that she would know my photographs anywhere for a distinctive approach that I seem to have developed.

"You can see it here as well with the photograph of women gathered outside vendors' stalls. The photographer seems to have a talent for catching just the moment when one of the women looked up and he took the shot."

I did see what he was talking about. Photographers as artists, indeed. Were we dealing with someone who considered himself an artist?

"Then it could be possible to determine who the photographer might have been from a photograph?" I suggested.

"Perhaps. Each has their own style."

I pulled the second photograph of Amelia Mainwaring from my bag, the one taken of her on the park bench at Hyde Park.

"What can you tell me about this photograph?"

Mr. Whitby studied the photograph. "Minimal light, the subject thoughtful, caught at just the right moment..."

Thoughtful was not a word I would have used to describe the photograph of Amelia Mainwaring— unless she was contemplating her own demise.

"Oh, my..." Mr. Whitby exclaimed.

Precisely. But what did that tell him about the person who had taken the photograph?

"Do you recognize who might have taken this photograph?" I asked.

I had a name, or rather a possible name. But it made no sense.

Paul Laughton— the photographer who had been at my aunt's All Hallows party?

"It does look familiar..." he replied. "I've seen something very like this— the angle of the subject... It could be, Paul Laughton, although he's not known for this sort of photograph."

Admittedly, Mr. Whitby at the British Museum wasn't certain.

There were similarities, but there were also differences and with the absence of appropriate lighting...?

If indeed, Paul Laughton had taken those photographs, what was the motive?

I had another thought, someone else I wanted to see, someone who had shown a definite response to the photographs. But what did that response mean?

Thirteen

JEFFERSON TALBOT'S studio was in Stepney, one of the boroughs in the East End, an area of markets with a few scattered shops and an immigrant population that that included Spital-fields near Whitechapel where the murder of five women had taken place.

I found a driver and gave him the location.

"Stepney, miss?" he repeated, perhaps thinking he hadn't heard correctly. "Are ye sure of the address?"

I heard the unspoken in his voice, that it was not the sort of place someone who had just left the museum might request to be taken. I understood his hesitance, and I could almost hear Brodie's objections.

However as it was still very near the middle of the day, I was fairly certain that Brodie wouldn't yet have returned from his own inquiries, and it was important to the case.

"Quite sure," I replied.

Stepney was part of the Tower Hamlets, with the river in the near distance that included the London and West India docks. It included a varied immigrant population from across Europe and the Far East as the city of London had continued to grow to the east.

My driver turned from Mile End Road onto Stepney Green that lined the marketplace with row upon row of outdoor vendors. They sold everything from food to clothing, to chickens and pigs with the gothic tower of St. Dunstan's Church in the distance. There was also a brewery, with loading docks for wagons.

The marketplace bordered adjacent streets of brick row houses with second floor casements. The windows looked to be a couple hundred years old. According to the information I had, Jefferson Talbot's studio was located on the ground floor of one of those houses.

My driver stopped to inquire as to the location from a man who carried a round tin container and appeared to have just left work. He spoke only broken English and my Italian, learned while asking directions when on my travels, was hardly better, however he was familiar with the photographer's studio.

Between the two of us, he provided directions— always something to be cautious about in an unfamiliar place. However, he seemed most gracious as well as I could make out.

My driver followed his directions down the next street, then stopped before a row house at Number 24 at Stepney High Street. A sign in the window on the ground floor of Number 24 that faced the street, announced that we had found the studio of Jefferson Talbot.

In contrast to the other parts of Stepney we passed near the marketplace, the houses on the High Street were well kept. The front steps were clean of any debris as well as the street in what was obviously a working-class area.

"Do you want me to wait, miss?" my driver asked as I stepped down.

I nodded. If Jefferson Talbot was in, it shouldn't take long for the questions I had.

He nodded and secured the lines of the rig.

There was a second sign at the door— *Customers please enter. Deliveries to be made at the back.*

The door was not locked, and a bell overheard announced my arrival as I stepped into Talbot's studio.

I had been in a photographer's studio before that included a tent on the beach at Brighton with my sister. Most studios were quite formal, much like a formal parlor where the photographer met with those there for his services.

There were also those who preferred to meet with the photographer in their home, most particularly during a social event such as a wedding or other celebration, or in the event of a death.

Talbot's studio contained a sitting area with photographs of various sizes and subjects on the wall, apparently his own private gallery.

The subjects were varied and fascinating I thought as I waited for Talbot to appear. The photographs were of common street scenes of some of the poorer parts of London in juxtaposition to photographs of Kensington, St. James Street, and Hyde Park.

There were also photographs of people on the street caught in some unsuspecting moment— a gentleman in top hat and tails at the Exchange, sellers at Covent Garden, women selling a different sort of accommodation on a street corner, and then there were other stark images.

There was a train wreck in another part of London, rail cars scattered like a child's toys with victims on the platform. There was another of a victim lying in the street outside a tavern in what appeared to be a pool of blood. And then there were those startling photographs of three of the Whitechapel victims that had appeared in the crime pages of the dailies.

"Forgive me, I was in my dark room," Talbot said as he finally appeared and removed a long apron much the same as I had seen Mr. Brimley wear when he was mixing chemicals and powders in his shop.

"Miss Forsythe..." he then greeted me with surprise and something else? "It is a pleasure to see you again. What brings you to my studio? A photograph perhaps? Or murder?"

That was putting it quite bluntly, and then the faint smile that reminded me of my first impression of him when he had met with us at the office on the Strand. It did seem as if there was a great deal going on behind those gaunt features and pale eyes. Secrets? Or playing at some game, perhaps?

I wasn't here to play games, but I was curious if there were secrets. Most particularly about the photographs in my bag.

"I have questions."

"Ah, yes, the lovely amateur sleuth out to solve crimes. Would you care for tea though it is past the hour?"

I didn't, however I saw no way around it, particularly if I was going to ask questions.

He left for a few moments, then returned. A small woman eventually appeared with a pot and two cups on a tray.

"My sister, Agatha," he introduced the woman who set the tray on the table in the parlor. We waited until she had poured both cups and then removed the tray.

"You have questions." Talbot angled me a look as he dropped a cube of sugar into my cup before I could protest.

I didn't usually take sugar in my tea... For that matter I didn't drink tea, but preferred coffee.

"I've been told that it might be possible to identify a photographer by his particular style." I took the photographs I'd brought with me from my bag and laid them on the table.

"Have you now? You've been quite busy, Miss Forsythe."

"What can you tell me about the photographer who took these pictures?"

He picked up the first photograph of Amelia Mainwaring taken, I was quite certain, at Wimbledon.

"A pastoral scene that one might find at a park or in the country. The young lady is handsome, though not a beauty."

This was apparently for my benefit as he looked over at me with that smile that made me recall our first encounter and the feeling now that I needed to get very far away.

"I'm told that artists often recognize the works of other artists," I added. "Does it remind you of any photographs you might have seen by another photographer?"

He continued to study the photograph. I handed him the second photograph of Amelia Mainwaring, sitting on the park bench in Hyde Park.

"What of this one? At night with very little light, yet quite clear? Taken with a glass plate camera?"

He looked at me with surprise. "Very good, Miss Forsythe." Then studied the photograph once more.

"Very obviously a death photo," he replied. "Such a shame."

"Is there anything about either photograph that is familiar? Something that you might have seen before in another's work?"

There was that look that I had first seen in the office on the Strand; slightly amused, secretive, as if it was something that only he and the person who had taken that photograph shared.

"Most interesting... The position of the body..." he said then regarding the second photograph.

"And the position of the hands folded together, almost as if in prayer or supplication."

Supplication? As if asking for forgiveness?

That seemed most strange, yet as I looked at the photo, it did seem as if Amelia Mainwaring's hands had been deliberately folded before her. She most certainly wouldn't have folded them after she was dead.

I showed him the photograph of Catherine Thorpe. Her hands were positioned exactly the same way.

"Do you recognize who may have taken the photographs?"

He continued to study them both with interest. "You are quite right, Miss Forsythe. One can usually see a certain style in photographs, much like paintings. Though there are those... artists, who would argue with you that photographs are not art at all.

"I would argue, however," he continued, "that the photographer must wait for just that moment with the light and the subject, even one who has... passed on. The challenge as well as the art is then the ability to capture that perfect moment. And artists don't like to share their secrets."

That seemed an odd thing to say.

Once again I asked if he recognized who the photographer might have been.

"In due time, Miss Forsythe. In due time." He pressed a finger against his lips much like someone quieting a child.

"I've been working on a particular subject that may interest you," he added. "I've taken several photographs." He stood then and took hold of my arm. "Let me show you some of my latest work."

His hand tightened slightly as I stood. "And do bring along your photographs."

...Said the spider to the fly?

I hesitated. Still if he could identify the photographer... I freed my arm.

"Of course." I replied, pushing back that uneasy feeling I had experienced at the office when he first met with us.

"It is at the back of the house. I will let my sister know, should a client arrive."

I followed him, at a distance, through the house down a hallway to a door under the stairs in spite of that feeling, aware of the way his sister stared after us as he spoke with her.

The knife Munro had given me some time ago when I first set off on my adventures was comforting in the pocket of my skirt.

My first impression when he opened the door was that smell resembled rotten eggs that I heard about.

My next impression was of the surrounding darkness with a single electric light over several pieces of paper that had been hung along a wire over two long basins on the counter below.

"My sister complains that it smells dreadful and insists that I keep the door closed." Talbot reached around and closed the door behind me.

"These are my latest endeavor, taken a short while ago down

at the docks," he explained, quite proudly I thought as he took down one photo and pinned it to a board.

"Such an opportunity to capture life... and death."

The light was faint from that single overhead lamp, but it was easy to see the subject— several men gathered about, no doubt from one of the ships with various expressions that were amazingly clear.

"Taken with the glass plate camera as I was out and about. I was able to quickly set it up and take these."

In the next photograph the men had stepped apart, two of them looking back over their shoulders at the camera, and in the third...

"This should be of particular interest to you, Miss Forsythe."

He reached across in front of me, the back of his shoulder brushing mine as he retrieved a third photograph.

I stared at the picture. The men in the previous photograph had stepped aside to give him the view of the man who lay at their feet.

The details were excruciating. The man was young, perhaps no more than twenty, and had obviously been pulled from the river by the pool of water that surrounded him. His eyes were wide open, the upper part of his head mangled as well as one arm, his clothes shredded. The horror of it reminded me of that first case when I had first gone to Brodie to assist in finding my sister.

"He had fallen overboard in a scuffle with one of the other men, unfortunate fellow, and drowned before they could reach him. And then, it seemed that he was crushed against the pilings on the dock." Talbot explained matter-of-factly, as if discussing a bird or some other poor creature. Certainly not a human being.

His hand closed over my shoulder. "Are you quite all right, Miss Forsythe?"

My fingers closed around the handle of the knife in my pocket.

"I thought to show you this, as an example of my own work,

which you can clearly see, the way the light is angled at each shot for a specific effect.

"I always try to show the victim in the perfect way so that anyone looking at the photograph will feel a certain emotion."

"I understand," I managed to reply, battling twin emotions of anger and revulsion. "And the photographs I showed you?"

I turned, his features stark from that single light— a particular effect perhaps?

"You are most persistent, Miss Forsythe..." he smiled.

"The photographs are quite excellent, don't you think? And the emotion is there. There is after all emotion even in death, wouldn't you say, Miss Forsythe."

The way he kept saying my name was irritating in the least, unnerving in the extreme. I felt increasingly uncomfortable, the promise Brodie asked me to make, there as well.

He looked back at the photograph of the young man who had been pulled from the water at the docks.

"Women are so very vulnerable these days, wouldn't you agree, Miss Forsythe?"

An answer that was no answer at all. Or was it? I needed to leave.

"Thank you for your time, Mr. Talbot."

As I turned toward the door, he blocked my way with his arm.

"There are more to see. Or perhaps a photograph of yourself? You would make a wonderful subject for my camera, Miss Forsythe."

More photographs? I had no desire to see more as my hand tightened around the handle of the knife.

"Thank you, no. I must be going. Mr. Brodie is expecting me."

Of course, he wasn't, and I had no idea where he was at present. And even as I said it, I thought to myself— coward. But it was more than that. It was that tiny little voice that whispered a warning.

Just as I would have pulled the knife from my pocket, his arm dropped.

"Of course, Mr. Brodie."

I was finished with polite conversation and immediately went to the door of the dark room.

Talbot's sister was standing in the hallway as I quickly passed by and returned to the front of the studio.

It was already dark out, in that way that the days shortened this time of the year, and a bone-chilling cold had set in.

There was only a single street lamp across the way, and I was relieved that my driver was still there as I hastily climbed aboard.

I didn't know what to make of my encounter with Jefferson Talbot.

What was the purpose of showing me those photographs he had obviously recently taken? Merely an artist, as he obviously considered himself, showing his works?

Or was there more to that display in the dark room? A threat perhaps?

"Is everything all right, miss?" the driver called down.

No, everything was not all right, I thought, as I gave him the address of the office on the Strand.

With the weather and the fact that it was well past the time that workers filled the streets at the end of the day, the traffic was less than it had been earlier, and we arrived at the office in good time.

I paid the driver and included extra fare for his time. "Thank ye kindly, miss. And a word of caution, that ye might not want to be in that part of London late of the day."

I appreciated his concern. He tipped his cap and set off. I turned to find Mr. Cavendish and Rupert on the sidewalk.

"Mr. Brodie asked about you earlier," Mr. Cavendish commented as I bent to scratch the hound's ears. "You might take that as a word of caution, miss."

I thanked him, and climbed the stairs.

"Where the devil have ye been?" Brodie demanded as I entered the office.

I had discovered over the past several months that there were two different types of anger when it came to Angus Brodie.

There was the quiet, intense sort of anger, even cold with little said, thoughts working how best to confront a situation. Munro had once explained that was the side of Brodie that came from the streets. And he should know well enough.

"Best to leave him to himself when that happens. Not that there would be any harm to ye, only that ye might see things ye wish ye had not."

And then there was the other sort of anger, as now. He was furious and made no attempt to hide it. I had experienced that as well on a few occasions, admittedly when I had perhaps, and I emphasize the word perhaps, given him some reason.

"I was at the museum." Not exactly a lie as far as it went. "And then I had a brief encounter with Jefferson Talbot, and one thing led to another."

I didn't explain that *one thing or another*. Now was probably not the best time to explain all of it. Nor was it the first time that I had been out and about on a case. Always best to pick my moments.

Unsettling as my meeting with Talbot had been, it did seem that Brodie's reaction was a bit over the top.

He sat at the desk, chin propped on his hand. I felt that dark gaze on me that saw far too much as I removed my coat and hung it on the coat stand then went to the stove.

"Excellent, there's coffee," I commented in an attempt to redirect the conversation. "It is quite cold outside."

"Aye." A single response, not a good indication.

I poured myself a cup of coffee. It looked strong, more than strong, the sort my friend Templeton described might stand up a spoon— something she had heard on her travels to the United States.

This certainly did seem that it could. I needed that.

I turned, cup in hand. That dark gaze was still fastened on me. That other sort of anger was there— intense, thoughts hidden, and far too quiet.

"The information from the curator at the museum was most informative," I began. "The man is quite knowledgeable. He has a background in photography as well." I continued on with what Mr. Whitby had explained.

"According to him, most photographers have a particular style that might be identified, very much like a calling card."

The coffee was hot and fortifying. I was also starving, I hadn't eaten since breakfast. However, it seemed that Brodie had been warming himself with a bit of Old Lodge whisky.

"It is often quite easy to identify a particular photographer once one is familiar with their work."

"And yer *encounter* with Mr. Talbot?"

Brodie emphasized each word, most particularly the word *encounter*, as if I had just happened to see Talbot on the street.

He didn't believe it for a moment. That was the problem with knowing me quite well.

As I also knew him? That little voice whispered.

That was beside the point.

"Informative, as well," I replied. That was all quite true as well. "The man is very talented. It seems that he's working on a particular project."

I thought it best that I didn't go into details on how I knew that.

"I was most interested in his thoughts about the photographer who took the photos of Amelia Mainwaring and Catherine Thorpe. If he saw something in them that might indicate who had taken them."

"Did he?"

"There was a moment when I thought perhaps he had, but he refused to reveal what he was thinking..."

Brodie leaned across the desk and handed me a copy of the Times daily. It was the late edition from just a few hours earlier.

There was a photograph just below the title block on the front page. It was vivid and startling, the headline across the top equally shocking.

"There's been another murder."

Fourteen

THE VICTIM'S name was Eleanor Strachan, of the Strachan-Ward family.

Her father, Sir William Strachan, had attended Sandhurst, retired from the military, and had been appointed head of the War Office by the Queen. He was also a founding member of the Carlisle Sporting Club, and was on the board of the Wimbledon Racquet Club.

Eleanor was engaged to be married to James Allendale, a man from a notable family and also a member of Wimbledon. The photo in the police report in the newspaper had been delivered to Sir William Strachan the previous evening.

Eleanor Strachan was the third young woman in that original photograph taken at Wimbledon, and she was very obviously dead.

"Oh, dear." Seemed so very inadequate.

"I've also had a call with Sir Avery regarding the case," Brodie quietly added. "And I was able to speak with Inspector Mayhew."

The chief inspector's man.

"I can imagine how that might have been received."

"The man has decided to cooperate with what he has learned."

I could also imagine what might have persuaded him. Abberline was undoubtedly going to have a fit and fall in the middle of it over that.

"Abberline has been informed," Brodie continued. He continued to watch me with that dark gaze.

"I am to keep him updated on what we have learned in the matter."

I have discovered in the few but glaring moments of silence that the office is given to other sounds and noises— the creak of the wood floor underfoot, the snap of fire in the coal stove, and the sound of rain on the window as it turns to ice.

"Now, do ye want to tell me what happened with Talbot? It's quite obvious something has ye upset."

It did seem that he knew me quite well.

And then there was the tight control in his voice that I imagined more than one criminal had heard over the years.

I seriously considered staying with my story as far as it went and not getting into the rest of it.

However, I also considered that Brodie was most accomplished in dealing with lies and deceptions. He'd grown up with it, and then made a career of unraveling lies and deceptions in his time with the MP, and knew a deception when he heard one.

And then there was that other part of it...

I had no use for lies myself, however a slight stretch of the truth or an omission was useful from time to time.

I decided to go with the truth, and told him about my visit to Talbot's studio. I did omit the part about the dark room although I did share with him about Talbot's new project and his apparent fascination, even excitement I might say, about photographing dead bodies.

Brodie was quiet when I had finished, far too quiet, that dark gaze still watching me. I was prepared for the anger and undoubtedly a lecture about *taking myself off without him,* or in the very least with someone else— Munro perhaps or the hound for protection, as in the past.

But there was something else there as well. He stood as if he couldn't remain confined to the chair, and poured himself another dram of whisky. He didn't offer any to me, and quickly drained his own glass then poured another.

"Do ye know what it does to me when you don't return as ye said ye would, the sort of things that go through my head that might have happened to ye? It's like a madness because I canna control it, I canna help ye if something should happen... and because I know what's out there."

He stopped me when I would have spoken. He obviously wasn't through and poured another bit of whisky and just as quickly downed it.

"Ye tear my heart out, lass," he said softly. "In a way I've not felt for a good many years. And I know that I canna change ye, nor do I want to as much as it terrifies me that I might lose ye, because I know that's who ye are— brave and strong, and that's part of the reason I want ye so."

He walked toward me.

I have never been afraid of Brodie, and wasn't afraid now. However, I was afraid of the words as if they were being ripped from his throat.

"I've never known anyone like ye and I want more than anythin' to have ye in my life, to share my life with ye. But it if means that I might lose ye because of it and what's out there..."

I stopped him. I was prepared to be logical, to argue that I had found information that was valuable, and that I wasn't really in any danger at all. I was prepared to be angry, to defend what I had done, and not apologize for it.

All of that disappeared like smoke on the wind.

I knew the rest of what he would have said when I stopped him, that he was prepared to end it— our association, the inquiries... and his proposal.

"You're right, I should have told you..." I had no chance to get the rest out.

He kissed me, fiercely, passionately, with a taste of whisky, heat, and Brodie.

I had never been kissed like that before, not even by him, as if he might take the breath from me, his hands in my hair, his beard scraping my cheek, refusing to let me go.

I fully expected him to pick me up, carry me into the adjoining bedroom, and have his way with me as he had once promised. He did not.

Instead, his hands were gentle now, his forehead against mine, his fingers tender on my face, and somehow that undid me more than if he had carried me off.

Well, if I couldn't persuade him into the bedroom...

"More please," I whispered, wanting very much for him to kiss me again.

He cursed softly. "Ye try a man's soul, Mikaela Forsythe."

"I do try..."

~

Brodie had contacted Sir Avery as soon as he read that article in the late edition of the daily. Sir Avery had in turn contacted Sir William Strachan, the young woman's father, and made an appointment for first thing in the morning. Apparently there had also been a conversation about Abberline.

The delay was frustrating, however there was nothing to be done about it. The young woman's mother was at their country estate and Sir William had set out to meet her and bring her back to London.

Eleanor Strachan was last seen at another All Hallows party where she had departed with a friend just after midnight. After leaving the friend at the girl's residence, Eleanor never arrived home.

The two families lived only a few residences apart at Portman Square near St. James Park. Sir Strachan had also been out for the evening. Upon his return the servants had informed that his daughter had not yet returned.

He had thought that she might have decided to stay over and so had not learned of her disappearance until the morning, and then learned of her death in the afternoon daily with that horrible photograph.

Horrible. That was the only word for it.

In the photograph, Eleanor was still in the costume she had worn the evening prior, that appeared to be that of a witch. She had obviously been murdered then positioned at the curb of the street, head slightly bent at an awkward angle that spoke to the method of her death. And the same as the other two young women. Her hands were folded before her in that same pose for the photograph.

Three young women, three deaths. The only reason that all of London wasn't in a complete terror as they had been and still were with the Whitechapel murders, was that the murders of Amelia Mainwaring and Catherine Thorpe had not as yet appeared in the dailies. That brought me back to Abberline.

The chief inspector had used the article about the latest murder as a political statement, though he'd refused to reveal the other murders as he openly campaigned for the criminal reform that he was determined to achieve. He had also mentioned that Brodie had once been part of the MP, but had since departed.

He then went on to extol the accomplishments of the MP, including his investigation into the matter of Lady Lenore Litton's disappearance the year before.

"Despicable."

I detested the man and his aggravatingly inept methods of investigating a crime, motivated by his own self-interest. He had been a plague upon our inquiries from the beginning.

"It was bound to happen," Brodie commented, seemingly not bothered by the man's arrogance.

"He has certainly boasted of his part." Which was no part at all as it had turned out. I did wonder how the man lived with himself.

I had to admit that my opinion of Abberline had nothing to do with Brodie's history with the man when he was a member of the MP. Brodie could take care of himself.

It had everything to do with Abberline's bungled investigation into my sister's disappearance that might well have ended in her death. Not that I carried a grudge against the man, however...

A favorite saying of my housekeeper, Mrs. Ryan, came to mind:

"May those who love us, love us. And those that don't love us,
May God turn their hearts, and if He doesn't turn their hearts,
May He turn their ankles, so we'll know them by their limping."

Brodie looked up from the desk. "A bit of wisdom?"

"An old Irish curse," I replied. "Although I had something more in mind for Abberline."

"Ah, Mrs. Ryan," he concluded as he pushed back his plate after the late supper we'd brought back from the Public House across the Strand.

"Hmmm," I replied, standing before the chalkboard where I'd added the name of the latest victim.

"Eleanor Strachan was also in the photograph," I said, thinking aloud. "The one taken of the young men and women at Wimbledon."

"A possible connection," he replied.

Yes, but what was the connection.

"And there is another young woman in that photograph, standing next to her."

"Aye."

It was late, and obvious that there was nothing that could be done until we were able to speak with Sir William in the morning. He was to meet us at the Agency office at the Tower with Lady Strachan.

After two meetings with grieving parents, this one would undoubtedly be just as difficult.

"There's nothing more to be done tonight," Brodie said then. "I'll have Mr. Cavendish call for a driver and see ye home."

"That's not necessary," I replied.

"Aye, it is. I'll not have ye goin' about London this time of the night, in spite of yerself."

Well that was certainly a different way of putting it. And what was this over-protectiveness on his part?

Not that he wasn't mindful of my going into certain areas of the city, and had even appointed Rupert the hound as personal guardian in the past, much to Mrs. Ryan's displeasure at having the hound as a house guest.

I did have to admit that a most unpleasant odor usually accompanied Rupert depending on recent wanderings about the streets and which disgusting things he had tracked down.

But still, there was definitely something different in Brodie's manner and I wondered if it had to do with his proposal.

I would usually have been put off by such a thing and simply ignored it and gone on about my way as I was accustomed. Surprisingly, I wasn't put off, merely curious.

"Yer coat, lass," he said, retrieving it from the coat rack. His hand lingered as he held it for me then settled it over my shoulders, and a question in that dark gaze. Perhaps *the* question that I had not yet answered.

"Yer scarf. It's colder tonight," he gently wrapped it about my neck. "There may be a storm comin' in."

~

A storm indeed, I thought as we met in Sir Avery's office at the Agency that next morning. A storm of anger, grief, and then anger all over again as Sir William and Lady Strachan sat across from him, and he provided details he had received from Abberline.

Sir William rose and paced the office. "Within steps of our home! How is that possible in that part of London?"

Lady Strachan sat still as a statue, as if it was all she could do to hold herself together and any movement might shatter her. She was pale, her features drawn. There had undoubtedly been little sleep the night before, if any, as she returned from their country home after learning of her daughter's disappearance and then that horrible photo.

I sympathized remembering the first days after my sister's disappearance and that horrible death that had first sent me to Brodie's office.

"Three murders? How is that possible?" Sir William said, his voice breaking. "And to have this in the dailies, like some common...? What is being done?" His voice rose with each question. "I want answers!"

"Mr. Brodie and Miss Forsythe were brought into the investigation by Sir John and Lady Mainwaring, and I have supported that due to their successful resolution of other inquiries in the past."

"And Abberline?"

"I have informed him that Brodie is to have the lead on this after his people found the second young woman, whom I believe is known to your family. He has overstepped in this and that will be dealt with."

I could only imagine how that would go over.

Sir Avery and Sir William continued to discuss what was now a third murder in the case with Brodie, that included what we had learned about the first two murders, Brodie's conversation with the constables who were on the watch at Hyde Park, and his conversation with Mayhew.

Lady Strachan sat quietly throughout, refusing to be left to the outer office, as details were discussed, including that of the method by which their daughter had been killed.

As I listened to the conversation between the men and

provided information that we had been able to determine, I was aware that Lady Strachan was watching me.

"Lady Mikaela Forsythe," she repeated the introductions that had been made. "I know your family."

Considering my father's somewhat dismal exploits, I wasn't at all certain what she might know.

"Lady Antonia Montgomery is my great aunt. My sister and I were raised by her." I left it at that as my aunt was the only one I truly considered family, after my sister, and our mother.

"Your sister is Lady Litton?" she replied.

"Lady Forsythe now. She has once more taken our family name."

She nodded. "I remember that unfortunate situation."

That unfortunate situation being the first inquiry case I had taken to Brodie when Linnie disappeared.

"I heard that was resolved quite dramatically. I seem to remember... that you were injured."

Dramatic was one word that might describe that situation. In the process of following clues and desperate to find my sister, I had the misfortune to be shot, though I had obviously recovered.

I didn't go on and on about such things, but many of the details of that case had been included in the dailies in spite of the royal family's best efforts to prevent it.

"Mr. Abberline was involved?" Lady Strachan asked.

Abberline had been a constant obstruction in the matter, and I had feared that my sister may become the next victim due to his blundering and negligence.

Even though Sir William's initial response to Abberline was quite critical, there was no way of knowing if there were other *connections*. It was one of those matters that needed to be handled... diplomatically. Abberline was known to have been appointed chief inspector by someone high up as they say, although Brodie had never learned the person's name or position.

Whatever Sir Avery Stanton might know in the matter, he had remained discreet, although there was obviously no love lost for the man and when needed, as in our present case, he made it clear to Abberline that Brodie and I were to lead the investigation into the murders.

It did seem that either Mr. Abberline had not received the memorandum regarding that, or deliberately chose to ignore it to his own advantage.

How best to answer Lady Strachan's question?

I caught the look from Brodie as he had obviously heard that part of our conversation.

Be careful, that look said.

Careful, when what I would have liked to do was drop the man into the river tied to a sack of rocks.

Oh, dear. See Mr. Abberline flailing around in the river. Oh, my, he just went under! I imagined, but of course didn't say it.

"Mr. Abberline is a very busy man. There are many crimes to investigate," I replied diplomatically. And that was as much explanation as I was willing to share.

Lady Strachan nodded. "Do you have thoughts as to who might have done this?" Her voice broke softly.

"I believe that it may have to do with a photograph that was taken much earlier. We have been following information on that."

"Another photograph?" she asked.

In for a penny, in for a pound, I thought. While I understood perfectly how dreadful the situation was, I also knew that Sir William and Lady Strachan might be able to provide additional information that could be very helpful.

I proceeded carefully as I knew this might be the only opportunity to ask our questions with everything they were going through that included the publicity from that dreadful photograph in the daily and now with arrangements to be made for their daughter's funeral.

"I have seen a photograph of the young ladies that was very obviously taken at Wimbledon some time earlier. That photograph appears to be connected to what has happened."

"Our daughter belonged to a ladies' club at Wimbledon. She is... was quite athletic, and loved to participate with her friends."

There were more tears now that Lady Strachan wiped with a handkerchief.

"I remember the photograph... four of them, Eleanor's friends and the young men, including her fiancé. Oh, dear, I can only imagine how difficult this is for him, seeing that in the newspaper."

I was afraid she was going to collapse entirely with this new wave of grief, but she surprised me as she straightened in her chair.

"We have had nothing from Chief Inspector Abberline," she spoke with a much stronger voice than moments before. "Only what is shown in the newspaper along with... that photograph. Nothing, about what he has done to find who did this, no communication whatsoever."

"My dear..." Sir William replied and crossed the office to take her hand.

She shook her head. "You were once with the Metropolitan Police, is that correct, Mr. Brodie?"

He nodded. "I was an inspector with the MP."

"Why did you leave?" she then asked.

True to his character, Brodie did not hide the facts or gloss over them.

"I served under Mr. Abberline. We disagreed on several matters including a final case where I determined I would not work under his authority again."

Lady Strachan nodded, obviously satisfied with his answer.

"I want to know who did this! And I want you and Lady Forsythe to continue. You have shared far more this morning, than..." She took a deep breath and continued.

"Mr. Abberline has shown his purpose. The man is most ambitious. However, I insist you proceed in this, and we must assist in any way that we can."

When Sir William would have cautioned about making a hasty decision, she refused to hear it.

"Are you in agreement?" she asked Sir Avery.

"I am." He left it at that.

"Very well," Sir William agreed. "How may we assist you, Mr. Brodie, Lady Forsythe?"

～

We accompanied them back to their London residence. There they were met by tearful servants and we were introduced in turn.

Their residence was a townhouse at Portman Square, near St. James Park. They lived there in the winter months, the residence convenient to Sir Strachan's position in parliament. In the summer months when the heat became unbearable, Lady Strachan and Eleanor retreated to their country home.

That is after their daughter's competitions at Wimbledon. It seemed she was quite the athlete, something she shared with her fiancé, James Allendale.

He was there, pacing the floor of the front parlor. He had sent round no less than a dozen messages, and rang them up only to be told that Sir William and Lady Strachan were not there.

Obviously devastated, he barely made it through our introductions, before demanding what was being done to find whoever had murdered Eleanor Strachan.

This was the part I was not fond of, having experienced much the same myself— the shock, fear, anger. And the unknown.

Who was doing this? Why? And the terrifying possibility that there might very well be more deaths before the murderer was found.

Brodie had warned me quite early on, that not all crimes could be solved. The best we might do was... the best we might do, and perhaps bring some sense of closure for victims and their families.

I understood, however refused to accept that. It was a source of several conversations.

Brodie had called me idealistic while he was far more realistic. Be that as it may... I still refused to accept it.

I looked at each aspect of a case as if it was but a piece in a puzzle that eventually revealed another piece, and then another.

Sir William and Lady Strachan's staff provided tea and coffee while Brodie spoke with Sir William and James Allendale about what we knew, what we had discovered, and what we now needed, and that included access to Eleanor Strachan's body for evidence.

"There has still been no word from Abberline," Sir William commented. "However," this with a look over at Lady Strachan, "I've made arrangements and will provide you with the information."

Arrangements, of course, indicated information where Eleanor Strachan's body might be attended. I was impressed with Lady Strachan's fortitude in what I knew was an emotionally difficult situation.

Brodie then wanted to see where the young woman's body had been found at the curb in front, just down the way from the residence toward St. James Park.

The men departed so that Brodie might make his investigation there while I remained with Lady Strachan.

"Might I perhaps see that photograph of the young women at Wimbledon?" I asked.

It was an exact copy of the one I had first seen in Amelia Mainwaring's room, and included four young ladies as well as four young men that also included James Allendale.

Brodie had grown suspicious when two young women in that photograph were murdered. Now, it did indeed seem as if someone was deliberately targeting them. But whom, and for what reason?

If he was correct and it certainly seemed so, then the young woman standing next to Eleanor Strachan might be in danger as well.

So far, Sir Avery had managed to prevent news of the first two deaths from appearing in the newspapers. Once it was made known, there would be a new wave of panic about London.

"Anne Pemberton," Lady Strachan provided. "She and Eleanor attended school together and then traveled to France before Eleanor became engaged. She will be devastated."

I then told Lady Strachan that it was imperative that Brodie and I speak with the Pemberton family as well.

"As I remember, there were supposed to be five girls in the photograph," Lady Strachan added. "Another member of the club."

She didn't remember the name.

A fifth young woman who might also be in danger?

"Who would have that information?" I asked.

"I suppose that would be the manager at Wimbledon. He's only been there a few years, but quite instrumental in developing the site and the club. Is that helpful?" she asked.

When Sir William and Brodie returned, I then inquired what he knew about the manager of the club as he was one of the founding members.

It seemed that Albert Hughson, was an avid sportsman from a respectable family, who had been injured in an accident that prevented his further participation in sporting activities.

He had, however, channeled his expertise as well as his enthusiasm into the management of the fledgling organization, taking it from a casual lawn sport to a very competitive venture that had grown substantially.

Brodie was circumspect. "Has there been any contact of any sort received by yerself in this matter?" he asked Sir Strachan. "A request for financial compensation perhaps?"

Sir Strachan shook his head. "No. We have provided substantial contributions for the purchase of additional land surrounding the courts as well as provided for the hiring of an architect to design a permanent clubhouse."

"And Mr. Hughson has not expressed difficulty of any kind?" he suggested.

"No, absolutely not. You think that he may be responsible?"

I knew the reason for Brodie's questions and as I had learned through our past inquiries *absolutely not*, did not always mean that.

Albert Hughson could most often be found at the clubhouse or on the grounds according to the information Sir Strachan provided.

"And I would prefer that ye do not contact the man regarding this," Brodie insisted. "However, we will be speaking to him. He may be able to offer information that could be useful."

"I refuse to believe that Mr. Hughson would be involved in this," Sir William replied. "I have known him for years, and his family as well. His father is a physician."

Physician? I immediately thought of those traces of ether crystals we had noted on Amelia Mainwaring's body. Would we find the same with Miss Strachan? And where might that lead us?

"Well ye might trust Mr. Hughson, sir, however, we cannot ignore the possibility at this time. Ye have requested that we find those responsible for yer daughter's murder. Until we have questioned the man, I must consider that he could have some knowledge of the matter."

Sir William reluctantly agreed.

As we were about to leave, their butler announced that a note had been received while they were away.

Sir William opened it. He looked up with a frown.

"*And then there was one?* What the devil is that supposed to mean?"

I exchanged a look with Brodie.

Sir William and Lady Strachan had not been made aware of that chilling note received by the other families. Brodie said nothing, and I realized that it served no purpose to discuss the other murders.

"May I have the note, Sir William?"

I tucked the note into my bag.

That first murder had now become three, and the promise of more?

I told Brodie what Lady Strachan had told me.

"There was a young woman missing from the photograph. There could be two more young women in danger. Mr. Hughson might possibly have information regarding that," I speculated.

Brodie nodded. "I found something it appears Mr. Abberline missed with his initial investigation into Miss Eleanor Strachan's murder. There were traces of white crystals on the sidewalk where she was found.

"Residue from ether?"

"Perhaps."

"Then that would mean that she was drugged when she first encountered the murderer."

"Aye..."

We made the sad ride to the police morgue with handwritten instructions that we were to be given every courtesy in the matter of viewing the body of Miss Eleanor Strachan as Sir William Strachan's personal representatives. This was not to be questioned for any reason as there would be far-reaching consequences.

Abberline would have a fit and fall in the middle of it, I thought. Better that, I supposed, than being tied to a sack of rocks.

"A sack of rocks?" Brodie commented.

I had not realized that I had spoken aloud. I did need to be more careful with my thoughts.

I refused to think of it as a murderous thought considering how many instances Abberline had been far more concerned about his own future prospects rather than the criminals we had pursued on behalf of our clients.

"He is the most arrogant man I have ever met, and quite short."

"What might his height have to do with it?"

"My aunt insists that it has everything to do with it. I have chosen not to ask for specifics in that regard, although she has assured me that she has proven it to be true."

"A scientific observation on her part, no doubt," Brodie replied.

I angled a look over at him in the coach.

"She did say that she once conducted an experiment regarding that sort of thing. When she was much younger of course."

"I'm afraid to ask the details of her observations," he commented.

Fifteen

ANNE PEMBERTON, the fourth young woman in the photograph, lived within walking distance of the Strachan residence at Portman Square. Sir William put through a telephone call of introduction for us.

The Pembertons had learned about Eleanor's murder in the same manner as Sir William, in the daily when it was delivered. They were shocked, while Anne was devastated at the loss of her friend.

She was taller than the other young women in that photograph with dark hair, and green eyes. I could see the athleticism in the way she carried herself as she stood when we arrived.

We asked the same questions we had asked before of each of the families— had there been any threats, had anyone approached Anne in a threatening manner, had she noticed anyone about whom she didn't know, and had the family received any strange messages?

The answer in each instance was the same. No.

"Who would want to do such a thing?" Anne asked.

She refused to sit, instead pacing across the front parlor with a restless energy that I could imagine on a tennis court. And then there was the anger that came with it.

"Ye attended a party with Miss Strachan?" Brodie inquired.

"Yes," she replied. "Last evening. It was at a mutual friend's residence." She looked over at Brodie.

"Do you think it might have been someone at the party?"

"We need to look at every possibility," I explained. "Did you notice anyone you weren't familiar with? Was there any sort of disagreement among any of the guests?"

"The people there were from our circle of friends and from my brother's school. However, everyone was in costume," she added. "I suppose it would have been possible for someone to slip in unnoticed."

She had held up well until then. Now there were tears.

"Poor, dear Eleanor," she whispered. She gathered herself.

"We returned together from the party. Then, I walked on, as we have dozens of times since we live only a short distance apart. To think that someone..."

I knew what she was thinking, that it would have been quite easy for someone unknown to be waiting just there. I knew it could easily have been either one of them, or possibly both.

"I know this is a difficult time," Brodie sympathized. "However, I suggest that ye take all precautions whenever ye leave the house until this matter is settled. It would be best," he continued, "that ye do not go out alone. For whatever reason, it seems that the young ladies in that photograph have drawn this person's attention."

There was no need for him to explain the rest of it— that Anne Pemberton might well now be the next target for the murderer.

"Lady Strachan remembered there were to be five young ladies in the photograph that day," I then mentioned something she had told us. "Would you know who that was? The young woman and her family will need to be warned as well until we find whoever is doing this."

Anne shook her head. "There were several players there that

day, over a year ago now. It was an exhibition of sorts with several rounds in a tournament."

"The purpose was to promote the planned expansion at Wimbledon," Mr. Pemberton added. "The sport has grown, particularly for young women, and the directors were hopeful to encourage investors."

"Ye are one of the directors, sir?" Brodie asked.

"Yes, myself and three others, including Sir William Strachan, of course."

We thanked the Pembertons for their time. As we rose to leave, Anne Pemberton reached out.

"You will find who did this?" she asked and I saw that strength there as well as felt it in the hand on my arm.

"Most certainly," I replied.

After leaving Portman Square, Brodie directed our driver to the private morgue where Eleanor Strachan's body had been taken.

This sad experience was becoming far too familiar.

She still wore the costume she had worn to the All Hallows party the previous evening, her delicate features in contrast to the black gown. The owner of the morgue had been contacted by Sir William and advised that we would be calling on him.

He had medical experience and pointed out the injuries that had caused Eleanor's death, the bruising about the neck as in the other murders. However, there were no traces of the crystals Brodie had found at the location where the body was found.

"Was she perhaps wearing any other garments?" Brodie asked. "A neck scarf or shawl perhaps?"

There was a shawl, also black, that had been neatly tucked into a bag to be returned to Sir William and Lady Strachan.

Brodie examined it. I knew, of course, what he was looking for.

Due to the handling of the shawl it was impossible to determine if there was any trace of those crystals on the wool fabric. He then overturned the bag on a nearby steel cart, and shook it. A faint dusting of white crystals fell to the top of the cart.

"I would appreciate if you could tell us what those crystals are, sir," Brodie asked of the owner. "And we will wait."

The result was not surprising. It was the same as in the other two murders. Someone was drugging the victims with ether, before the murder was committed. Was it supposed to be some act of mercy?

The previous cases I had participated in had been equally brutal, but this new aspect was disturbing.

What did it mean?

"It's very much like the Whitechapel murders, except it's as if the murderer doesn't want to cause them any pain."

I thought of those young women. There had undoubtedly been those last moments of confusion, then fear before the drug took effect.

"Who would do such a thing?"

It was a question for which there was not yet an answer.

The weather matched my mood after we left. It seemed that we were chasing down a serial murderer.

There was rail service on a spur connecting the southwest of central London to Putney, that connected with the small rural station at the town of Wimbledon.

We arrived late of the afternoon, then hired a driver to take us out to the Wimbledon Tennis Club where that photograph had been taken.

The afternoon was dreary and soggy. This time of year there were no tournaments and the grass tennis courts had turned brown with the change of seasons.

A light glowed from the brick cottage, that presently served as the clubhouse, where Sir William indicated Mr. Hughson lived.

Brodie deployed his umbrella and held it over me as we approached the cottage. The door was answered by Mrs. Hughson.

We explained that we were there on behalf of Sir William and she directed us to a workshop behind the cottage.

Brodie introduced us and explained that there had been a situation, and Sir William had indicated that he might be able to answer some questions for us.

Mr. Hughson was a stout, energetic man, frustrated by the weather when he needed to keep the courts groomed for a men's competition that was to be held the following week.

Mrs. Hughson provided coffee, which was much appreciated as I warmed my hands, and then her husband took us on a tour of the *cottage*.

It was small but with a large receiving room where the business of the tennis club was conducted, a counter with a board on the wall behind where it appeared the last tournament had been announced.

There was also a table with architectural plans laid out and Mr. Hughson explained the expansion that the directors hoped for.

The present half-dozen courts would be expanded at least twice that much more. But he was obviously most excited for the new clubhouse that had been designed.

The reception room also included a dedication wall with portraits of the founding members of the Wimbledon Club including Sir William Strachan, as well as photographs from competitions that had been held there, and that original photograph of the club members, including the women's team after their first tournament the year before.

"Most interesting," I commented as I studied the photograph. "I understand there were supposed to be five women in the competition, but I only see four."

"You are well informed, Miss Forsythe."

"An acquaintance of Miss Pemberton," I replied.

"That was an unfortunate situation with one of our members, as I heard it described. I was away at the time to oversee a new variety of turf for the courts. The daughter was a member of the women's club."

"What sort of situation?" Brodie asked.

"It had to do with some damage here at the park to two of the courts, and an altercation with one of the young men in that photograph.

"The young woman's brother had something to do with it. Rather than bring in the authorities, the directors chose to simply ask the father to withdraw his membership for some reason, and nothing more was said in the matter."

"Who was the member who was asked to withdraw from the club?"

Mr. Hughson gestured to that photograph.

"The photographer, quite well known for portraits of the royal family, I'm told. By the name of Laughton, as I recall."

Paul Laughton was the photographer who had taken that photograph as well as others at Wimbledon. Then, he had withdrawn his membership after an incident that involved his son.

"He was there," I commented as we returned to the rail station to await the next train back to London.

"Who was there?" Brodie asked.

"The photographer, Paul Laughton, was at my aunt's party. I saw him only briefly. His daughter was there as well."

Both the son and daughter had also been members, according to what Mr. Hughson told us.

What would have prompted damage to the courts? And then being asked to withdraw their membership from the club?

We arrived back in central London, then continued on to the office on the Strand.

It had been a long, difficult day. However, far more difficult for the Strachans and our other clients. Murder was a nasty business.

I returned with Brodie. I thought of the Whitechapel murders that still had not been solved.

I had wondered if there might be a connection, however

Brodie, far more experienced in these things, thought not. The method of the murders simply was not the same.

Whereas the Whitechapel murderer had been most brutal, even methodical in his attacks, the victims had all been poor, working-class women, as if the murderer was making a statement, leaving his own calling card as it were.

There had even been suggestions that the murderer might be a physician by the precision of the wounds that were made. All to no end as the murders had abruptly stopped.

The deaths of *our* young women, as I thought of them, had been far different. Methodical to be certain, even appearing to be planned, the women in the photograph specifically chosen.

And the fifth young woman who had not appeared in that photograph? Her father relinquishing his membership after an incident that the other directors chose not to pursue?

Was it possible that Paul Laughton had decided to take some sort of revenge for the incident? I hardly thought it was cause for murder.

"There's more to this," Brodie commented. "There's something that we haven't discovered yet."

It was well into the evening by the time our driver turned onto the Strand with the usual overhead electric sign lit up along the way that advertised the latest plays at the theaters, including my friend Templeton's latest play at the Drury.

Quite recent, the addition of electric signs in the window of a tavern tucked back from the Strand that informed they were open, as well as a sign in a window with an electric light at the Public House across from the office that lit up the street.

However, it was the brightly lit windows at the second-floor landing that now caught my attention.

"Did you leave the electric on?" I asked Brodie.

He had not. He was after all, a Scot, known for their frugal ways.

How then was the light now on? And other lights along the street, including those carried by the police?

I was out of the cab before it stopped, Brodie just after.

A small group had gathered just off the street near the alcove below the office, including Mr. Dooley.

"What is it? Has something happened...?" I asked.

It was then Munro appeared.

What was he doing here? And then I saw Mr. Cavendish on the sidewalk just behind him. He had been badly beaten, his face bloodied and the platform he used to get around left in splinters.

I knelt beside him. His lip had been split, his beard caked with blood, and one eye was badly swollen.

"I tried, miss," he said, looking up at me. "But I couldn't stop 'em. They was on me afore I knew what had happened, and then they got poor Rupert."

The hound lay nearby, sprawled on the sidewalk.

Such things were not unusual, I knew. Most usually for robbery. But Mr. Cavendish had no coin, at least none that anyone knew of. He lived on the streets with Rupert, and was well liked by all. Who would harm a crippled man, and a mongrel dog?

Brodie knelt beside me. "Can ye describe the one who did this?"

Mr. Cavendish shook his head. "Sorry, Mr. Brodie."

"There were two of 'em. They wore costumes according to what he told me when I first got here," Munro explained. "Impossible to know who they were. And they used this on the hound."

A white cloth, smelling sharply of something now very familiar. Ether!

"It was good that ye came along when ye did," Brodie told him as I adjusted the bandage at Mr. Cavendish's head that someone had provided.

"It might have been worse."

"Aye," Munro replied. "The lass was here... The ones that did this have taken her."

I was immediately on my feet. "What are you talking about? Who was here?"

"The girl, Lily," Munro replied.

How? What reason did she have to be there?

But I knew. Curiosity for certain. She had asked me about my work with Brodie. And then there was that stubbornness and daring learned on the streets of Edinburgh.

My sister's words came back to haunt me. "*She reminds me of you...*"

"Brodie...?" I couldn't say anything more for the sudden tightness in my throat.

"I arrived just after," Munro told us then. "Yer sister was concerned after a conversation they had regardin' that first inquiry case of yours, and sent me to find her.

"She told Miss Lenore that ye might need her help," Munro added. "And there's more..."

He led the way up the stairs to the office while Mr. Dooley tended to Mr. Cavendish.

"This was found, nailed to the door."

He handed an envelope to Brodie from the desk.

Brodie opened it, took out the contents, and swore.

"What is it?"

He looked over at me. I took the envelope from him and the photograph that had been inside.

I stared at it, then looked up at Brodie.

"It's a warning," he said. "That we've gotten too close... and the next victim."

I stared back down at the photograph. It was a picture of me!

By the background and the clothes I was wearing, it appeared to have been taken that very morning at Portman Square as we called on Sir William and Lady Strachan.

Bold. Reckless. Or mad? Perhaps all three...

~

"No." Brodie was quite adamant. He was also angry, but the sort of anger I hadn't seen in him before— quiet, methodical as he retrieved a second pistol that I had carried in the past and put it in the waist of his pants, then with a look over at Munro with a silent message between them.

I was seeing something in both men that I could only guess came from those years on the streets together, the silent words that passed between them, and Munro's response.

"Aye."

Brodie had gone into the adjacent room and I heard the sound of a drawer being opened then closed.

"What are you going to do?" I asked. Munro looked up at me from the desk where he had laid out the knife he carried, and another one he slipped from his boot.

"We're going after them."

"I'm going with you..."

Munro shook his head. "Ye donna understand, Miss Forsythe. It's not just the girl, foolish bit that she is. That photograph... It's verra personal now and they won't stop until they're found."

I was angry and scared. Not for myself, but for Lily. Yes, she was brave and had lived on the streets as both men had, but as Munro said, this was personal.

I had brought her to London, and now she'd been caught up in this through no fault of her own. I supposed that it was arguable considering she'd taken it upon herself to go off on her own...

As I had, countless times. It didn't matter.

"I am going with you." This for Brodie as he stepped back into the office. "You can leave me here, but I will still find a way to go after them."

Oh, bloody hell. I was very near tears, and I never cried over anything.

By the expression on Brodie's face, I thought he might tie me to the chair. But he didn't.

"Ye're to do exactly as I say. The minute you put yerself at risk in this..."

The rest of it went unspoken.

"Here, take this." He looked at me as he handed me one of the revolvers. Then he was out the door.

Down on the street, he spoke briefly with Mr. Dooley. "There is to be no interference in this from Abberline. Do ye ken? And ye're to see that Mr. Cavendish gets to the Public House where the woman will take care of him."

"I understand," Dooley replied.

At the sidewalk near the opening to the alcove there was a sudden sound, very much like a snarl as the hound suddenly leapt to his feet, and began barking furiously.

I went over and calmed him. He licked my hand as I stroked his head and ears, grateful that he was alive.

He was wobbly, a bit like a drunken sailor but coming round with great determination. He shook himself again, then dashed off, stopped and sniffed the sidewalk, then bayed quite adamantly.

I looked at Brodie then had Mr. Dooley wave down a cab...

Rupert had proven himself most capable in the past. It might be argued that I owed him my life. At the very least he had proven himself to be quite a tracker. It accounted for all the disgusting things that ended up in the alcove.

Thin as the possibility was, I was willing to try anything to find Lily. These people had already proven they didn't care about killing someone. I wasn't about to let her be their next victim.

"We need to follow him," I told Brodie as Rupert bounded away again, then returned, quite anxious as though waiting for us.

"That mangy beast?" Munro exclaimed.

"Aye," Brodie replied, then told the driver as he pulled his coach to a stop at the curb. "Follow the hound."

The people who had attacked Mr. Cavendish and taken Lily had left on foot, traveled for some distance, then either hired a coach or had arrived in one of their own some distance away.

It was then that Rupert lost the scent, circling about, whining with what I could only interpret to be frustration, then trotting back to our coach. However, it was enough to tell us the most likely destination the ones who had taken Lily— Laughton's studio very near London Bridge.

Brodie made one last effort to send me back to the office. I told him what he told me at the office.

"No."

I didn't need to say more. He simply shook his head.

Rupert had done his job. He knew the streets of London better than most people who lived there, and I was confident he would find his way back to the office on the Strand.

"Do you think she's still alive?" I asked Brodie as we set off.

"She's a Scot," he replied. His voice softened then. "She's a good deal like yerself, lass. I pity those who have her."

My sister had said the same thing. I hoped they were right.

Sixteen

LAUGHTON'S STUDIO was just off the High Street, very near London Bridge.

The area was a blend of two-story houses, shops, and taverns. The studio was on Tooley Street, adjacent buildings alight at the windows, others darkened.

We arrived and left the coach to continue afoot with Munro moving on ahead. Eventually I heard a faint whistle, and Munro appeared through the misty darkness on the street with only an occasional street lamp.

He had found the studio at the corner, with a sign that over-hung the sidewalk, and announced *Laughton Studios, Paul Laughton, proprietor*. At the opposite corner of the window was a sign that displayed the royal warrant.

The studio inside beyond that bow window was completely dark. Munro motioned for us to follow around the corner to the back of the building. I felt Brodie's hand on my arm, as he moved past keeping me behind him.

An alleyway behind the building was dimly lit by a street lamp across along the street adjacent to the alley. The back of the studio and a door were darkened to make it almost impossible to see anything.

I felt Brodie's hand on my arm once more, and waited as a sound came from near that back entrance to the studio. Brodie looked at me through that murky light, just enough to see the expression on his face.

There was a faint flicker of light and I caught a glimpse of Munro at that back entrance with a hand-held lamp. Then he silently stepped inside the back of the studio, a reminder that he and Brodie had obviously done this many times in their previous life on the streets.

Brodie's hand found mine, and we followed Munro into the building.

The back of the studio was steeped in shadows with only the beam of the handheld light that outlined boxes, a crate, and various other things that might be found in a storeroom.

Munro slowly moved forward, stopping, listening, then moving forward again, and much reminded me of the hound on a scent.

As we moved quietly down a hallway that led to the front of the studio, I caught the faint glow of light that came from under a door on my left.

I held back as Brodie and Munro moved forward.

I hesitated and listened, my hand on the doorknob. There were no sounds coming from the room beyond. I slowly opened the door, the revolver Brodie had given me in my other hand, then stepped inside the room.

I had seen it before at Jefferson Talbot's studio— the projection machine that cast those glass plate images at a screen, the red tinted light that prevented over-exposure of the image, the basins with those noxious chemicals, and a line overhead where photographs were hung to finish the process.

There were photographs there.

They had been hung there recently, perhaps only within hours, still shiny with the last of the chemical bath, Talbot had described. On the wall were other photographs that had apparently been taken much earlier. They included photographs of Sir John Mainwaring, Sir William, and Mr. Pemberton.

There was also a photograph of myself, then one of Brodie and I together, and another of Lily. There were also photographs of each of the young ladies, including Anne Pemberton.

It appeared that she had been followed for some time, along with the other young women in that group photo taken at Wimbledon.

A glass jar sat on the counter alongside the basins with those noxious chemicals. The lid had been removed. I smelled it even before I picked it up— ether, sharp, pungent, and unmistakable.

It was all there, everything the murderer had planned and intended to carry out, and the means to do it.

Sheer madness! It was the only word for it. But who was doing this?

Laughton? He most certainly had the expertise and the knowledge... But for what reason?

I went after Brodie and Munro. I found them in the front of the studio with floor screens set about for background and props much like a stage production. And there was someone else there, sitting in a chair in that fake setting, like a stone statue, head bent forward, unmoving. Another victim?

My heart leapt into my throat.

Please, no! Not Lily!

It wasn't.

It was an old man, the same man I had seen at my aunt's party — the photographer, Paul Laughton!

He was alive, but breathing with great difficulty, the sound painful in the dark gloom of the studio, with pale sunken features in the beam of the light Munro held. And there were bruises on his throat, identical to those we had seen on each of the young women who had been murdered.

"Who did this?" Brodie asked with a hand on Laughton's shoulder. "Where are the others?"

There was a faint stirring and Laughton opened his eyes. They were dark, dilated, and filled with pain as he stared up at Brodie.

"Where are they?" Brodie again demanded. "Where is the girl? Where have they taken her?"

Laughton made a feeble gesture toward the second floor.

The scream that followed was shrill, a sound I'd never heard before, followed by a growl as I was seized from behind. A hand closed around the collar of my jacket as I was spun around.

I recognized Laughton's daughter from my aunt's party, only now she was dressed in far different clothes. Costumes Mr. Cavendish had said, and she wore make-up as well, cheeks vividly painted with an equally vivid, cruel smile that streaked across her lower face.

Madness— it was there in the crazed look in her eyes as she then lunged at me with a knife.

It all happened in seconds and there was no time to retrieve the revolver Brodie had given me.

Instead, I reacted instinctively, with just one thought— Lily. Was she already dead?

I pivoted from the hip as I'd been taught, and brought my left arm up in a sharp blow that knocked the knife from her hand. I then slammed the heel of my other hand into her face.

It wasn't enough, not nearly enough to satisfy me as I moved on her again and gouged at her eyes. That brought another maddened snarl.

Before she could recover, I swept her feet from under her. She landed on the floor with a sharp sound and lay perfectly still.

Munro was already past and moving toward the stairs in the hall. Brodie stopped, bent over Laughton's daughter and nodded.

"Stay here." Then he went after Munro.

Of course he would say that, and of course I didn't. Not if Lily was up there and in danger. I stepped over the woman, who was quite out of it, and followed them.

I followed the beam of that light as it played along the walls at the second then third floor landings. Then sounds of fighting, from somewhere at the top floor. I followed those sounds with the revolver now in hand.

That room was in chaos when I arrived. Munro was across the room, kneeling beside Lily. Her head wobbled, her eyes glazed, then much like the hound she came up fighting and landed a blow to Munro's chin.

"Get them both out of here," Brodie shouted as he was slammed back against a wall by the other person I had seen at my aunt's party.

He was dressed like some medieval character, his face blacked out, but not so that it disguised the grim determination as he moved on Brodie, pinning him against the far wall.

As they struggled, it was impossible to take a clear shot, as Brodie said once more, "Get them out."

"No!" I protested as Munro grabbed hold of my arm, his other arm around Lily.

I refused to leave Brodie.

I might as well have been shouting into the wind as Munro pushed me toward the doorway and then toward the stairs.

"No!" I shouted again, but there was only his grim expression as he forced me down those stairs, then to the ground floor.

"Don't you dare leave him!" I screamed at Munro.

"His choice, not mine... Think of the girl!" he replied.

Lily had barely roused, no doubt from the ether used to subdue her. And then...?

Those photographs in the dark room told what her fate would have been if we had not found her. But she was safe now with Munro.

When I would have pushed past him and returned to the stairs, his hand tightened.

"His choice, miss. Ye must accept it."

There was a loud crash from inside the studio as we reached the street. Flames could be seen through that bow window at the back of the studio in the direction of the dark room.

Fire? And a warning that slipped back from days past when we had first met with the chemist, Mr. Brimley.

Ether was highly flammable and extremely dangerous, and now fire?

I glanced over at Munro. His expression was grim as he supported Lily.

I ran toward the studio...

The explosion threw me back into the street, clouds of flames following as Munro grabbed me and pulled me farther away as shattered glass rained down onto the street. Then the fire turned back on itself like a ravenous beast that filled the hallway and then spread.

I stared up at those upper rooms, as fire reached the third floor. Briefly, sickeningly, I saw the two men struggling.

"Come away, miss," Munro pulled me back from the heat of the fire that had now engulfed the entire main floor of the studio.

"I ain't never seen nothin' like that," Lily managed to say, the words as wobbly as she was.

"No!" Through my tears, I refused to believe that Brodie wouldn't somehow manage to get out. And I never cried!

The alarm had gone out and there were distant sounds of the fire brigade. There would be little left by the time they arrived.

"Miss...!"

I felt Munro's hand on my arm. There was something more but I didn't hear it over the roar of the fire, the shouts of people nearby as they came out into the street, and the clang of the bell as the fire brigade arrived and began their efforts to prevent the fire from spreading to the adjacent building.

"There was something I wanted to tell him..." My throat was tight from the smoke and something more, as people swarmed around us.

And those damnable tears!

I wanted to scream...! I wanted to run back in there!

Damn you, Angus Brodie!

I went to Lily and wrapped my arms around her. She was safe, in spite of herself. Dear girl, she did remind me of me...

She was somewhat steadier now, although smudged and disheveled no doubt from the fight she had put up. Her hair was a wild tangle down her back and there was an ugly bruise on her cheek. But she was alive and safe.

"Miss?"

She pointed through the chaos of firemen, a water wagon, and the tangle of hoses and other wagons to the figure of someone who made his way through the snarl of people and debris in the street.

He moved slowly, favoring his side, features smudged with soot, that mane of dark hair wild about his head in the wind from the fire. And those dark eyes...

I gathered up my skirt and ran to him.

We very nearly both went down as I reached Brodie, desperate to make certain it was in fact him.

It was, an arm going round me and pulling me against him. He winced but he was alive. Very much alive.

Oh, bloody hell! I thought as more tears came.

"Ye're all right?" It was barely more than a whisper.

I nodded, my throat suddenly tight. Damn bloody Scot!

"Yes!" I finally managed.

He nodded. "Aye."

"No...!" I held on to him. "I mean the answer is yes!"

I thought my life was laid out before me. I had my novels and my travels. I made my own choices and decisions, and right in the middle of it was this somewhat bruised and smudged Scot!

"Do ye mean it took a damn explosion and verra nearly gettin' meself killed for ye to say it?"

There was just one word of course...

"It occurred to me that life would certainly be quite dull if you did manage to get yourself killed." I realized that was several more than just one.

He winced and swore again.

"Yes," I repeated.

He kissed me, there in the street, smudged, bruised and battered, and quite shamelessly.

I could have sworn my toes curled...

Seventeen

BRODIE SHIFTED in the chair across from Sir Avery Stanton of the Special Services Agency, against the pain.

He was fairly certain that he'd broken at least one rib in that struggle during the fire, and there was the burn on his hand. Minor, he thought, compared to the other losses.

The man was Laughton's son, they now knew, some twenty odd years old, but with the mind of a child. Both innocent and dangerous, in the things he had experienced at the hands of others, including those at the Wimbledon Club and then in the way the young man had been used by his sister to take revenge. Weak and infirm, it seemed that their father was not part of the daughter's scheme.

It might never be known how much Laughton knew of what his daughter had done— the other deaths she was responsible for.

It seemed that he had tried to stop her the night before by the bruises about his neck.

Revenge.

As Brodie knew only too well, it could be a brutal task master, and often left others, including the one who would take it, another victim. Once set on the course, there was no going back. It could only end badly, and it had for the Laughtons.

That night at the photographer's studio had been the end of it for Paul Laughton, his son, and daughter. They had all perished in the fire that engulfed the studio.

But more importantly, it was also an end and brought closure for the families of the young women who had been murdered.

It was all there in the report he had written and given to Sir Avery, and then the rest of it they had learned afterward as the pieces of the puzzle, as Mikaela referred to the case, finally came together.

There had been years of abuse as the son had been shunned, even feared, due to his size and habit of grunting a response, then becoming frustrated when people didn't understand, and he had lashed out physically, even dangerously.

The photographer sought to protect him, refusing to send him to one of the asylums in London, and Brodie couldn't find a reason to argue the decision having briefly seen the inside of one of the places when caught stealing when he and Munro first arrived in London.

The daughter, Sara, younger by two years, had become her brother's keeper and protector. She was well educated and had sought ways that he might be *healed* of the affliction, although she was eventually told there was no cure for something he had very likely been born with.

Paul Laughton, the photographer, had been highly successful and had received a royal warrant. He was also accepted at the Wimbledon Club where he had taken that photograph of the club team.

His daughter, quite accomplished in the sport of lawn tennis, might have been the fifth woman in the photograph if not for her father submitting their resignation from the club after the actions of her brother.

It was not the first time there were issues, as the young man struggled with a disability that he could never overcome. In the aftermath of the damage to the courts, the photographer withdrew his membership as his son had become too dangerous.

The situation had been painful, the young man's dangerous actions an equally painful reminder that there were those who would never accept him.

It became a motive for revenge against the members of the club and their families, and an obsession for revenge that bordered on madness. The photographs, taken by the daughter, were a way of striking back.

It was a sad outcome, and Brodie supposed the argument could be made that Sir John Mainwaring, Sir William Strachan, and the other gentlemen of the club perhaps shared some responsibility in what had happened.

Whatever their thoughts in the matter when he and Mikaela had called on each family to tell them the case had been solved, he knew well enough it was something they would have to live with.

"There is still Mr. Abberline," he commented. "He will want to know the facts."

Sir Avery nodded. "I will have Alex make a copy of your report and see that he receives it." He looked over at Brodie.

"Well done. And Miss Forsythe? She is quite well?"

Brodie nodded with a faint smile. "Well enough and interviewing tutors at present."

"Tutors?"

"The girl, Lily. She has taken her on as her ward and is determined to see her educated."

Sir Avery chuckled. "Having met the young woman and Lady Forsythe, they seem much alike. That should be most interesting."

Interesting?

Not the word he had used, but it would do. It would most certainly be that, and more.

"Will that be all, sir?" he asked, rising from the chair.

Sir Avery nodded. "You will need time to heal from the ordeal," he commented. "A few days at least, and then I may have something for you. And Lady Forsythe, of course."

Brodie nodded with a half-smile.

"I was thinking a bit more than a few days..."

Sir Avery nodded. "Take the time you need. Contact me when you're ready to proceed. You are needed out there, Mr. Brodie."

More than a few days, Brodie thought, as he took the stairs and left the Tower offices of the agency.

He walked to High Street, signaled for a driver, then gave the man the address when he pulled to the curb.

"Sussex Square."

It was well into autumn now, frost on the window ledges and trees as they left the hustle of the city behind and approached that stately part of London with houses and manors, some that were several hundred years old.

Then, the house at Sussex Square with its Georgian façade, or some other thing that Mikaela would know well enough, came into view.

"Is this the place, guv'ner?" the driver called down as he pulled the team to a stop just outside the gates.

Brodie signaled for the man to continue on and he swung the rig through those gates and up the circular drive.

He had heard it before, of course, that slight hesitation because of his manner and clothes, not precisely what the lord of the manor might wear, but more the simple long coat and trousers of someone with business for the family.

He stepped down from the coach, uncertain what he would find inside the manor; there seemed to be some difference of opinion between Mikaela and the girl, Lily, precisely what was intended for her education.

It had been said by Munro after the conclusion of the case at Laughton's studio, that they were two of a kind.

Of course Mikaela had denied it.

"Ridiculous," she had announced.

He smiled at that as he pulled the bell cord and heard the sound from inside the entryway. And a great deal more as Lady Montgomery's butler Mr. Symons answered the door.

"Good afternoon, Mr. Brodie..." he was greeted. "We are most pleased to see you."

Unless he missed his guess, there was some desperation about the man.

"Miss Mikaela," Brodie told him.

"Oh, I do hope so, sir."

"Mr. Brodie!" Lady Montgomery exclaimed. "You are just in time."

She took his arm. "You are quite well recovered?"

He assured her that he was, even though the ribs still bothered him and would for some time.

"Do come along then. The girl is of an opinion that she doesn't need further education. Quite adamant about it. It's most entertaining. And how is Mr. Cavendish?"

"On the way to recovery and with a new accommodation courtesy of Mr. Munro," he replied.

"I will not!" met their ears in a thick Scot's accent, as Brodie escorted her into the formal parlor.

"And ye canna make me!"

Lily was squared off with Mikaela and quite flushed as she stomped a foot.

"The man is a pig and smells like one," she announced. "And he put his hands on me. I donna allow anyone to do that."

Brodie looked across the *battlefield* in the middle of the room at Mikaela, equally flushed and striking in a dark green gown. He did like the view *verra much* and the argument that much more.

"I am tempted to send you back to Edinburgh!" Mikaela responded.

"I will not go. Lady Antonia has said that I may live here as long as I earn my keep."

"And just how do you propose to do that without an education?" Mikaela fired back.

Lady Antonia patted his arm. "It is a bit like the pot calling the kettle black, or some such thing like that. You really must do something about them, Mr. Brodie."

"Ye received my earlier message?" he asked.

"Yes, quite. And I must say about time." She smiled coyly at him and he could only imagine what she had been like as a younger woman.

"Her sister has taken care of the details," she continued with a sly look. "You know, I predicted this quite some time ago," she said then, with a look back at the two embattled in the middle of the parlor.

"Mikaela can be quite... stubborn. I told her that if she didn't accept, that I would..."

There was that sideways glance again, and a smile.

"Here you are," Lady Lenore arrived and greeted him. "Oh, dear, they are still going at it."

"The first of many, I predict," Mikaela's aunt commented. "It will be good for both of them."

"A moment, Mr. Brodie?" Lenore Forsythe asked.

Brodie followed her into the adjacent sitting room. She poured them both a drink; some of her ladyship's whisky from Old Lodge in the north of Scotland.

"We haven't had the chance to speak before... Not about this." She handed him a glass, and smiled almost shyly. "I've acquired a taste for it. It's quite bracing."

"Courage?" Brodie suggested.

"Yes, well, what I wanted to say is that I know my sister can be strong-willed at times. But there's a reason, you see." She took another swallow.

"Our father was..."

"Mikaela has spoken of it," he replied when it seemed she was having some difficulty.

"It's that she has always been the one to take care of me," she continued. "I do believe that is where the stubbornness and that damnable determination to see a matter set right... Forgive me for cursing. It's just that she has such strength and courage, and has quite imagined her life as a single woman, you see."

She took another swallow. "And the truth is that there was

never a man that she trusted after everything that happened when we were children." She made a gesture through the air with the now empty tumbler.

"More please, Mr. Brodie."

He smiled to himself and did as requested.

"And there was also that other aspect... And I'm certain that she must have spoken of it."

Brodie continued to listen.

"It's just that it would be expected, and..."

"Here you are," Lady Antonia announced. "The dispute has been resolved without injury. Lily and I will proceed to the sword room where she will apply herself as best she can. I fully intend to best her."

"Then, she has agreed to the tutor?" Lenore Forsythe asked, quite surprised. "I thought they might bring the walls down with their shouting and bickering."

"She has. You and I will see to the young lady's education. We are both well read and had the finest tutors," Lady Antonia went on to explain. "If there is a disagreement it will be settled in the sword room. I do believe she is beyond a spanking." She smiled. "Do close your mouth, Lenore. You look like a cod." She turned then.

"We must have appropriate costumes for duels. I must contact Madame for her suggestions. And it will mean cancelling my plans for safari... Although Lily might enjoy that very much."

Lenore Forsythe downed her second dram of whisky. "I do hope we have an ample supply. I must remember to have Mr. Munro check on that."

Brodie turned as Mikaela came into the sitting room.

Stubborn, forceful, with courage and a temper to match. And he wanted her *verra much*.

"Her ladyship seems to believe the matter is settled," he commented.

She shook her head. "Ridiculous. She is eighty-five years old. Lily is fourteen, as well she can remember."

"I would place my wager on her ladyship. She seems to have done quite well before." Brodie replied.

Mikaela frowned. He liked her frowns as well as her smiles. Although the frowns were usually a warning.

"How are you?" she asked.

"Well and good," he replied. "I've given my report to Sir Avery."

"And Abberline?"

"He will not be pleased, though not for the first time."

"Nor the last," she added. She glanced toward the stairs.

"I don't know what's to be done with her."

"Lily."

"She is quite impossible."

"Her ladyship seems to have the situation well in hand."

"That's what worries me. She's talking about taking Lily on safari."

"Aye."

"You agree?"

"I do not disagree." He knew when to pick his battles, and it seemed there would be many.

"Miss Lenore has packed your clothes and the coachman is waiting," he reminded her, half expecting that she would make some excuse.

"What if Lily burns the place down?" she said with a worried frown.

"My money is on Lady Antonia, and yer sister. And there is always Munro."

She wasn't convinced. This was a new side to her and one that he suspected he was going to take pleasure in.

"Eighteen days, though?"

"Aye. Eighteen," he replied.

Eighteen

OLD LODGE, SCOTLAND

THERE WAS A GREATER wisdom about Scotland in the winter, I had heard, what with the incessant rain and wind, and the frost and snow that might blow in from the loch, cattle in the pasture at Old Lodge like enormous shaggy snow creatures going about their way as if the storms were no bother.

Eighteen days, Brodie had declared and tolerated no argument.

It was, he informed me on the train north, the requirement for a civil license, avoiding the reading of the banns and the requirements of the Church.

I suspected he might have considered that he would not be let into the Church for such things. Myself included.

Now, twenty days, and counting, and it was done.

"Ye said aye. I'll no allow ye to take it back," he had told me on that trip north, effectively carrying me off with the bag my sister had packed while my aunt looked on with a smug expression. I did detect a conspiracy afoot.

Those long hours from London to Edinburgh and then farther north to St. Andrews and still farther north by local rail as the coach roads became impassable, we had spoken of the case, our meetings with the families of the young women who were lost, and had then attended their funerals.

There were no funerals for the Laughtons. The fire from the explosion had taken care of that.

I had gone with Brodie to the Port of Southampton, to personally let Captain Mathison know that the persons responsible for Amelia Mainwaring's death had been found and would not harm anyone again.

So many shattered lives.

There had been other conversations as well. Sir Avery Stanton had approached Brodie about joining the Agency. He had discussed it with me. The decision seemed to be his, not mine. Though, he insisted otherwise.

He preferred to maintain the office for the time being, and I was pleased with that. I couldn't imagine not having Mr. Cavendish to greet me, or the welcome nuzzle of the hound, foul smelling beast that he was.

Then there was *the conversation*', difficult as it was. Something that I shared with him earlier. "There is something, I've spoken of it before," I had said, during one of those moments when our private car was warm inside with frost on the window and the passing countryside.

He had listened, in that way that I had come to know him and trust him. When I stopped to think about that, I wasn't at all certain when it had happened. Only that it had, when I had convinced myself there wasn't anyone for me like that.

And a bloody Scot as well!

He continued to listen as I spoke again of things I had already spoken of in the past at one time or another— my mother's death, the loss of our family home, then my father's death by his own hand.

Other things he had learned from my great aunt; there was that adventure on the Isle of Crete, one of my first adventures where she had me retrieved as it were. And other things, of course.

"There is something rather important to some people," I had

begun then. "Important to most men it seems... That whole passing on the family name, titles, the family jewels, sort of thing."

He had not spoken and I looked over to find him watching me with that dark gaze that I found so very fascinating and more than a little disconcerting the way it softened. A reminder of other things...

And I had just blurted it out. Get it over with, and then if he chose otherwise, there was always the return train to London. Perfectly understandable...

"I've spoken before of the fever going round when Linnie and I were quite young. She avoided it entirely, but I came down with the miserable thing. Afterward, the physician told my aunt that I would very likely be unable to have children. I would certainly understand if you changed your mind."

And certainly proof enough of it what with our relationship of the past year, even with certain precautions.

Then absolute silence except for the sound of the train, a passing attendant in the passageway, the wheels beneath, the rocking motion of our private compartment. And Brodie.

I looked up once more to find him staring out the window, chin propped on his hand and for a moment I was certain he hadn't heard me...

"Ye know well enough that I grew up on the streets. I only know me name from me mother. My father was... not there. As for a title, there is none, nor family fortune, unless ye consider the hound or Mr. Cavendish."

He turned then and looked at me. "I asked ye because it's yerself I want, and I accept ye as ye are, Mikaela Forsythe, verra possibly the better part of meself. You.

"That's the way of it. But have ye considered that ye already have a family? I think it's not always a matter of having given birth to a child yerself, but those who need ye and those ye care for."

"Lily."

"Aye. Ye've made a commitment to the girl, no different than if she was blood relation, and more a mother, or older sister, than she's ever had."

He was right, of course. I simply hadn't thought of it that way.

"And that would make you... her father?" I asked.

"It's more than I ever expected, although two of ye will probably be the death of me."

So there we were, a different sort of family but a family nevertheless. Not unlike the one my great aunt had created with me and my sister.

Now that it was done, I looked down at the ring Brodie had placed on my hand after the eighteenth day and our appearance at the local magistrate's office.

It was a simple circlet made of bronze and fit my right hand perfectly. It matched the medallion that had once been his mother's.

"She would come back to haunt me if I didna give ye a ring, though there are no stones. I didna know what ye would prefer," he had said that day.

Now, I heard the cottage door slam and the sound of Brodie stamping his boots.

Mr. Hutton, caretaker at Old Lodge with his wife, had brought supper over earlier and I had lit the fire in the fireplace. As I had reminded Brodie, I did not cook. It was one of those details we had yet to navigate.

He dropped an armful of wood at the hearth.

"It's bloody cold outside," he said as he placed more wood on the fire.

I poured us both a dram of whisky.

"But there should be enough wood to keep us warm for the night."

He downed the whisky, then looked at me with that dark gaze. Warm indeed, I thought as he took hold of my hand and pulled me against him.

"Mikaela Brodie," he said, his beard brushing my cheek, obviously enjoying the sound of my new name.

His mouth found mine. The taste of whisky and cinnamon and Brodie was delicious.

"Actually," I said as the kiss ended and just as another began. "According to Mr. Cavendish, the new sign on the office will read Brodie and Forsythe."

He nipped at my bottom lip... most delicious!

Author Note

I carefully research anything referenced in the Deadly Series. I find it fascinating that sayings and certain things we take for granted or use every day have actually been around for two hundred years or more.

To share a few... Wimbledon, originally known as the All England Club, was established in the mid 1800's for those— both men and women, who played the sport of lawn tennis. The membership was exclusive, much like private men's clubs at first, however, women participated more and more in sports, beginning in the 19th century. Bravo.

The term, "fuzzy little balls", actually referred to rubber balls wrapped in flannel, then later as we know them today. Mikaela simply appropriated the saying in the moment...

Photography was rapidly becoming an art with developments in Germany (glass lenses), Britain (chemical development process-es), and in the United States with rolled film courtesy of a gentleman by the name of Eastman and his Kodak company.

The flash mechanism had been around for some time, enabling the photographer to take pictures at night. Death photos of loved ones were common among all classes who could afford them, particularly those of infants and children.

Ether as an inhalation anesthetic had been introduced in 1846. It was also used in the development of photographs, one of the solvents used to thin collodion to obtain the desired and appropriate physical properties of wet plate film photography.

All Hallows or Halloween, is celebrated all over Britain, with parties, elaborate costumes, and all sorts of spooky entertainments. The Legend of Sleepy Hollow, a short story, was first published by Washington Irving in 1820, something that Mikaela would have been familiar with.

Poker was a popular past-time that made its way across the pond from the United States to England in the mid-19th century. Women and men both played in private clubs. Mikaela's aunt is quite accomplished, however it does appear she has been outdone by a streetwise chit of a young girl.

Those are just a few, with more adventures to come...

Preview: A Deadly Obsession

ANGUS BRODIE AND MIKAELA
FORSYTHE MURDER MYSTERY, BOOK VII

Prologue

THE SHADES of the window were hastily lowered. Then a light glowed in the room.

It gleamed off glass jars, the steel surface of the table, the chair, and the surgical instruments on a steel tray.

"It is too soon. I told you... you must give the incisions time to heal."

"Six weeks! It has been long enough!" Then, "You have been well paid for your time and your expertise."

"I cannot guarantee there won't be repercussions..."

He cut him off. "I have not paid you for guarantees. Only results. Now, get on with it, and I will be on my way."

"You must continue to rest. To do this now might well ruin everything."

"I do not need your advice, only that you finish this now."

It began, slowly, carefully, each bandage loosened then removed. One by one, discarded.

Then another bandage removed as the face of the man in the chair gradually emerged. Another bandage just below the eyes was peeled away and revealed high cheekbones and a patrician nose.

One more, the hand that held the bandage trembling, as full lips were revealed, and curved in a smile after the weeks of waiting, and the chiseled chin beneath with a sparse growth of beard on the barely healed skin.

Six weeks he'd waited... Longer, truth be known.

The search, the risk, and the deception was close at hand.

"Mirror!" he demanded as the last bandage was removed.

It was thrust into his hand and he stared at the reflection, the arch of the brows, the nose, cheeks with only thin scars remaining at the hairline.

He slowly smiled, testing the feel of it, the look of it. Perfect.

For weeks he'd waited, planned, fought his way through the pain, paced the flat where he'd hidden himself away, going out only at night to come here so that the bandages could be changed.

A genius, he was told of the man he'd found. A man who could work miracles. And he had.

Only one thing remained to be done, he thought, as he grabbed the man by the front of the surgeon's coat, seized the knife from the steel tray and plunged it into the man's throat.

The surgeon flailed, a stunned expression on his face, blood spurting from the wound as he stared at his creation.

He slowly lowered him to the floor.

The surgeon wouldn't be found right away, in this secret place where he worked his little miracles. But it didn't matter.

There were no records, no names written anywhere. He had seen to it with each payment that bought the surgeon's skill and his silence for the experimental procedure.

What was one more death, when the most important one waited?

He seized the bandages and threw them in the coal stove, then discarded the surgical gown that he'd worn each time before should there be any blood then slipped on the pristine white shirt from the exclusive tailor's shop. The only blood was in a pool surrounding the good doctor.

Then he scattered the other instruments, threw the jars to the floor, and tore books from the shelves— including the book he'd read about the procedure, as old as the Egyptians.

When he was finished it looked as if there had been a robbery, the physician murdered in the midst of it. Not uncommon in that part of London.

He donned the cravat then his long coat and hat, taking care with the freshly healed skin on each side of his head and neck.

Then, out the door, the misty night air redolent with the stench that was almost constant in London, the sliver of dawn on the embankment.

After months, countless meetings, planning, painful surgeries and recovery that had followed, it was finally time to set their plan in motion...

Also by Carla Simpson

Angus Brodie and Mikaela Forsythe Murder Mystery

A Deadly Affair

Deadly Secrets

A Deadly Game

Deadly Illusion

A Deadly Vow

Deadly Obsession

A Deadly Deception

Merlin Series

Daughter of Fire

Daughter of the Mist

Daughter of the Light

Shadows of Camelot

Dawn of Camelot

Daughter of Camelot

The Young Dragons, Blood Moon

Clan Fraser

Betrayed

Revenge

Outlaws, Scoundrels & Lawmen

Desperado's Caress

Passion's Splendor

Silver Mistress

Memory and Desire

Desire's Flame

Silken Surrender

Angels, Devils, Rebels & Rogues

Ravished

Always My Love

Seductive Caress

Seduced

Deceived

About the Author

"I want to write a book... " she said.

"Then do it," he said.

And she did, and received two offers for that first book proposal.

A dozen historical romances later, and a prophecy from a gifted psychic and the Legacy Series was created, expanding to seven additional titles.

Along the way, two film options, and numerous book awards.

But wait, there's more a voice whispered, after a trip to Scotland and a visit to the standing stones in the far north, and as old as Stonehenge, sign posts the voice told her, and the Clan Fraser books that have followed that told the beginnings of the clan and the family she was part of...

And now... murder and mystery set against the backdrop of Victorian London in the new Angus Brodie and Mikaela Forsythe series, with an assortment of conspirators and murderers in the brave new world after the Industrial Revolution where terrorists threaten and the world spins closer to war.

When she is not exploring the Darkness of the fantasy world, or pursuing ancestors in ancient Scotland, she lives in the mountains near Yosemite National Park with bears and mountain lions, and plots murder and revenge.

And did I mention fierce, beautiful women and dangerous, handsome men?

They're there, waiting...

Join Carla's Newsletter

Printed in the USA
CPSIA information can be obtained
at www.ICGtesting.com
CBHW032234021224
18348CB00027B/324

9 781648 395369